PENGUIN BOOKS

Bad Apples

Moïra Fowley-Doyle is half French, half Irish and lives in Dublin, where she writes magic realism, reads tarot cards and raises witch babies.

She spent several years in university writing about vampires in young adult fiction before leaving to concentrate on writing young adult fiction with no vampires in it whatsoever.

Moïra's first novel, *The Accident Season*, was shortlisted for the Waterstones Children's Book Prize and received widespread critical acclaim. Her second, *Spellbook of the Lost and Found*, was shortlisted for an Irish Book Award.

MOÏRA FOWLEY-DOYLE

All The Bad Apples

PENGUIN BOOKS

PENGUIN BOOKS

UK | USA | Canada | Ireland | Australia
India | New Zealand | South Africa

Penguin Books is part of the Penguin Random House group of companies
whose addresses can be found at global.penguinrandomhouse.com.

www.penguin.co.uk
www.puffin.co.uk
www.ladybird.co.uk

Penguin
Random House
UK

First published 2019

001

Set in 11/16.5 pt Sabon LT Std
Typeset by Jouve (UK), Milton Keynes
Printed and bound in Great Britain by Clays Ltd, Elcograf S.p.A.

A CIP catalogue record for this book is available from the British Library

ISBN: 978-0-241-33396-9

All correspondence to:
Penguin Books
Penguin Random House Children's
80 Strand, London WC2R ORL

MIX
Paper from
responsible sources
FSC® C018179
www.fsc.org

Penguin Random House is committed to a
sustainable future for our business, our readers
and our planet. This book is made from Forest
Stewardship Council® certified paper.

For my daughters

After the funeral, our mourning clothes hung out on the line like sleeping bats. It had rained in the cemetery and everything was muddy. Wet grass clung all the way up to our knees and clumps of muck stuck to the heels of our best shoes.

'This will be really embarrassing,' I kept saying to anybody who would listen, 'when Mandy shows up at the door in a week or two.'

Rachel gave me a pitying look, but my best friend, Finn, was uncertain.

That's the problem with having a funeral for your sister without really knowing whether she's dead. Without a body in the coffin, how can you be sure she won't come back?

1. A *nice, normal girl*

Dublin, 2012

On my seventeenth birthday, two things happened.

I came out to my family (somewhat by accident).

And my sister Mandy disappeared.

Died, Deena, Rachel said – our other sister, the middle sister, the one who came between us. *Died, not disappeared*.

But I knew Mandy wasn't dead.

It was raining that morning. I'd woken early, surfacing with a shock from dreams of drowning, of cliff faces with sharp teeth and gaping mouths. Rachel was already up when I came downstairs, frowning at her phone.

The table was set with the best china, the plates we saved for Christmas, and on mine were two strawberry Pop-Tarts – the birthday breakfast I'd loved when I was little. They were still hot; my sister must have heard the shower running, timed it perfectly. She had spread the good tablecloth, red with white polka dots, and had set a bunch of violets, my favourite, in a vase in the centre. The birthday card beside my plate was the expensive pop-up kind. Rachel was always trying to make up for my lack of a mother by mimicking some ideal fantasy version.

'This is amazing, Rachel.'

But Rachel was distracted, still reading the text she'd just received.

'What's wrong?' I asked.

'Dad's on his way,' she said.

'What?'

'He messaged just now to say he's getting the train. He'll be here this afternoon.'

'*Dad?*'

'Yes.' My sister's mouth was a thin line.

'As in our father?'

'Yes, Deena. Dad as in our father.'

I hovered in the kitchen doorway, watched my sister sigh and tuck a stray red curl – a darker, neater version of mine – behind her ear, rub her forehead with one finger like she was trying to erase the lines there.

'What do you think he wants?'

'Maybe he wants to wish you a happy birthday,' she said with a shrug. 'Happy birthday by the way. Sorry. Should have led with that.'

I couldn't find the voice to answer. I had a theory as to why our absent father should feel the need to visit this week. I didn't think it was anything to do with my birthday.

He knows.

My face must have betrayed me. 'Is everything OK?' Rachel asked.

I poured myself some tea. 'Nothing,' I said. 'I mean, yeah, I'm fine. Are you sure Dad didn't say why he's coming to Dublin today?'

Rachel sank a mixing bowl into the sudsy sink, wiped the batter left around the edges. 'It's your birthday,' she said, not quite answering the question.

I gave my sister a *come on* look. 'And when's the last time he visited for any of our birthdays?'

'I don't know, Deena.' Rachel sighed. Her impatience was probably more about Dad's impending arrival than my question. 'Maybe he has business in town.'

Or maybe the rumours that had been floating around school recently had somehow got back to him and he wanted to come over and confront me about them himself.

Our absent father all but abandoned us – his three motherless children – when I was less than a year old. He oversaw from afar our education (in the strictest, single-sex Catholic school he could think of); he only called us if he'd heard rumours that we were not upholding the Rys family name; he only ever dropped in on us unannounced, as if to try to catch us out, so determined was he to make sure we were the good, traditional, God-fearing daughters he expected us to be. All the while clearly not caring enough about us to actually stick around.

Which left me with my sisters.

My sisters were fraternal twins. Mandy was older by twenty-four hours, although she neither looked like the eldest nor acted like it. Rachel had always been impossibly adult – practical and mature – and was now positively ancient at thirty-four. But while Rachel raised me, did her best to tame me, Mandy wilded me, carelessly undoing all of Rachel's work: muddying my shoes, tangling my hair, making me question authority.

Mandy and Rachel were night and day, fire and frost, chaos and logic. They were opposites in so many ways their few similarities were shocking.

They were my family, these sisters, this strange push and pull.

Our father had long since given up on Mandy, and I knew exactly how he would react if he ever found out about me.

Sitting across from me, Rachel narrowed her eyes. 'What is it?' she said.

I attempted a breezy tone. 'Nothing really,' I said. 'It's just there've been some rumours going around school. For the last week or so. About me. I'm a bit worried they might have come back to Dad. Through one of his friends on the school board or the parents' association. You know.'

'What kind of rumours?'

'All kinds. You know my school.' I wrapped my fingers round my teacup, made the decision to say it almost before I realized the words were coming. Deep breath, dive in. 'But mostly there are rumours that I'm. Um. Gay.'

Rachel squared her shoulders. 'Our father would know better than to believe a rumour like that.'

I never understood why nerves were described as butterflies in your stomach. This was more like a prolonged electric shock.

'They're true,' I said softly. 'The rumours. I'm gay, Rachel.'

My body could have set off sparks. Rachel opened her mouth to speak.

It was at that perfectly unfortunate moment that our father walked unexpectedly into the kitchen. Panic rooted me to the spot. I could have been felled by a single axe stroke, falling with limbs askew like branches.

For half a second, I thought he hadn't heard me, but all the wishful thinking in the world couldn't change the

7

way his face – neutral, lined, neat red hair gone mostly grey – had twisted in fury.

When he spoke, his voice was low and dangerous. 'What,' he said, 'did you say?'

My voice froze in my throat.

'Nothing,' I whispered, the word sounding strangled and strange. I could feel the colour leach from my face.

'Dad!' Rachel jumped up from her seat. 'You're early! I thought you'd still be on the train.'

Our father ignored her. 'What do you mean, nothing?' he said to me. 'Nothing what?'

'Deena was just saying,' Rachel said in Dad's direction, fast and nervous, 'that sometimes girls say the most horrible things. That's bullying, you know. I'm sure it's against school policy.'

'Don't you go covering for your sisters again,' Dad shot back at her. 'That school's feckin' policy is the reason I'm here in the first place. Getting people in to talk about deviant lifestyles with impressionable kids.' He gestured at me, grimacing. 'It encourages this kind of disgusting talk.'

'I'm not—' I said. 'I didn't mean—'

Dad's voice lowered, had that dangerous edge to it again. 'You're damn right you didn't mean,' he said. 'And you'll say nothing like that ever again, you hear? I'm giving you one last chance. If I get even a whiff of this off you again, I'm sending you to one of those camps. Sort this nonsense out once and for all. I won't have another bad apple in this family. Mandy's bad enough already. No daughter of mine—'

'Dad,' Rachel said peaceably. 'This is all just a big misunderstanding. Everyone knows Deena is a nice, normal girl.'

'Then she'd best start acting like it,' Dad said to Rachel as if I wasn't in the room, as though I was a naughty child needing to be taught some manners.

I could neither speak nor stop the tears that had sprung up the moment my sister – the one whose opinion actually mattered to me – had said the words *nice, normal girl.*

I wanted to speak up, defend myself, tell the truth. Instead, I did the only thing my body seemed capable of doing, something that probably proclaimed my guilt even more than my tears. I turned and ran out of the door.

2. Please stand for morning prayers

Dublin, 2012

The words drummed on my umbrella like raindrops. *Nice, normal girl* fogged up the air in the crowded bus. *Nice, normal girl* formed puddles on the school grounds that my shoes threatened to slip in. *Nice, normal girl.*

I walked into the hall for Friday assembly, drenched despite my umbrella, shivering. I draped my dripping coat over the back of my chair and took two long puffs on my inhaler. They didn't help unknot the panic in my chest.

The hall filled slowly. Girls in green jumpers and tartan skirts sat in small clusters: the prefects and class reps to the front, the rebels at the back, the popular girls in the exact midpoint of the hall – the centre of our small universe. The rest of us branched out from them, groups of friends chatting together or yawning, scrolling on their phones or showing off their renegade nail polish, strictly forbidden by the school dress code.

2. *Please stand for morning prayers*

I sat alone.

My phone lit up with a message from Finn.

> **Many happy returns on this the day
> of your birthday which I wish I was
> spending with you instead of in
> maths test purgatory. Pretty sure
> Mr Geary is going to fail me. Approx.
> 5 hours of homework dished out
> already and it's not even 9. Me and
> some of the lads are considering an
> uprising. How's your stats looking?**

My best friend, by virtue of being a boy, was unable to attend the same school as me, which would have made the long hours I spent there infinitely easier. As it was, we had to be content with narrating the tedium of our weekdays via text. Finn was smart, and well liked in his school, so his tedium mostly consisted of being overworked by admiring teachers who only wanted the best for him.

> **Bleak. Stats as follows. Dirty looks
> received: two. Whispers directed at
> me: three. Possibility of nasty
> rumours circulating: mid to high.**

I didn't mention anything about my dad.

Stay strong, Finn messaged, his usual parting words.

I got in a **You too** before the vice-principal called for us to please stand for morning prayers.

I could recite the Our Father in my sleep so I let my voice go to autopilot and looked around at the other girls, noticing that two sixth years a few rows behind me stayed seated, kept their mouths clamped shut during morning prayers in silent protest.

They were stone warriors, chins raised defiantly like statues of queens. One had long earrings, two bright purple plastic Venus symbols. The other wore two pins on her collar: one was a large, enamel rainbow flag. The other said DON'T HATE, EDUCATE.

Nobody gave these girls dirty looks. No rumours circulated about them the way they did about me. They were untouchable; they radiated cool. Unlike me – ill-defined and self-conscious, plump, freckled and bespectacled like the bumbling best friend in an old children's book – these girls announced themselves, chins high, daring anybody to challenge them. We may have sheltered underneath the same umbrella, but, in the many judging eyes of the school, we were completely different species.

Our prayers ended to a chorus of amens.

2. Please stand for morning prayers

'All right, girls.' The vice-principal's voice came through the mic in front of her. 'As you all know, there has been some hullabaloo about the cancellation of the Schools Out Loud workshop last week.'

It had been all over local news and radio:

'*Dublin school calls off LGBT youth group's anti-bullying workshop.*'

'*Sixth-year girls organize protest against school's cancellation of LGBT group lecture.*'

Those sixth years, soon joined by a couple of the more confident younger girls, had been quick to criticize the school's decision. When I'd tried to do the same during lunch break on Monday, my classmates' eyebrows had immediately shot up.

'You have probably seen our statements on school social media,' the vice-principal went on. 'Our Lady the Mother of Immaculate Grace Secondary School has a zero-tolerance bullying policy. We are proud to have a diverse student body. However, some parents expressed concern over an activist group speaking without a fair and balanced counter-argument present. The school board is looking into speakers who could represent the other side of the discussion. In the meantime, the Schools Out Loud workshop has been postponed, not cancelled.'

I chanced a glance behind me. One of the two sixth-year girls had bent her head to whisper in the other's ear. They both rolled their eyes, then glared back at the stage, sitting even straighter. A girl in my class, sitting close by, noticed me looking and elbowed her friend. They both giggled.

There had always been rumours about me, but this week in particular they'd got a lot louder. And my father now knew they were true.

Face flaming, heart pounding, I turned to the vice-principal again.

'I would also like to remind students of our school dress code,' she was saying. 'No pins, badges or garish accessories will be allowed during school hours and on school uniforms. As always, Our Lady girls are expected to be well groomed, well presented and uphold the reputation of our school. *Slán agus beannachtai Dé oraibh.*'

Goodbye and God's blessings be on you. Provided you weren't wearing a rainbow pin.

The two sixth years stood at either side of the assembly-hall doors as the school trickled out, proud sentinels handing out printed leaflets calling for a student protest.

I hung back. One of them beckoned me over. Her earrings had just been confiscated and she kept reaching up with her free hand, feeling their absence.

'You joining the protest?' she asked. I wondered if she could sense it on me. 'The details are on the event page.' She pointed to a link printed on the flyer.

I couldn't join the protest. It would be like painting a big rainbow target on my back. Still, I felt my cowardice like a toothache, sharp and constant.

'I'm sorry your earrings got confiscated,' I said to the girl instead. 'They were awesome. It's completely unfair.'

The girl looked surprised for a moment, then smiled, as if she was pleased I had noticed. 'Thanks,' she said. 'I made them myself.'

'What? Really? They're amazing.'

She pushed the flyer into my hand and I took it automatically, grinning stupidly.

'Monday morning,' she said. 'Scheduled walkout. See you there.'

She turned to wave her leaflets at a group of fourth years behind me and I carried my flyer and my smile halfway down the corridor, thinking that maybe things could be OK, that maybe I could even talk to pretty older girls who made their own earrings, that maybe if I joined the protest nobody would suspect a thing.

Until I slowed by the toilets and overheard four girls from my class talking about me in front of their lockers.

'Oh my God,' one of them was saying. 'Did you see Deena Rys drooling over that sixth year? Scarlet for her.'

A flurry of whispers erupted in the wake of her words. I shoved through the door towards the toilets, to splash cold water on my burning face.

When the door closed behind me, I thought I could hear one of them saying, 'OK, you win. I'm changing my vote.'

I didn't wonder long what vote she meant. When I walked into French, before the teacher but after most of the other girls, it was right there on the whiteboard at the front of the class.

It said, in glaring bold black letters:

IS DEENA RYS A LESBIAN?

Underneath the words were three columns. The first said **Yes**. The second said **No**. The third said, in somewhat squashed writing, **She's too ugly to get a boy so she may as well try dykes.**

In the first column there were ten votes. In the second there were three. In the third there were twelve.

It was every nightmare I'd never even thought to have, and I was so mortified I didn't even feel it. I stared at the board for a long moment, loaded silence coming from the desks behind me.

2. Please stand for morning prayers

I could have said something. I could have gone to the vice-principal with her 'zero-tolerance bullying policy'. Instead, I walked out of the classroom and nobody stopped me. Tears trailed hot and shameful down my cheeks, but still I slammed the door so hard the crucifix above it fell off the wall and crashed to the floor.

3. The Rys family curse

Dublin, 2012

Without it being a conscious decision, I walked all the way to Mandy's, crying in the rain, my umbrella forgotten under an assembly-hall chair.

Mandy had never lived with Rachel and me – not since a little after I came along anyway. I, the afterthought, the accident, the small slip of the tongue, born seventeen whole years after my sisters, the final straw that killed our mother. At around the same time that our father left, Mandy and Rachel fell out, loudly and dramatically – at our mother's funeral no less, or so the family always said. Mandy had left Dublin, to who knows where and doing who knows what, but she came back after I'd started school. Since then, Mandy had lived in a dingy flat in Fairview with two friends and a revolving cast of couch-surfers with varying degrees of personal hygiene. As far as I was aware, she'd given back her key to the family home.

3. *The Rys family curse*

Whenever I asked what they had fought about so seriously, my sisters were uncharacteristically united in their silence. But there was nobody else to ask; the rest of our family had had very little to do with us since that very fight.

Mandy had quit school at sixteen, told me she'd learned everything she knew from the Marino public library. She had once been fired from a job in a bar because she had punched a man who'd groped her. She'd had a scandalous affair with a married banker, spent two weeks in his penthouse apartment in Marbella. She'd toured with a punk band for a few months in her teens. She'd joined a cult, briefly, in her twenties, had lived off the land with other white-clad, barefoot women, until she grew weary of their rules, said they were just as bad as the church she'd left as a girl.

She'd let me smoke a joint with her last year, laughed when I told her that her grey eyes were exact mirrors of mine, fed me chocolate digestives until I fell asleep. She snuck me into concerts and burlesque shows, convincing the bartenders I was over eighteen, slid sugary cocktails across the table to me. She let me borrow books that Rachel would undoubtedly have considered unsuitable, which I read curled up wherever I could find a clear bit of space in her bedroom, sipping coffee, listening to the rain.

I had never come out to Mandy, but I had long suspected I didn't have to.

'Our family tree blew down in a gale and we are the bad apples it shook off,' Mandy said, the moment she opened the door of her flat.

'What?'

'Bad apples,' Mandy repeated. 'Isn't that what Dad always says?'

I stood open-mouthed and dripping in the hallway, unable to tell my sister that Dad had used those exact words that very morning, that her saying this, specifically, right at that moment, was eerie.

'Bad apples don't have history,' she went on, handing me a towel. 'They don't have roots. They just sit in the grass where they fell, rotting alone.'

Or they walk all the way to Fairview in the pissing rain without an umbrella to knock at their sister's door.

'Speak for yourself,' was all I could say, but I knew she already was. Mandy was the baddest apple in our bunch, and I loved her for it.

Drying my hair, I followed my sister through the dusty, dimly lit flat into her bedroom. The floor was covered in notebooks and folders and library books about nineteenth-century landed gentry. She flopped cross-legged onto her unmade bed and gestured at her cluttered bedside table, upon which was a fresh mug of coffee, perched next to a pink-frosted cupcake topped with a flickering candle.

'Happy birthday,' she said, cigarette-scratchy. 'I hear Dad's in town. Have my coffee – you look like you need it.'

'Thanks,' I said, warming my palms on the full mug, still thinking about her saying we were bad apples. 'So Rachel called you? What did she say?'

Mandy threw an arm over her eyes. Her hair, the signature Rys red, more auburn than my orange, fell in messy curls halfway down her back, several strands, once bleached and dyed purple, now faded to a dusty lavender, red at the roots. There were shadows of sleepless nights under her eyes. 'Not much over the phone. She says she wants to see me later, to "have a chat",' she said. 'I need a drink.'

'You're not the only one,' I muttered.

My sisters had very different reactions to meetings with our father, but both seemed to come from the same place. Rachel's mouth would tighten so much her lips disappeared, and by evening the house would be spotless, sparkling, and her hands rubbed raw from scrubbing traces of dirt from the bathroom walls. Mandy's mouth would only tighten when it was round a bottle and she'd be messy drunk by evening. If the interaction was particularly bad, she might disappear for a few days.

'Did Rachel say what she wants to talk about?' My heart beat in my throat.

'No, but don't worry about it.' She pushed the cupcake across the bedside table. 'Make a wish.'

My stomach tightened. I made a wish and blew out the flame.

'Do you feel different?' my sister asked me.

'What? Because of the wish?'

Mandy barked a laugh. 'If you like,' she said. 'But I meant now that you're seventeen.'

Seventeen was hardly the age of spindles and spinning wheels, but to Mandy it still seemed to mean something. I wanted to lie, tell her I felt no different than I had the day before, assure her that there was nothing unusual about this day, no pivotal moment that had sent me running to her. I was suddenly unsure I could tell even her, could risk saying the words again.

'A bit, yeah,' I said.

'Your present's on the floor beside you,' my sister said.

I pulled a heavy box wrapped in newspaper and kitchen twine onto my lap. When I opened it, it was filled with books.

'Mandy! Thank you!'

'Have a look,' she said.

I took the books out one by one, stacked them on Mandy's overflowing little desk with her library books and refill pads and folders full of who knew what. After

I'd taken the third book out, I understood my sister's present.

These were more than just the kind of books I couldn't find in my school library. Than those I'd read, illicitly, at Mandy's since I was little. These were books I would never have had the courage to let anybody but Finn see me read.

There were silhouettes of girls holding hands on a couple of the covers, and on one – a shiny, hardback American edition – two girls kissing. I shook my head at the audacity of my sister, at my own embarrassment, at the sheer perfection of both her timing and her gift. From *Tipping the Velvet* to *Cameron Post*, an entire library of girls like me.

'You can keep them here if you like,' she told me. 'If it's easier.'

I didn't want to put the books back in their box.

Mandy was watching me carefully. 'Was I wrong?' she asked gently.

I felt strange, nervous, choked up, tearful. 'No,' I croaked. 'You're not wrong.'

'I have another present for you,' she said, brushing aside my garbled thanks. 'But it isn't ready yet.'

'This present is perfect,' I said, voice shaky, still overwhelmed. 'You don't have to get me something else.'

'I want to,' said Mandy. 'It's just not quite finished.'

'That's OK. It can be a surprise.'

'I'm shit at surprises,' said Mandy. 'So I'll tell you. I thought we could take a little holiday, just the two of us. A road trip. What do you reckon?'

On my tenth birthday, Mandy had picked me up from school unexpectedly. We drove to the westernmost part of Donegal with a tent, two sleeping bags, a backpack full of books, enough candles to light a small church and the horned skull of a bull. (Even at ten, I was aware that Mandy was a little eccentric.) We set up our tent in a campsite on the dunes facing the ocean and we spent our days reading on the windy beach, talking to the cows in nearby fields and going for long walks, upon which Mandy always seemed to be looking for something. We were constantly covered in sand and salt that scratched when we slept, we'd forgotten to bring a brush so our hair was all tangles, we washed our knickers by hand in the sink of the camping-ground toilets – and I'd never had so much fun in my life.

At night we'd howl at the waves and when we got tired Mandy would wrap us up in blankets with a thermos of tea and tell stories about Tír na nÓg, the fairy land far west across the water – to which the poet Oisín was carried on the back of a white horse in the myth everybody knew – where nobody gets old or sick and no one ever dies.

On the last night she drew a large circle on the sand with salt from a shaker she'd stolen from the local pub. She sat me in the middle with the bull skull and the candles, which didn't blow out even in the strong sea breeze.

'He'll protect you,' Mandy told me. 'Keep you safe.'

But I always felt safe with Mandy anyway.

It was only when we returned to Dublin a week later, barefoot and dirty, bright-eyed, windswept and tangle-haired, that I learned Mandy hadn't told anyone else she was taking me on our camping trip.

After several days without a word from Mandy, Rachel had called our father. At the time I thought Rachel had overreacted, had betrayed us by involving him, but, now that I've thought about it, she must have been so worried. That she hadn't called the police meant she'd trusted Mandy that much at least.

When we returned, there was all manner of uproar. Dad called constantly for the next few days with criticism and unsolicited advice. I sat on the stairs in the hall and listened to Mandy and Rachel argue, listened to Mandy shouting at our father on the phone before storming out, then listened to the phone ring and ring unanswered when his number kept coming up.

I'd snapped and snarled and told Dad those seven days had been the best in my life, and he told Rachel, 'She'll turn out just like her if you don't do something.'

'What is it?' Mandy's eyes now searched my face like spotlights, illuminating all the hidden corners. She'd started doing that. For weeks, I'd catch her watching me, as if she was waiting for something. As if I would break out in blisters, spontaneously combust, disappear.

'Nothing,' I said, my traitor cheeks flushing the same pink as my cupcake. 'A road trip sounds brilliant. Where will we stop along the way?'

'That's why it isn't ready yet. I'm still working out the route.'

I smudged a finger into the icing, licked it. 'It's a great birthday present,' I told my sister. 'Thank you. And for the books.'

'I'm glad you like them.'

I puffed out my cheeks and said, 'Your timing is kind of spooky actually because I kind of accidentally came out to Rachel this morning.'

Mandy's face went through several expressions that I couldn't read before settling on a sort of resignation. 'Don't worry, Deena,' she said. 'Whatever she said, Rachel will come round eventually.'

'Mandy, Rachel didn't—'

'She's just still trying hard to hold on to her plan for you, but she'll understand it's changed soon enough.'

'Her plan?' I repeated.

'You know,' Mandy said. 'She likes to think of you as the perfect blank slate for everything she never got to be. A wife and mother with a worthwhile career. She's probably planned your and Finn's wedding and picked out your babies' names already. She just wants you to get the life she couldn't. As a *nice, normal girl*.' Mandy made air quotes; these were Rachel's words, not hers. A lump formed in my throat at hearing, for the second time today, the very phrase I couldn't get out of my head.

Mandy brushed her hair behind her shoulders with one sweep of her arm and said, rather grudgingly, 'It's because she loves you, you know.'

'I know she does. It's just I *am* a nice, normal girl, you know?'

Mandy laughed. 'If you say so, kid.'

'I do.' I stroked the spines of the books. 'Although – I'm not sure Dad does any more.'

Mandy stared at me. 'What do you mean?'

The fury on my father's face flashed into my mind. 'He heard me,' I said, the words heavy. 'He came into the kitchen as I was telling Rachel.'

She sat up abruptly. 'He *what*? Are you sure?'

Our father's words echoed round my skull. *Deviant lifestyles. Disgusting. No daughter of mine.*

'Oh yeah,' I said. 'I'm sure.'

Suddenly Mandy's face was stricken. 'No. *No.* No, no, no. Deena, you can't tell anyone else. Nobody else can find out.'

'What?'

She clutched her head, shook it, her hair tangling in her fingers. 'If it were just me and Rachel . . . but if Dad knows—' Mandy took a breath. 'Do you remember when we went up to Donegal for your tenth birthday?' she asked.

'Of course. Our infamous road trip. I was just thinking about that a few minutes ago actually.'

Mandy sat forward, hands on her knees, bracing. 'Do you remember what I told you on the last night?'

Sand and salt, fire and bone.

'No?' The word was a question. I remembered the bull skull. I remembered her telling me the bull would protect me, keep me safe. I remembered feeling enchanted, but mystified.

'Do you remember what I told you about our family?'

'Not really. Sorry.' But a memory was dredging itself from my subconscious, ringed in salt. 'Yes,' I said. 'Sort of. Did you tell me some kind of story about a family curse?'

Mandy nodded deep. 'The Rys family curse.'

We knew next to nothing about the Rys side of the family because Dad never talked about them. When we spoke about our family, my sisters and I, we meant the MacLachlans, our mother's kin. We rarely saw them – each as self-righteous, pious and judgemental as the last. They'd taken Dad in with approving, welcoming arms.

I shrugged, bemused. 'The Rys family curse. Remind me.'

'Bad things happen to the bad apples in our family,' Mandy said, her eyes unfocused, her voice trance-like. Small pinpoints of unease prickled along my skin.

'You were saying something about bad apples when I first got here, right? What was it again?'

'You know the kind,' she went on as if I hadn't spoken. 'You'd know them a mile away. The ones who don't look like the others, don't act like the others. The ones who don't conform, don't follow the rules, don't go to church on Sunday. The ones who run away, make their own lives. The ones who drink too much, talk too much, don't work enough or at the right things. The ones who dress differently, love differently, think differently. Our family tree protects its good seeds, keeps them safe. But the bad apples get shown the door. Shunned, ignored, talked about in hushed whispers. They get pushed off the tree, breaking every branch on their way down. And once they've fallen, once they've been cast off the family tree, that's when the curse comes to them.'

'The curse.'

'It happens at the age of seventeen. Like some kind of fairy tale. If you've lived a life on the straight and narrow, the curse may never find you. But, if you're considered rotten by the rest of the family, you're doomed.'

I stared at her. 'Doomed? What does that mean exactly?'

Mandy stared right back. 'It means deaths and disappearances. Terrible losses and tragedies. Things you'll carry with you always.'

'But, Mandy—'

'I'm telling you, Deena, if the family think you're rotten, you're doomed.'

The rain battered at her bedroom window.

'You'll know for sure if you hear the banshee scream.'

The icing of my birthday cupcake was pastel paste on my fingers, sticky and too sweet. 'The banshee,' I repeated. 'This is a metaphor, right?'

'It's not a metaphor. There are three of them. The first is the one whose screams mark you as cursed. Then you'll find grey hairs fallen from the second's bone comb tangled on the threshold of your home. You'll know there's no hope left when the third scores your skin with her sharp nails as you sleep.'

I placed my half-eaten cupcake back on Mandy's bedside table. This was not how I'd expected this chat to go. Mandy believed in many things – ghosts, UFOs, conspiracy theories. It made sense that she would believe in banshees, in family curses. But what she was telling me now I didn't understand. I didn't want to understand.

'I'm afraid,' said Mandy. 'I'm afraid this is the curse. I'm afraid you're another bad apple ready to fall from the tree.'

My heart was hit with hammers. 'I'm not a bad apple,' I whispered. 'This doesn't make me a bad apple.'

Mandy stared right through me. I wanted her to say *Of course not.* I wanted her to say *I know that.*

'You're cursed,' she whispered. 'This has to be the curse.'

'Mandy, I'm gay, not cursed. I didn't know Dad was home yet. I didn't know he would hear me. I would never have said anything if—'

Mandy was speaking too fast and too loud. 'I didn't think it could happen to you. I've made a huge mistake. If Dad heard you— You can't tell anyone else. Nobody can find out. Maybe if you keep your head down this year, maybe if you just pretend—'

'*Pretend?*' The books on the desk mocked me, unboxed, covers loud.

'It's going to be OK,' she said. 'Don't worry. I can fix this.'

I stood and went with heavy feet to her bedroom door.

I could have sunk all the way to the ground floor. 'I don't need fixing,' I said to my sister, but she just let me walk away.

Finn found me later, down by the beach past the wooden bridge. The rain had stopped and the world was wrung out and blanketed in puddles. I was sitting on my jacket underneath the statue at the end of the walk down to Dollymount Strand: a seventy-foot-high Virgin Mary towering over the bay. Our Lady, Star of the Sea. I was on my third coffee (which wasn't helping the pace of my heartbeat), the paper cups stacked neatly on the ground beside me, and I was scrolling on my phone, dangling my legs above the water.

Finn dropped down to the ground beside me.

'How long have you been here?' he asked.

'Since half past twelve.'

A ferry rolled slowly out of the port at East Wall, and Finn and I watched it – this colossal monster of a thing – sending waves washing towards the strip of land we sat on, under the feet of the Virgin Mary.

'Are you going to tell me what happened?' he asked.

I put down my phone and kicked out my legs. Softly, I sang, '*Happy birthday to me, happy birthday to me.*'

'Deena.'

'*Happy birthday, dear Deena, happy birthday to me.*'

'You cut class, for the first time in your life,' Finn said. 'You go dark online for the whole day until you ask me to meet you here. You're acting weird. Er.'

'Very ha.'

'So either you're deciding to try out a bit of good old-fashioned teenage rebellion on your seventeenth birthday, in which case I applaud you and wish you only the best, or—' Finn paused for breath. 'Or something happened today.'

The ferry picked up speed.

'So far,' I said slowly, 'I think it's safe to say that this has been the worst birthday in the history of birthdays.'

'Did something happen in school?'

'I can't go back there,' I told him. 'Ever, probably.'

Finn turned to look at me, his features blurry in my peripheral vision. I stared in silence through my glasses at the sea.

'OK.' He rubbed his hand twice over his close-cropped black hair. 'So what's the plan?' he asked. 'You go on the run? Get Rachel to home-school you? Good luck with that.'

Three tears ran silently down my cheeks before I could stop them. 'I might not be able to go home either.'

'Shit,' said Finn. 'Come on, Deena. What happened?'

'They had a vote at school.' Of everything that had happened so far, this was the easiest to open with.

'What? Who had a vote? Is this about the talk they're protesting?'

'No,' I said. 'No. They had a vote about me.'

Finn shook his head. 'You're going to have to fill in the gaps for me here, Rys.'

I filled in the gaps. I started with school. I began to cry when I told him about my dad. By the time I'd got to Mandy's reaction I was having trouble breathing. Finn put a careful arm round my shoulders. There were certain things that only my best friend could understand, being bi himself. He may not have completely understood why I was so terrified of my father finding out, seeing as how Dad didn't even live with us, but Finn did understand not wanting to be out loudly and publicly at school. Only a small handful of his friends in class knew. Until this morning, I hadn't been out to anybody but Finn.

When I had finished, he stood abruptly and said, 'That's it, I'm buying you a chocolate muffin. And when you've eaten it we're going to get my cousin to buy us some cans. Screw those bitches in school. And screw your whole damn family. It's your birthday. Tonight we're going to get drunk and talk about girls.'

He strode purposefully back to the little coffee shop by the car park, his hips lean in his grey uniform trousers, his head high. I understood why Rachel had always wanted me to end up with Finn (apart from the obvious fact that he was the only boy who'd ever shown interest in me, romantically or otherwise). Life would be so much simpler if I could just fall in love with my best friend.

Above me, Our Lady, Star of the Sea watched the ferry slide slowly out of sight. When I turned back round, ahead of me in the water there was a woman.

Not a swimmer. Not somebody who'd jumped into the bay on a dare. An old woman so pale her skin seemed grey, submerged past her mouth, her long silver hair tangling through the foam of the small waves around her. A woman with a ravaged, skeletal face, cheeks sunken, eyes set deep in wrinkles, their irises as grey as her hair.

She wasn't treading water. She wasn't moving at all. She was staring right at me, unblinking.

A long grey hand came out of the water. Its twisted fingers beckoned.

I couldn't explain what happened next, only that I must have started so hard I slipped off the rocks at the base of the statue and into the water. There was nobody close enough to push me. The woman was too far from me to have pulled.

A split second and I went under. Not even enough time to feel real fear. Water whooshed around me, filled my ears with roaring and my mouth with salt. I kicked wildly towards the surface.

When I came up, the woman's face was a hair's breadth from mine. She opened her mouth and screamed.

Suddenly Finn's hands clamped down on my upper arms and he dragged me out of the water. I helped hoist myself up onto the rocks and I spluttered and coughed and hacked up salt water. Finn pushed my inhaler into my hand and I puffed until I could breathe again.

The second I could find enough air to speak, I said, 'Did you see her? Oh God, did you see her?'

'See who?'

'The woman. The woman in the water.' I craned my neck but there was no one there. 'Oh God.' My teeth chattered. 'Her face. Her fingers. Did you see her?'

'There's no one in the water.' Finn brushed me down, flicking water on the rocks. 'What happened? Did you fall in?'

Shock sent shudders through me.

'Are you OK?' said Finn. 'Let's just get you back to your place. Get you dry.'

'I was sure I saw her,' I said. 'Clear as day. Cold and grey. Those eyes.'

'Did you hit your head or something?' Finn asked, concern threaded through his words.

'I'm fine,' I told him, eyes still on the water. 'I didn't hit my head.'

'Then you need to change out of your clothes or you'll catch pneumonia or whatever.'

I gave the rocks below us one last searching look. 'Yeah,' I said vaguely. 'Yeah, you're right.'

There was nothing there. No one. The scream must have come from me. The vision of the woman must have come from the stress of the scorn of my father's rage, from the stares of the girls in school, from the fall, from the coffee. From Mandy, who I'd always thought would understand, would love me no matter what. It couldn't possibly have been real.

Couldn't possibly have been a banshee, like my sister told me.

Finn and I walked back together along the wooden bridge to the seafront and up the residential roads towards my house.

All the way home, for some reason, I smelled apples.

4. *Bad apples*

Dublin, 2012

When Finn and I walked through the kitchen door, with
me leaving trails of seawater behind me in the hall,
Rachel was sitting at the table, smashing apples with a
mallet.

I thought I was hallucinating. After all, I had possibly
just seen a banshee in Dublin Bay. Yet somehow the
concept of Rachel smashing apples with a mallet (where
did Rachel get a mallet?) was almost more unbelievable.
Rachel did not smash apples with mallets. Rachel
bought apple pies from Marks and Spencer and heated
them in the oven in their foil trays. Rachel did the dishes
before sitting down to dinner. Rachel kept her sharpened
knives neatly lined up in their knife block and got cross
if I just shoved them into the cutlery drawer.

My feet squelched. Rachel looked up from the table,
mallet in hand.

'Deena!' she said. 'What in the world happened to you?'

'Got wet,' I said. Apple bits dripped from the mallet head. 'What's . . . going on here?'

'The juicer broke,' Rachel said.

'OK.'

'I really wanted some apple juice. And then the juicer wasn't working, and we had all these apples that were going to go to waste.' Rachel waved the mallet and laughed a little unsteadily. 'I guess this isn't really working,' she said. 'But it sure is therapeutic.'

'Right.' This wasn't about the juicer. This was about Dad, and this morning. Rachel carefully avoided mentioning it, though.

She put the mallet down, started to scoop the apple mess onto a wooden chopping board to dump in the compost. 'You should change out of those clothes,' she said, back to her busy, bustling self, not even looking at me as she doled out advice and commands. 'Bring them down when you're done, would you? I'm going to put a wash on. Your birthday cake is in the fridge. Banoffee pie, your favourite. I know Finn is staying over tonight so I'll leave you to it, but I'll be home before eleven, just so you both know. There's money for takeaway on the hall table.'

Rachel said not a word about our father, not a word

about what I'd told her that morning, and I found I couldn't say anything either.

The entire kitchen smelled green and sharp.

That night, Finn and I celebrated my birthday with cans of cheap cider, banoffee pie and Chinese takeaway. We sat on the floor underneath my bedroom window, and outside a storm blew up from over the sea, sent gulls circling the suburbs.

One can deep, we wrote out the names of the girls I knew were behind that morning's poll and burned them in the bathroom sink. Two cans deep, Finn held my face and told me not to worry, my dad wouldn't do a thing, that I was wrong, I couldn't be cursed, I was the best apple of the bunch. Three cans deep, we swam between telling each other what our friendship meant, how much we loved each other, and comparing our taste in girls, despite me never having actually tasted one.

'Earth to Deena,' Finn said, four cans deep, his eyelids drooping, his smile lopsided.

Finn lived three doors down from me, had been my friend since we were kids, playing superheroes in the nearby church car park, then video games when we got a little older. In the tricky in-between pre-teen years, we drifted but still met up occasionally to borrow graphic novels, until the day Finn told me, at fourteen, shoulders pushed back and face defiant, that he'd kissed a boy on his summer holidays. I'd been filled with an indescribable jealousy, a recognition. We'd been best friends ever since.

I opened up the window to the rain. 'Storm to Deena,' I said. 'Sea to Deena.' I swayed.

Finn snorted. 'Bullshit to Deena.'

I closed the window. Under my breath I whispered, '*Happy birthday to me.*'

I woke with a feeling like a bone stuck somewhere in my windpipe, cutting off my breath. My sheets were all in a tangle. I could hear Finn's snores from the spare room next door. And, in the distance, something like a scream.

I sat up. There was a face at my window, one sunken eye in the gap where the curtains never properly closed. I bolted across the room. When I pulled open the curtains, there was only the quiet street outside and the rain.

The window was open a crack. Around the latch were some long grey hairs.

Three banshees. First a scream; then, when they get closer, grey hairs caught on the threshold of your home.

Fear was a big ship moving fast across the water.

*

I left Finn asleep, threw on some clothes and took the bus to Mandy's. I banged, loudly, on her door. After about three minutes of solid pounding, one of her housemates answered. The corridor behind him was black and he squinted as the daylight poured in.

'Hey, Deena,' he said. 'Looking for Mandy?'

I couldn't think who else I'd have been looking for, but I just nodded. He let me in. I opened Mandy's door and stopped dead.

The previous day, my sister's bedroom had been a mess as usual. Books and folders and notebooks, discarded shoes and dirty clothes on the floor, empty coffee cups and the wrappers of biscuit packets on every surface, the ashtray on the windowsill overflowing with cigarette butts and ash.

Now it was pristine. In the wardrobe, her clothes hung neatly, her towels folded, her shoes polished and stacked facing the same way. On her bedside table the coffee stains and cigarette ash and remains of yesterday's birthday cupcake had been wiped away, and her dog-eared books were arranged alphabetically on her shelves. The bed was perfectly made, with the sheets tucked in and the pillows fluffed up, and a white envelope sitting half camouflaged in the middle of the white bedspread.

4. Bad apples

Inside the envelope was a piece of paper, folded once: a note written in Mandy's hand. It was short. The ink at the end had run, as if from tears, and the last few words were smudged.

Going to the end of the world. Give all my love to my daughter.

5. A funeral for someone who was not dead

Dublin, 2012

I never knew my mother. She died of an aneurysm barely four months after my birth. It was sudden, unexpected and unavoidable. It was not my fault, but I carried it with me.

In the absence of a mother, I had two sisters. Rachel, especially, I told myself, with her busy, no-nonsense nature, her domesticity, her structure and routine, filled the role of mother in my life. Sometimes I even believed it myself.

But sometimes I saw her sitting curled up in an armchair and she looked so tiny, so tiny and still, reading a book or watching TV, that I felt huge looking at her. Huge and wild and restless. Blessed by salt and skull and horns.

If Rachel was like my mother, Mandy was my fairy godmother. The trickster spirit who showed me another world.

5. A funeral for someone who was not dead

Mandy might have been flighty, but she would never leave me. Mandy might have disappeared occasionally, but she said she'd always be there for me. Mandy told stories about ghosts and curses, but she wouldn't really lie to me.

But Mandy had never left like this.

And Mandy had never told me she had a daughter.

I went back home, dazed. Walked into the kitchen, clutching the letter.

Finn, slightly hung-over by the look of him, sat at the table with a plate of rashers and eggs, and a pint glass of orange juice. Rachel was frying mushrooms on the hob.

'Where did you come from?' she said, alarmed. 'I thought you were in bed.'

I stood in the doorway. 'Did you know that Mandy has a daughter?'

'What?' A mushroom slid from the spatula into the pan.

'Did you know. That Mandy. Has a daughter.'

'A *what*?' Finn said, despite himself.

'A daughter.' My face was expressionless, frozen like a thin sheet of ice formed over a puddle.

'Don't be silly,' Rachel said.

I handed her the note without a word and she opened

it with grease-coated fingers and immediately sat down on the floor.

'Oh,' she said, a lost sound. 'Oh.'

It took them a matter of hours to find her car. *Them*, the police, the Gardaí, whom Rachel insisted on calling, convinced that Mandy's letter was a suicide note.

It was parked at the edge of a cliff on the other side of the country, unlocked and empty. A woman out walking early that morning had seen a figure jump from the edge. Had rushed over and looked down, had seen nothing but what looked like splashes of blood on the jagged rocks below, torn clothes tossed by the crashing waves of the stormy sea. A body could be washed away in seconds, pulled under, never to be found. The woman had called the Gardaí to report a suicide.

Two officers came round to break it to us two days later, after they'd traced the car's owner, tracked down her next of kin. 'It's unlikely we'll ever find her body,' one of them told Rachel softly. 'I'm sorry.'

'OK,' Rachel said, her voice scratchier than Mandy's ever had been, her eyes glassy. 'OK.' She looked right through the Garda, said *OK* another few times, and called our father to tell him his eldest daughter was dead.

I locked myself in my room so nobody could make me hear it again.

It rained all through the funeral and the priest mispronounced our family name, thinning the y so that Rys (which we pronounced like the white grain: *rice*) sounded reedy and insincere: *reese*.

None of us corrected him.

'Amanda Marrrie Rrreeeese,' said the priest, the 'r's rolling drunkenly into his vowels in his Kerry accent, 'was a grrreatly loved, rrrespectable young Chrrristian woman who is now living at the rrright hand of the Lorrrd.'

None of us corrected him on that part either.

The rain battered at the stained-glass windows of the church. I turned to Finn, sitting in the pew behind me and Rachel.

'You know Shakespeare didn't invent pathetic fallacy,' I told him, one elbow leaning on the back of my pew. 'But as a literary device it's always been attributed to him. Which is typical really. Dead white guys getting all the credit.'

Finn, who is a guy but is neither dead nor white, said, 'What does that have to do with . . .' He trailed off, took a shaky breath and said softly, 'Are you OK, Deena? Do you need to get some air?'

'Pathetic fallacy,' I said, ignoring his question, ignoring Rachel softly shushing me through her tears, and my father's glare from the end of the pew, 'is when the weather reflects the mood of a play or a story. Sometimes it's nothing but a metaphor: a man walks sad and lonely in the rain. Sometimes it's an omen: the storm signals a battle about to be lost.'

Finn shook his head at me in sympathy. 'And what does this storm signify, Deena?' he asked.

'This one? Oh, that's easy.' I turned back to face the altar and said loud enough for Finn to hear me, 'This one means Mandy isn't really dead.'

6. *Happy families*

Dublin, 2012

After the funeral, we wrung out our wet black clothes. We brushed the mud from our best shoes. We tiptoed round the house so as not to rouse our father, who was currently in the spare room, sleeping off the five whiskeys he'd drunk at the wake.

In the morning, there was a sweet, fruity smell in the house. We thought it was one of our cousins' perfume, but it lingered after everyone left. Rachel opened all the windows, but in the garden the smell was just as strong.

I poked my head into every cupboard, trying not to think of the woman I'd seen in the water on my birthday, before Mandy left. The banshee. How afterwards all the way home I smelled apples, found Rachel pounding them into juice. 'Where is it *coming* from?' I slammed the door of the fridge; no apples in there.

Rachel rubbed her temples. 'Does it matter?' she said.

'It's driving me crazy,' I muttered, teeth gritted. 'Does he have some kind of fruity cologne? Is he just spraying it in every room like he's marking his territory?'

'I don't think it's coming from Dad,' Rachel said, exhaustion in every syllable.

'Well, it's not coming from anything in this kitchen,' I declared, apple search concluded. 'Maybe it's all in our minds?'

'Don't be absurd,' said Rachel.

'Did something, like, crawl into a wall and die or something?' I stared, tapping on the walls, pressing my ear to them as if the smell of apples could speak.

'Stop that,' Rachel said sharply. 'Nothing's died in the walls. It's probably one of our cleaning products. It's fine. It'll go away by itself.'

The kitchen door swung open and suddenly our father was standing in the doorway, an imposing stranger in slippers and a fleece dressing gown. His chin was stuck with day-old stubble, ginger streaked with grey, and he ran his hands through his thinning hair like he was surprised to have ended up here, in the kitchen of the house where he once lived.

I automatically scowled, but Rachel sprang from her spot by the counter, pulled out a chair for him and offered him tea. He sat like a guest in a banquet hall, waiting to be served.

'I want you to pray with me, girls,' said our father when Rachel poured his tea. 'For your sister's everlasting soul.'

'We don't pray,' I started to say, in a clear voice that surprised me, but Rachel shushed me gently by placing a peaceable palm on my shoulder. Dad bent his head to his clasped hands. The lines across his forehead deepened with every sigh.

'Our Father,' he began, 'who art in heaven, hallowed be Thy name.'

'Mandy's a good person.' I cut loudly through our father's prayer. Any fear I'd had of speaking out of turn around him seemed to have disappeared with my eldest sister.

Our father said, 'She was a troubled soul.'

'Well, *maybe*,' I said, before realizing I was speaking, 'do you think that *maybe* if her father hadn't abandoned her as a teenager she wouldn't have been quite so troubled?'

Rachel's eyes were saucers.

'I'm just saying,' I said, each syllable as sharp as knives. 'Might have been a factor.'

Dad looked at me like he'd never really seen me before. And he hadn't, not really. My sisters were around my age when he left us; he packed his things not long after our mother's funeral and got a job as far across the country from us as he could. I'd only just been born. He didn't know me, this man who'd given me life. He didn't know any of us.

'Deena,' he said finally, heavily. 'There's a lot you don't know about your sister.'

This was so exactly what I'd just been thinking about him that I snorted with laughter. 'Yeah, I'll bet,' I said. 'And there's a lot you don't know about me.' I grabbed my cup abruptly and tea sloshed over the side and pattered onto the kitchen tiles. I stalked out into the hall, tea dripping down my fist as I walked.

But I stopped at the bottom of the stairs, suddenly out of steam. I tiptoed back through the dark hall, following my trail of tea drops. The kitchen door was open a crack and from inside I heard our father say my name, say Mandy's, say, 'She puts her on a pedestal. It isn't right.'

'Let her process,' came Rachel's voice, slow and tired. 'She's in denial. She hasn't cried. Let her put her sister on a pedestal if that's what helps her mourn.'

'One day you'll have to tell her. Or she's going to end up exactly the same.'

I waited for Rachel's usual deference, for the way she always showed her throat to our father, rolled over backwards so as not to step a toe out of line. But her soft, peace-keeping voice didn't come. Instead, she said, 'If Deena ends up as half the woman Mandy was, she'll be better than I could ever be.'

There was silence for a long moment, then our father said, 'You girls were put on this earth to test me.'

Rachel spoke, strong and clear. 'Dad, I think you should leave.'

After he left, we covered cakes and sandwiches from the night before with cling film. Rachel drove the empty beer and whiskey bottles to the bottle bank. I changed the sheets on the spare-room bed. Neither of us said a word all morning until Rachel came back with the box, now empty of bottles, and slammed it down so hard the kitchen table buckled. Then she sat heavily on a chair as if that one display of anger had exhausted her completely and she would never be angry again.

So I got angry on her behalf. '*Fuck* him,' I said. '*Fuck* him and his prayers.'

'Deena,' Rachel said.

'What? Deena *what*? You were right there with me.' I put on a gruff voice, quoted, '*She was a troubled soul*. What absolute bullshit. This is Mandy we're talking about.'

'That's right,' said Rachel, her voice breaking like a heart. 'This is Mandy we're talking about. And honestly I can't say this was entirely unexpected.'

For a moment, I couldn't speak.

'We needed to be there for Mandy,' Rachel said, and

her voice was strangled. 'But we weren't. This is all my fault.'

I shoved the plastic bottle box off the table, where it fell on the kitchen floor and cracked all down one corner. 'This is *fine*!' I shouted. 'This is *stupid*. She'll be back in, like, a week. She'll laugh at how Dad just came home for one night. She'll laugh at how he wanted to pray for her immortal soul. She'll laugh at how all these random aunts and uncles turned up and didn't say a single word to us. She'll laugh and tell us she could well have guessed all that. And I'll be saying I told you so. What we need to do now is find Mandy's daughter. She told us about her and you've been completely ignoring that for days – *that's* your fault. *That's* your fault.'

I couldn't read Rachel's face. There was something stricken to it, something broken. Like I'd smacked her. Like I'd sworn inside a church. Like I'd smashed through the table, not just accidentally cracked a plastic box.

I couldn't stand her. I couldn't stand the lot of them.

When I slammed the front door behind me, I could hear my sister start to cry. The air was still sweet with the smell of apples.

I stormed down the garden path, seething. Rachel was right, I hadn't cried. I hadn't stared blankly at things, like she had, whenever I moved. Sometimes, mid-task, she would stop, bend over at the waist as if from cramps. Like she was giving birth, or dying.

My mind was a clear, smooth lake. Whatever Rachel said, I wasn't in denial. I was a woman on a mission. I knew Mandy was coming back. And, in the meantime, I had a secret niece to find.

Online searches thus far had yielded nothing so that day, the day after the funeral, I resolved to go to Mandy's housemates and friends, anybody who might know of her whereabouts, or about the daughter nobody seemed to know she had.

I threw open the garden gate and stood on something that crunched underfoot. I stopped short. Under the sole of my shoe was what looked like a piece of broken comb. Rough, off-white, the teeth jagged and sharp.

My breath caught in my throat and I held on to the gate to steady myself. Tangled round the curling handle of my garden gate were wisps of long silvery hair. My arms prickled, goosebumps rising among the freckles.

Maybe it wasn't a comb. Maybe it was just a bone left by a dog. Maybe it wasn't really made of bone. Just white plastic, broken and yellowed. I didn't want to touch it, to find out.

Stories, I told myself. *Just stories*.

I reached down to pick up the piece and saw something bright white lying on the grass.

An envelope. Inside the envelope was a letter.

Dear Deena, it said.

I knew Mandy's handwriting. It crowded the margins of the books she lent me, it covered every one of my birthday cards in poems and memories, it was scrawled across the notes she left me in her flat if she'd already left when I arrived: *Coffee's still hot, close the window when you head off, love you, Mandy.*

I read the letter, hardly blinking, hardly breathing, start to finish. It was long. Pages and pages of that rushed, spiky handwriting.

Reading it made me dizzy. And when I'd finished, I knew. Knew what I'd suspected ever since the Gardaí came to tell us they had found our sister's car.

Mandy wasn't dead.

Mandy was alive and she wanted me to find her.

This is what the letter said:

Dear Deena,

I want to tell you a story. To explain the curse. To explain our family tree. To explain where I'm going. To help you understand why.

This story starts in London in 1858 with the birth of the first Rys who would come to Ireland, although our family was here forever before

*him – funny how history only remembers the
fathers. But our family curse begins with him – so
I'll begin with his mother.*

*Her name was Marie Lefèvre, épouse Rys. She
was French, married to a wealthy Englishman and
living in London. And from the moment she
conceived her son, our great-great-grandfather,
Gerald Rys Jr, she had the strangest craving for
apples.*

7. A craving for apples

London, 1858, and Donegal, 1879

Marie had a craving for apples. It began with the first small lapping wave of nausea and grew stronger until the waves became an entire sea storm inside her that would not allow her to keep anything down, as if the baby was pushing against the bread, the cheese, the meat and greens with its tiny hands, throwing it all back out.

Our great-great-great-grandfather, her husband, Gerald William Rys, brought her King Pippins and Ashmead's Kernels, the tartest strains he could think of, but none tasted sharp enough to his wife's tongue. He brought her cider apples, crisp and bitter. He brought her cooking apples too sour to eat. But everything she tried tasted too sweet. The bones in her face grew sharper by the day. Finally, her husband bought an orchard west of London and had his gardeners pollinate acre upon acre of different cultivars to find the exact apple his wife craved.

It takes about seven years to grow an apple tree, in the right conditions. The gardeners knew this, knew that at the rate she was going Marie and her baby would be dead within the month, but they did as they were told. They planted seeds and saplings, crossed tart dessert apple trees with those of the sourest cooking strains. They swept pollen into blossoms by hand with paintbrushes, they set up hives and let loose the bees. Meanwhile, Marie lay in bed, rocked by stormy seas. She dreamed of a grey-faced, wild woman with bone combs stuck in her wild hair, a wild baby suckling at her breast. When Marie screamed, it was in the woman's voice. Glass shattered and windows cracked. The doctors shook their heads and sighed.

'She'll be dead by morning,' they said. The servants closed the drapes.

The next morning, in the middle of the newly planted orchard, among the spindly saplings and tiny shoots of seeds, there was a tree. A chance sapling: the cross-pollination of a common English russet with a particularly acidic French *reinette* that resulted in an apple so bracingly tart one had to grit one's teeth to eat it.

It takes around seven years to grow an apple tree. This one had sprung up overnight.

When Marie first ate an apple from the new tree, the baby kicked for the first time, and he continued kicking for the rest of her pregnancy. When he was born, the room smelled of apples.

Gerald William Rys, who was not a man of great imagination, named the cultivar the Rys Russet. He named the baby Gerald William Rys Jr. Marie called the apple *le Lendemain*, which means the next morning. She called the baby *mon amour*.

Gerald William Rys Jr arrived in Ireland at his father's request in the autumn of 1879, holding a letter from his mother (in her native French), a lock of his sweetheart's hair (thin, fair) and a small sapling.

'The juice of these apples runs in your blood,' Marie told him as he climbed aboard the PS *Violet* at Holyhead. 'Plant the tree on your land and your children's blood shall run with it too.'

Gerald tried again and again to plant the sapling, but it would not take root. The problem, he thought, was that the land was not *his* land. The Big House at Glenliath in the barony of Banagh, County Donegal, with its 800 acres of dismal bogs and granite hills, sheep and small stone shacks, belonged to his father, who until now had overseen its tenants from afar, from the warmth and comfort of his London home. But with the bad harvests of the previous years, the hunger and unrest of the tenants, and the rumours of further Land Acts blowing in from Westminster, Gerald William Rys Sr decided to send his eldest son as his agent to supervise the estate. His eldest son had had very little say in the matter.

The place was bleak, grey and cold. Every night the wind howled past the windows and every night it sounded like a woman's screams. The tenants were sullen. The food was bland. Gerald couldn't imagine bringing his sweetheart here, couldn't imagine lasting in this landscape for more than a year.

The land to the west of the estate was too sandy for the sapling, the land to the east too rocky. Everything smelled of the sea. As the months passed and the apple tree refused to take root, Gerald began to associate the smell – salty, fishy, wet with rain – with the unrest of the estate and his unease at the helm of it.

At night the screaming kept him awake.

He took to wandering the hills with the sapling in his arms. The staff of the Big House hushed when he came near. The tenants in their small stone huts averted their eyes when they caught sight of him. When he was out of earshot, the men spat on the ground.

'It's the apple-tree man,' he could hear the children whisper. 'It's the madman. It's the ghost.'

And Gerald did feel ghostlike, as if he might well disappear. He thought of his mother at seventeen, who almost died with him in her womb, brought back to life by the bite of an apple, a fairy tale in reverse. He thought that if only he could persuade his sapling to take root then the tenants would cease their angry simmering, then the rain would stop, then the winds would die down and he would no longer hear the screaming.

One night, after a visit from another local landowner, Gerald got lost. His guest had drunk his way through most of Gerald's wine cellar and had complained all night about taxes and tenants, and Gerald had been desperately, desperately bored. Not entirely sober himself, he picked up his sapling (the branches drooping now, the buds shut tight, the bark growing dull) and set off across the bog in the middle of the night in search of the right spot to plant his orchard.

He had walked for almost an hour in the near-dark of the cloudy sky, under relentless drizzle and through never-ending mud, when he saw the light. A wink, a glimmer, like laughter up ahead. When he ran to the spot, the light appeared to blink out, then reappear further away. Gerald followed it. It danced and twinkled, flitting like an insect, a flickering candle, and Gerald, encumbered with his apple tree, turned his ankles on rocks and stumbled over hillocks, splashed through mud and puddles deeper and deeper into the bog. Then the light went out and did not appear again.

Gerald took another step and the firm ground beneath him gave way to wet, sucking mud. It rose round his ankles, pulling him down, and the more he thrashed and tried to run, the more he sank. Thigh-deep in the bog hole, Gerald cried out, knowing full well there'd be nobody to hear him but the ancient bodies buried under the turf. The wind screamed as he shouted louder, trying to drown him out. For hours Gerald struggled, the sapling thrown to the grassy rocks too far for him to reach, his strength waning, his voice fading, the darkness his only constant.

Then he saw the girl, candle in hand. He'd heard the chambermaids talking about banshees: the howling women, the ones with bone combs and ashen skin, the ones whose voices – wordless screams – if heard, foretold death. He waited for death to take him.

Of course, the girl was not death. The girl that Gerald saw that night in the bog was Mary Ellen Boyle, our great-great-grandmother, which means you now know exactly how this story is going to go.

When the girl pulled Gerald out of the thick black mud, the heavens opened and the misty, drizzly air became sliced through with cold, hard rain. Mary Ellen grabbed Gerald's hand, he hoisted the sapling into his other arm, and they ran through the deluge to the edge of the cliff, to a tiny cottage that might once have been a shepherd's hut, staring out at the stormy sea. It had no windows, doors or roof, but a cluster of hawthorn trees had grown over it, making a canopy to keep out the rain.

Gerald was racked with tremors, shivering so hard his teeth clacked inside his mouth. He could not tell if this was because of the cold, the effort of having struggled inside the bog for hours, or if it was simply the effect this beautiful, ghostly woman was having on him.

When he spoke, his voice was hoarse from having shouted half the night. His voice was faint from wanting.

'Are you death?' he asked the girl.

She only smiled and shook her head, and her hair, under a damp woollen shawl, escaped in copper tangles.

She took him in her arms to warm his bones, to calm his quaking, and if he truly believed she had come to take him to his death he would have gone willingly. He left his mud-covered clothes on the dirt floor of the hovel and she threw down her shawl for them to lie on. If the rain came through the hawthorn roof, neither of them noticed.

In the morning, Gerald put his damp and muddy clothes back on, retrieved his sapling from behind the tiny cottage, and returned to the Big House with the full intention of forgetting this whole misadventure completely.

But he couldn't stop thinking about Mary Ellen. Never mind his wan blonde wisp of a fiancée. Her face drifted in his memory. Did she have green eyes or blue? Mary Ellen's were sea-grey, as light as clouds before dawn. Her face was freckled, flushed with the abrasive salt air of the coast. She was all the more lovely for it. Her arms were roped with muscle, her thighs sturdy where his fiancée's were slim and soft. Mary Ellen looked like she could easily survive the end of days, no matter how starved and pinched her cheeks were underneath their half-apple cheekbones.

While Gerald ate in a warm and comfortable dining room, his workers went hungry, were soon ready for revolt. Inspired by others around the country, Gerald's tenants organized a rent strike. It did not go well. There weren't enough of them for the strike to be effective, and Gerald evicted seven families from his land in one night, calling on the constabulary to break the cottage windows to ensure the families could not return.

The screaming got worse. He could hear it in the daytime. He could hear it as he took his tea. He could hear it as he sat on the lavatory. He could hear it as he wrote a hundred letters to his half-forgotten sweetheart that he never sent, and plaintive missives to his mother to persuade his father to reconsider and send his younger brother here instead.

As the weeks went on, the only light in his constant dark thoughts was Mary Ellen. He went to the abandoned cottage on the cliffs across the bog every night, waited like a shadow by the entrance. And, every night, she met him there.

His heart was pulled by his sheer hatred of this godforsaken place and his obsession with the young woman. Strong arms, strong thighs, freckles in places he'd never before thought that freckles could be. Rough lips chapped by the cold and the sea. Calloused hands he longed for more than his sanity. For a few stolen hours in the middle of every cold and rainy night, the couple kissed and whispered, touched and held and dreamed.

Perhaps he truly loved her, but he hated her country more. At no moment in their secret meetings did he ever mention his sweetheart back in England. The woman to whom he was engaged to be married. The woman who was his ticket out of this awful place, away from the screaming wind and never-ending rain and the sour-faced peasants. Because, once he was married and his new wife was with child, it would simply not be possible to stay on at the Big House. These cliffs, these rocks and bogs were no place to raise a baby. His father would surely agree: the next generation of Ryses would have to return to England, their feet never to touch Irish soil again. He would be more glad of this than he had words to say.

But, until that happened, he met Mary Ellen every night when the moonlight was shrouded in cloud. He kissed her and whispered nothings that were as sweet as ripe apples, but that meant far less to him. What was love, he asked himself, when he would not be here for more than another season? What was love when she was a peasant and he her landlord? What was love when not state nor church nor family would ever bless their union?

Back home, his mother and his fiancée made wedding plans. Their letters to Gerald were full of lace and beads and invitations. They felt to Gerald as though they came from a world away. Far from the tenant agitators, the political unrest, the scowls of the workers, the rain and the screams. Far from the hovel in which he met a girl each night, knowing well that he could never make an honest woman of her.

Meanwhile, Mary Ellen was craving apples.

8. Exit, pursued by a bull

Dublin and Galway, 2012

I turned the last page of the letter over, wanting to be told what happened next. I now realized that Mandy had been researching the family curse. This was what all her notebooks and folders, her library books about nineteenth-century landed gentry had been about. But her letter didn't explain the curse. Barely mentioned it. And it didn't finish the story. Instead, on the final page, Mandy had written an address that was on the outskirts of Galway city.

She had been planning a birthday road trip for me. Cross-country, mapped out by her hand. *I want to tell you a story*, her letter had started by saying. *To explain the curse. To explain our family tree. To explain where I'm going. To help you understand why.*

Mandy had started the journey without me. And it

seemed that she wanted me to follow. Obviously, Galway was the first stop on the map.

I snuck back into the house and packed a small bag. Rachel was in her bedroom with the door shut so I left a note on the kitchen table telling her I was staying with Finn for a few days, then stared blankly out of the top-deck window of the number 130 bus to Dublin city centre, where I would change and get the bus to Galway.

I'd been to Galway a few times before – once with Mandy for some hippie harvest festival her friends were performing at, and a couple of times with Rachel for the Christmas market – but I didn't recognize the address Mandy had written down, had no idea why she'd send me there.

Stopped at a set of traffic lights, I glanced down at the street below and there, standing in front of a small petrol station missing most of its sign, was a bull.

A horse I would have expected. It wasn't unusual for Dublin traffic to slow behind a horse. A cow would have greatly surprised me in the inner city, but I might have chuckled to myself and turned away. But a bull – enormous, slate-grey, with gleaming white horns – a bull was unheard of. I blinked, convinced I was hallucinating.

The bull looked up and met my gaze through the window. He nodded.

I snapped my own head round and stared straight through the front window, heart thudding. The traffic lights changed and the bus trundled on and I didn't look back.

My phone was hot with the map open and I was the moving blue dot. I didn't know what I was looking for until I found it.

The address Mandy had left me was that of a secondary school. Interdenominational by the looks of it. No statues of Mary in alcoves in the walls, no crosses above the doorways. The students didn't wear uniforms so I almost looked like I belonged, slipping through the front gates with my backpack and my earphones, looking for a sign, a reason why my sister had sent me here.

It must have been break time. Students thronged the corridors. I saw hoodies and jeans, hair both dyed and shaved, jewellery on wrists and around necks. Hockey sticks, guitar cases, schoolbags covered with enamel pins. A large noticeboard opposite the library announced music and drama club auditions, helpline numbers, and reminders of the school's LGBT society meeting times. A bumper sticker at the bottom of the board said RESPECT PERSONAL PRONOUNS.

My chest felt tight suddenly, heavy with a sort of

longing. I doubted the noticeboards in my school were aware that one could use a pronoun to which one had not been assigned. I thought about rainbow enamel pins, purple plastic Venus earrings, protest leaflets. My eyes ran over the notices. I wondered how I would have turned out if I'd gone to a school like this.

The wall beside the noticeboard was covered in A5 prints of students' pictures under the heading KNOW YOUR CLASS REPS. She was second from the left.

She had pale skin, light freckles, grey eyes. Her hair was auburn, a reddish chestnut, thick and curled. Her cheeks were like apples and she had a gap between her two front teeth. She was every picture I had ever seen of Mandy at sixteen. Underneath her smiling face, somebody had written *Class 5B: Ida Nolan*.

I had assumed that Mandy's daughter was a child. Eight or nine years old, her birth aligning with one of Mandy's longer disappearances, her gestation somehow gone unnoticed.

I had not imagined that my sister's daughter would be the same age as me.

I waited by the school gates and watched each student as they left. When I saw her, I stood. She was adjusting the strap of her backpack, mouth twisted in concentration, long plait tangling with the strap on her other shoulder.

When she saw me, she stopped. The crowd broke like waves around us.

Later Ida told me that for a second she thought I was Mandy. Less than a second. Just enough time to realize that I couldn't possibly be. That I was barely a year older than her. That there was nothing in my wide eyes to suggest that I had known she'd be here.

But here she was. And here I was. We were undeniably family.

9. A family reunion

Galway, 2012

I said her name aloud, to test it. 'Ida?'

I knew I'd mispronounced it by her slight wince. Not *Eye*-da, then. *Eee*-da probably. I wondered who had named her, her father or Mandy.

Emotions played over her face until she seemed to reach a decision and pulled out of the crowd to join me by the gate.

'You're her sister,' was the first thing she said to me. 'Amanda's.' Her knuckles were white around her bag's strap.

'Mandy.' My voice was faint. 'We call her Mandy.'

'Mandy,' Ida said. 'I'm sorry for your loss.' She winced again, spoke louder to cover it. 'Which one are you, Rachel or Deena?'

'I'm Deena.' My voice had almost disappeared. I wished I hadn't come here.

'Deena.'

We stood and stared at each other.

'Look,' Ida said, after several interminable moments of silence, 'why don't we go round the back of the assembly hall, away from the noise?'

I nodded mutely and followed my niece as she strode, purposeful and self-possessed, back through the gate against the throng, giving waves and short nods in response to the greetings coming towards her from students and teachers. She was tall, like Mandy, wiry where I was all softness. She led me to a set of stone steps round the back of the building, in front of a sign that said FIRE EXIT.

She dropped her bag and sat. I leaned awkwardly against the railings.

'I guess you saw me at the funeral,' she said to her hands. 'I'm sorry I didn't come over. Introduce myself. Maybe I should have, but it was already kind of too much, you know? I never met her, but I'm sure you know that. My dad barely even talks about her. I don't really know why I went. Dad still has no idea that I did.'

I let each scrap of information sink in. I hadn't seen Ida at the funeral. I'd been imagining her to be a little girl, perhaps unaware of her biological family, having been, I'd assumed, adopted as a baby. I could never have imagined this bright, vibrant girl my own age, tall and slim, popular and beautiful: a more wholesome version of my sister. This girl who was everything I wasn't. This girl who knew my name.

'She never mentioned you,' I whispered.

Ida closed her eyes, briefly, as if she'd felt a sudden pain.

'Then why are you here?'

I dropped down onto the step beside her. She wasn't what I'd expected, but I knew things she didn't. She was poised but nervous. I could tell by the way she twisted her hair round her fingers, brushed dust from her jeans, straightened her bag on the step, touched her hair again.

'I'm here because she sent me.' I looked at my niece as I said it. 'Ida. Mandy. Your mother. She isn't dead.'

The look she gave me was sharp, direct. 'I was at her funeral.'

Because there was no way of making any of this less surreal for either of us, I took out Mandy's letter, and the brief note she'd left on her bed before she disappeared. Ida read the note first. I watched her eyes take in every word.

Going to the end of the world.

I watched her eyes narrow to make out the second tear-smudged sentence, made all the less legible now by repeated foldings and unfoldings.

Give all my love to my daughter.

I watched her eyes fill with tears.

'I found this stuck in my garden gate this morning.' I touched the letter she held in her lap. Ida twitched reflexively, as if afraid I would take it from her. 'It's how I knew to come here.'

Ida said nothing. She started to read.

It was a long letter. A long story. She didn't rush through it, like I did, hands shaking, breath held. She took her time, drank it all in. She didn't once look up from the page.

In my pocket, my phone pinged. It was Finn.

> Where the fuck are you, Deena?
> Rachel's after calling Mam because
> you said you'd be staying here for
> a few days. I had to bullshit about
> you being up in my room but not
> wanting to talk. Mam's only
> buying it because of the funeral.
> Haven't heard from you all day.
> Starting to freak out here. Tell
> me where you are or I'm calling
> Rachel

> Don't freak out. I'm in Galway.
> Explanation forthcoming.

Finn's response was immediate and contained an uncharacteristic number of exclamation points.

> WTF ARE YOU DOING IN GALWAY
> THAT DOESN'T HELP IN THE
> SLIGHTEST!!!!!!!

A small sound from Ida, not quite a gasp. She turned over the last page of the letter, then turned it back again.

'That's where it ends?'

I put my phone down, ignoring Finn's incoming call. 'Yeah. With the address of your school.'

Ida took a breath, shook her head. 'She sure could tell a story, your sister.' She stacked the pages so their edges aligned perfectly, shushed the lot back in the envelope. 'What's the deal with this curse she talks about at the start?'

I tried to shuffle my thoughts into order. The deal with the curse was still a little blurry to me. 'Mandy believes there's a curse on the Rys family, heralded by three banshees.'

'Banshees,' said Ida, one eyebrow raised. 'Like ghosts who scream before somebody dies.'

'That's right. Only here the scream is part of the warning.' I had to swallow hard before speaking, brushing aside the scream of the woman in the bay, the long grey hairs wrapped round the gate. Nowhere in Mandy's explanations had she said anything about actually seeing these ghosts. 'And it doesn't necessarily announce a death.'

'So what is it then?'

'Before she left, Mandy told me that there's a curse on the bad apples of our family tree. That our family will cast off anyone who doesn't conform, and when these bad apples turn seventeen they fall off the family tree, metaphorically speaking, and the curse comes to them. You'll know you're a bad apple – that you've been cast off and cursed – when the banshees come for you.'

Ida's eyebrow was still raised. 'What happens when they come for you?'

'She says it's different for every bad apple. Losses, tragedies, even death maybe. Things that could be chalked down to bad luck, but that are really a curse on bad apples.'

'Do *you* believe this?' Ida asked. 'I kinda can't tell.'

I let out a sigh. I kinda couldn't tell either. 'I don't know. Mandy has always believed in all sorts of things that I haven't. But there are things I can't explain. And honestly there are things that are starting to scare me.'

Ida nodded at me to go on.

I recounted my vision of the banshee in the bay. How there were silvery-grey hairs caught in my window, tangled round the handle of my gate when I found Mandy's letter. As I spoke, I watched my niece's face carefully for signs of disbelief or scorn but found neither.

'Eyes play tricks sometimes,' she said.

'I know. I'm not discounting that. That's probably what's happening. My sister told me all these things and my imagination ran with them. I'm just telling you what I think I saw. I'm just telling you the things I can't explain. Like the fact that this letter appeared in our garden gate this morning, almost a week after she disappeared.'

'You know she could have sent this before she died.'

'She didn't.'

Mandy's daughter considered me. 'Is it crazy that I kinda believe you?'

'Only as crazy as this whole situation.'

Her gaze was unwavering, cool but curious. 'I think I saw her after the funeral,' she said.

10. *After the funeral*

I heard Ida's words but didn't understand them.

'It could have been someone who looked like her,' said Ida. 'Like you said about the woman in the water. A trick of the light.'

'Wait,' I said. 'Back up. After the funeral when? What did she look like? Where was she?'

Ida bit her lip at my eagerness, looked unsure. 'I *think* I saw her,' she said again. 'Yesterday after the funeral, a few hours after they buried her. In Dublin, in the street, in the dark, in the rain. I couldn't make her out very well. She was looking the other way. I just thought it might have been her.'

'No,' I breathed. 'You must have seen her. She must have been there. She's alive; I know she is.'

Ida twisted her hair round her fingers, frowned. 'I don't know, though, Deena,' she said. 'I mean, how could I be sure? I'd never seen her before in my life. All I had were a few pictures of her as a teenager with my dad.'

'You'd know,' I said. 'You'd know your own mother.'

'Up until two days ago,' said Ida, 'I knew nothing about my mother.'

From somewhere nearby, there came a sudden scream. I jumped, then told myself it was only children in the playground, kids messing about in front of the school. Ida didn't seem to hear it. She teased the end of her plait with her fingers.

'My dad was telling my aunt on the phone how he met Mandy,' she said. 'Except he called her Amanda. He thought I was asleep upstairs, but I heard everything he said. Everything he'd never told me.'

Ida stared at the end of her plait, at her fingers twisting the strands of her hair, and, echoing Mandy's letter perhaps without realizing it, told me what she'd heard like it was a story. Something happening to somebody else. This is what she said.

Ida's dad was nervous, breathless on the phone, didn't know what to do. For a week, Amanda Rys had been dominating his dreams. Every night he'd woken in tears, arms reaching for something he had never been able to hold. He hadn't looked her up in years, but that morning he typed Ida's mother's name into the search bar on his laptop. The first thing that came up was a funeral notice.

In his strange and sudden grief, he called his sister. And, while Ida listened in, he spoke about the woman he had once known.

Jeremy Nolan didn't know much about Amanda Rys, but he knew she was a liar. When they met in a crowded pub in Galway seventeen years ago, she asked him to buy her a drink to celebrate the end of her master's degree, told him she was in her mid-twenties.

Their time together was brief, electric: two weeks of deep intensity until he awoke one morning to find her gone, realized he'd never asked her surname, had no idea where she lived.

When Ida said that, I let out a little laugh. 'Mandy has that effect on people.'

'Yeah,' she said. 'I figured.'

'How did he find her then, in the end?'

'He didn't find her,' said Ida. 'She found him.'

Ten months later, one Sunday dinnertime, Ida's father answered the door to an infant in a car seat on his front porch, a taxi turning out of his driveway, red curls in the back seat. Under the child's blanket was a birth certificate for Ida Miranda Nolan, daughter of Jeremy Nolan and Amanda Rys.

In the years that followed, Ida's father taught himself

not to think of Amanda much. He now had a full name, had the means by which to look her up, to contact her, but as time went by he wanted to less and less. His parents and family rallied round him, became the village that helped to raise a child. Leaving Ida had been Amanda's choice, he told himself. There must have been a reason she had never come back to him, to her baby. He had to respect that, even if he would never understand it. She could come to him, he figured, if she ever wanted.

'You'd think he could have let me decide that for myself,' said Ida. 'You think he could have given me the choice.'

'He didn't tell you *anything* about her?'

'Only stories. Fairy tales.'

Ida's father built Amanda into a fairy spirit, at the same time larger than life and far too small to fit comfortably into Ida's world. Little by little, the myth that was Amanda grew smaller. Until two days ago.

Jeremy Nolan was unaware that his daughter had heard every word he spoke, that the moment he hung up on his sister Ida typed her mother's name into a search bar on her phone.

The funeral notice on RIP.ie was brief. Stark black pixels that stayed on the back of Ida's eyelids like a photo negative. She read them every time she blinked.

Ida thought it strange that she should cry. She hadn't

yet let herself imagine she might ever find her mother. But the thought must have been there, somewhere deeper down. When she realized she'd never get that chance, it tore a hole right through her.

When she left for Mandy's funeral the following day, Ida told her father her school had organized a last-minute field trip to Dublin. He had no reason to suspect his daughter was lying – other than the fact that she owed half her DNA to Mandy Rys. Ida was clearly a golden girl, bright and focused, friendly and open, so different to her summer storm of a mother. Even I could tell already that she studied hard, had plenty of friends. She probably never got in trouble, never talked back. She seemed unfailingly honest, to the point of bluntness, so it made sense that, to her father's knowledge, she'd never told more than a white lie in her life.

He signed her fake permission slip and asked no further questions, just told her to let him know when her bus came back to Galway in the evening so he could pick her up from the station.

After the funeral, Ida's head was a wild wood of words, each branch a sentence she'd heard in the churchyard: the drone of the priest in his rain-speckled robes, the whispers of the family (her family) in their damp mourning clothes, the condolences of strangers under large umbrellas.

Ida heard the words 'I'm sorry for your loss' so many times that the sentence was stripped of meaning, but nobody was saying it to her. She'd placed herself apart, hidden her hair under the hood of her raincoat, covered half her face with her scarf. She looked exactly like her mother but nobody saw her. She was sidestepped by pall-bearers, looked over by the blank-faced family, assumed to be a distant relative from out of town. Which was true, except for the distance.

And, from the sidelines, Ida heard the words whispered out of the corners of the mouths of neighbours, of teachers, of family friends: *suicide, crazy, bad apples, the lot of them.*

These words dug under her skin. Maybe this family, all held apart – nobody hugging, nobody crying but for the woman with the dark red hair and neat mourning clothes – really were nothing but a bunch of bad apples, not even worth her time. She had no history with these people. No kinship apart from a striking physical resemblance.

She left without telling us that she was Mandy's child.

After the funeral, Ida took a bus back to the depot in the city, wet to the skin. On her way to the station, she stopped at the statue of the four angels below Daniel O'Connell, staring out in four different directions. There were still bullet holes in them from the Easter Rising in 1916 – a pockmark on the breast, a shot straight to the stone heart.

Ida's heart was stone and every word she'd heard that morning was a bullet wound.

She climbed the slick marble and she watched the world melt. She held her face out to the blessed rain. That's how she spotted the only other person standing still in the downpour.

A woman on the bridge right in front of the base of the statue, half turned, staring at the river. A woman with wet red hair.

It was her. Amanda Rys. It was Ida's mother. Her mother, whose funeral Ida had just secretly attended.

Her mother, who was supposed to have died five days before.

Ida spoke for a long time, omitting nothing – not the words she'd overheard, not her rejection of our family, not her continual anger at having been abandoned by her mother, my sister. Tears welled up in my eyes, brushed softly down my cheeks when I blinked.

Our phones both vibrated beside us, at intervals, but remained untouched.

'They were saying at the funeral how they didn't find her body.' Ida said the words softly. 'How they found torn scraps of her clothes, blood on the rocks. How there was no chance she'd have survived. How they sent divers but she could have been washed far out to sea.'

'She wasn't,' I said, my tone matching hers, my voice thick with tears. 'Because she's still alive. You know that. You saw her.'

'I'm not sure what I saw.'

'But you *know*,' I insisted. 'You can feel it. You're her daughter. You'd know it if she'd died.'

Ida gave a small laugh. 'I don't think that's science.' She checked her phone. 'My friends want to know where I am,' she said, standing. 'I was supposed to meet them after class. Just give me a sec to talk to them so they stop freaking out. I've five missed calls already. Next thing they'll be ringing my dad.'

Ida moved away from the steps, towards the side of the building, phone to her ear. I watched how fast her mouth moved when she spoke, made the same shapes as Mandy's. I watched how she touched her hair unconsciously, exactly like her mother. I caught myself making the same gesture.

My hair was short and often tangled, carrots to Mandy's copper. And Ida's. I fluffed up my curls and shook my head to tousle them and in the corner of my vision something rustled. I jumped to my feet, imagining rats, but seeing – half a second later – the whisper of long silvery strands of hair floating down the high grey wall.

Sometimes shock is a splash of cold water.

The wall was blank concrete cracked with climbing weeds. The only other soul I could see was Ida, behind me, voice low and insistent on the phone. There was nobody here; there was no explanation. Although I had agreed with Ida that all this was surely my eyes playing tricks, I had to fight the urge to run away. And something else caught my eye, something that was neither tangled hair nor ghost: white paper, trapped beneath a small stone.

It was an envelope. Inside was a letter, bulging. Ten thick pages covered in rushed, spiky writing.

'What's wrong?' Ida called out behind me. She appeared at my elbow before I could find the words to speak.

Dear Deena, the letter started.

A letter from my sister, right there, basically nowhere, the place she'd sent me. Left under a stone as if she'd somehow known we would sit on the steps round the back of the assembly hall. As if she was watching us while we spoke.

Ida's breath warmed my shoulder. 'That's not—'

'It's Mandy.'

'But that's not possible.'

I walked five careful paces backwards until I reached the railings and slowly sat down on the top step. 'She said to come here. She gave this address. I thought it was just to find you. But she must have wanted me to find this too.'

'But, Deena, that's not *possible.*' I just about registered Ida sitting beside me, my eyes so focused on the page that nothing outside my sister's words existed. 'What if we'd just talked at the gate? What if we'd gone into an empty classroom? What if we'd just walked away?'

'Somebody knew we'd come here,' I whispered, a shiver.

Ida and I raised our heads to look around. A blank grey wall, weeds, rustles. Emptiness and silence.

'No.' Ida shook her head, touched her hair, rubbed at her arms. 'That's not possible.'

I breathed out. 'None of this is possible.' And I started to read.

Dear Deena,
I'm sorry. This is hardly the best way to tell you this
story, but it's all I've got time for. You'll
understand. You'll understand it all in the end. I
thought I wouldn't have to rush but here we are.
Rushing.

I told you to look out for the banshees who herald our family curse. To begin to fear if you hear them scream. You'll understand why I have to hurry.

There are three of them, I told you that. The first comes alone, but the other two soon follow. That seems to be the pattern. Reports are mixed. My sources aren't always reliable. But in my experience that's how it happens. When it starts, you'll hear the first one's screams. When the second joins her, she leaves grey hairs from her bone comb caught in your window or outside your door. You'll know the third has come as well when you wake up with scratches on your skin; you'll know it's too late when the three of them have touched you.

Mary Ellen was the first to learn this because it was she who cast the curse. She did it unknowingly, but still she did it, and now the three ghosts haunt our family. I don't know where they came from. Maybe they were always there. But, since Mary Ellen, the three banshees have heralded the curse that nudges each bad apple right off our family tree.

11. *Three banshees*

Donegal, 1880

Mary Ellen was pregnant. She was about to turn seventeen. She was only aware of one of those things.

On the eve of her seventeenth birthday, in the near-dark of crescent moonlight moving between deep grey clouds, she met Gerald at the cottage on the cliff. The night was cold and he had brought blankets: rough woollen things that were habitually used for horses, the only kind he could take from the house without raising suspicion. He had also brought two green-and-yellow-speckled apples, bought at the market that morning, especially for her. Mary Ellen saw these gifts – the blankets, the apples – as proof of Gerald's love. As evidence that he would soon ask her to marry him.

'Your sapling,' she said, her mouth full of the sweet, tart taste of his gift. 'Is it an apple tree?'

Gerald nodded, kissed her neck. Everywhere, the smell

of apples. That morning, before leaving for the market, he had received a letter from his mother announcing that she and his sweetheart would visit the following week. *Some plans must be made in person*, Marie had written. *And it has been so long since you have seen your love.*

Gerald knew that tonight, once Mary Ellen was asleep, he would slip away home, to continue his preparations for the visit.

'It was a gift,' Gerald told her, his mind still on the letter. 'From my mother. A tree to plant in this new land. She told me to cherish it like a prized possession, a family heirloom.'

He could have told her what his mother believed the tree symbolized, but in his short time administrating his family's estate Gerald had become a man of logic, fast in the footsteps of his father. A woman's flights of fancy – tall tales of seeds growing into trees overnight, of magical apples that had saved his mother's life – these were only stories. Things his mother told him to lull him to sleep as a child. The tree was just a sapling. Something sentimental. Still, he could not deny his deep need to find soil in which to plant it.

Mary Ellen was also a woman of logic. But her logic dictated that if all evidence seemed to point to magic then it would be unwise, logically, to discount it. Unlike

Gerald, Mary Ellen was at home in her wild landscape. A woman of rock and bog, salt and sea wind grating her skin. Mary Ellen had seen the wisps in the darkness, had heard the keening of grey ladies in the night before unexpected deaths. She knew not to walk inside a fairy ring, never to cut a hawthorn tree. Had Gerald told her the truth about the sapling, she would have treated it with the reverence it deserved. Especially once she knew about the baby.

Yet already Mary Ellen felt a strange connection to the half-dead, drooping sapling that sat inside the main door of the Big House in its round clay pot. And that night, wrapped up in rough blankets and in her lover's arms, the scent of apples still sharp on her skin, she dreamed only of the sapling. In her dream, it broke through the clay of its pot and laid down roots that ripped up the foundations of the Big House. It grew taller than the house by half, rained down apples like grenades that broke the windows and the roof, let in the rain and the harsh sea air, which mingled with the apples' sweet, sharp smell.

Mary Ellen woke to hailstones tearing through the overhanging leaves of the hawthorn tree, hitting the blankets hard enough to bounce back off again, sending shivers through her bones. She was alone.

When she threw off the blankets, she found long silvery-grey hairs tangled round her fingers. Strands were caught between the stones of the broken walls, were fluttering in the empty windows. A noise like a fox's scream sounded in the night. Mary Ellen shivered without quite knowing why.

And, at that moment, she felt something moving, deep inside her. Not her usual pangs of hunger, knots of muscle from working the land. This was a stirring, a quickening.

It did not take her long to understand what it was.

While Mary Ellen waited impatiently for her love to return so that she could tell him of her fate, Gerald was lost in preparations. He did not know how the excitement of her new knowledge thrilled her, filled her mind during long days toiling on the hard land and longer nights waiting for him.

For a whole week, Gerald did not leave the Big House to see Mary Ellen, only busied himself with making this inhospitable place as pleasing as possible for his sweetheart and his mother. He ordered new linen, washed and starched; he sent the servants for fresh flowers, fruit, fish.

Each night Mary Ellen sneaked out of her home and went to the cottage, and each night she waited alone. In the morning, when she untangled herself from the dew-damp blankets, rearranged her wrinkled clothes, she noticed raised red lines like scratches running over her legs and arms. She trembled in the morning light, told herself it was nothing but the brambles, twigs caught in her clothes that had marked her skin without her knowledge. She went back to work and returned again to the cottage after nightfall, when her family slept.

The night before his guests were to arrive, Gerald met Mary Ellen one final time at the cottage on the cliff.

'My mother is coming,' he told her, still unable to speak of the woman who would soon be his wife. 'I won't be able to sneak out like this. Things will have to change.'

Mary Ellen took his hand and placed it on the slight, tight mound of her belly. 'Things are already changing,' she said.

When Mary Ellen told him, Gerald smelled apples. A rotten, mulchy, sickly-sweet smell. He shook and shook his head. He backed out of the cottage, coat sleeves catching in the hawthorn branches, feet slipping in the mud.

'My love,' said Mary Ellen. 'Wait—'

Our great-great-grandfather turned and fled.

Mary Ellen stood in shock for so long a fox whispered right past her, and when his bushy tail had swished away she shook herself and followed her lover home. She knocked quietly on the back door of the Big House and stood for a long time before it was opened. When the light of the kitchen spilled out into the dark, the cook stood silhouetted in the doorway. She took in the sight of Mary Ellen: her cheeks flushed, her eyes bright, the small mound of her belly barely hidden under her dress. The cook knew that there was only one reason a pregnant peasant girl would come to the landlord's house in the middle of the night. But she didn't say anything, only called for the landlord, who wouldn't even let the girl into the kitchen, but sent the staff away while he spoke to her on the threshold.

Gerald's face was livid, scarlet patches on his cheeks and forehead.

'I told you never to come here,' he said.

Mary Ellen fought fury with fury. 'I'm carrying your child.'

Gerald could hear rustling by the door that led to the rest of the house, knew his staff were surely listening. Rumours spread on nights like this, under the cold darkness. Who knew what truths could reach the ears of his mother, his future wife? Who knew how long he would have to live out his penance in this godforsaken place if his sins were ever discovered?

Gerald allowed his voice to rise. 'Lying girl,' he spat. 'Little slut.'

Mary Ellen recoiled as if he'd struck her.

Gerald spoke louder. 'How dare you come here looking

for a handout? That bastard isn't mine, and well you know it. How dare you try to ruin my good name?'

'Gerald,' Mary Ellen said, her voice choked.

'Do not presume to know me, girl!' Gerald's voice boomed, his words theatrical, affected. 'Now go home and tell your family of your disgrace. You'll get no charity here.'

The next morning, he evicted her entire family. He sent the constabulary to break the windows and doors of their tiny cottage so they couldn't come back. There was nothing they could do but watch, shock still thrumming through their bodies.

When it was done, Mary Ellen's parents and siblings gathered up their meagre belongings and began the long walk south, towards what family they had left, towards survival of a sort. Mary Ellen stayed behind. She was seventeen, unmarried, pregnant; this was clearly all her fault. Her family did not expect her to join them. She was no longer one of them.

For the second time, she sneaked up to the back door of the Big House. She didn't know what she would do. She wanted to break the door down, climb the stairs to where Gerald's guests were sleeping. She wanted to tell them everything. Wanted to hear their cries and curses, wanted her lover to share in her disgrace.

Mary Ellen had lost everything. Gerald had lost nothing. But breaking into his home would do nothing but land her and her baby in the nearest jail.

Consumed with grief and frustration and rage, Mary Ellen spat on the ground. She creaked the back door open, crept through the long hall of the Big House and grabbed Gerald Rys's precious sapling. Then she ran away, hoisting the tree in her ropy arms with our great-grandfather kicking in her belly.

The night was dark, a closed door. The moon was new.

Mary Ellen knew the land she walked through. Unlike Gerald with his expensive boots, his hat, his belly full of wine, she had wandered these fields, these rocks and stretches of uncut peat, for years. She knew not to follow the wisps. Her feet found each steady tussock, every gap in stone walls to lead her away from the bog and towards the sea.

When she reached the cottage at the edge of the cliff where this baby had been made, she stopped and watched the waves crash far below her. Her heart was a jagged coastline. She dropped her pack of meagre belongings, what food she had scavenged, her woollen shawl. Her grip on the sapling was fierce and furious.

The wind tried to beat her back. Mary Ellen held the sapling high in her arms and went to throw it into the sea. From somewhere behind her, she heard a woman scream.

In shock, she dropped the sapling and it landed at her feet. The clay pot cracked and soil spilled out. She turned. Standing on the rocks before her, blurred by the rain and the darkness, blurred by Mary Ellen's own fear, were three old women, each with grey skin and wild eyes. The first's mouth was wide, filled with unnaturally sharp teeth. The second had long, matted grey hair with bone combs stuck in the tangles. The third had a wicked grin and pointed nails at the ends of her long fingers. They clustered close.

The stories said that the scream of a banshee foretold a death in the family. Mary Ellen clutched her belly, but the three banshees shook their heads. Their hair was all grey tangles, but it stuck out the way Mary Ellen's did. Their fingers were long like Mary Ellen's. Their cheeks, now sunken, could once have been apples. Their chins were just as sharp.

As one, the three women reached out their hands. They curled their fingers, beckoned. Mary Ellen's heart hammered like boots through a cottage door.

'No,' she said. She bent and gathered the sapling in her arms. 'No.'

She turned to face the ocean, churning dark green below her, so far down she could feel the pull, so stormy she could feel the spray. This cliff, this moment, felt like the end of the world.

When she threw the sapling down onto the crashing rocks, Mary Ellen heard the banshees scream.

The wind howled and the spray of the sea flew over the cliff face. Mary Ellen screwed up her eyes against the lashing rain. When she opened them again, the three old hags were gone.

Mary Ellen's stomach lurched. Her feet hurt. Her breasts were tender. Her head was tight.

She had done what she meant to do: she had stolen Gerald's precious apple tree, the one he carried around with him, the one he kept alive in its clay pot because it wouldn't take root on his land. It wasn't much punishment, but it was all she had.

She had no way of knowing how powerful the tree had been. What magical protection would have been found in its branches, in its fruit.

Slowly, she turned from the cliffside with her shawl wrapped tight around her and a packet of food in her arms, and she followed the road south.

And the curse she had unwittingly cast on the bad apples of our family followed her.

12. *Fine apple cider*

Galway and Sligo, 2012

Sometime during the reading – her head so close to mine her hair tickled my cheek – Ida had worked her plait loose, her fingers unconsciously smoothing, untangling, snapping split ends.

Her teeth worried at her lips. 'I just don't get how we found this,' she said. 'Lying there right in front of us.'

I didn't say anything. I simply pointed to the Sligo address on the last page of the letter. Ida eyed it suspiciously, then tapped the details into her phone.

'Two hours north by car. Looks like a house,' she said, her phone on satellite view. She zoomed in closer and read the words next to the little red pin. 'Market View Bar. Your sister wants us to go to a *pub*?'

'Us?' I said.

'You don't honestly think I'd let you keep following these letters all by yourself? I'm coming with you, Deena.'

Her eyes were the same grey as Mandy's, but lighter, brighter. 'OK,' I said, my relief like welcome rain on a hot day. 'Thank you.'

'Just let me call my best friend,' she told me. 'I definitely can't tell my dad about this, so I'm going to need an alibi.'

While Ida called her best friend, I called mine.

'Don't move,' was the first thing he told me. 'I'm coming to get you.'

'What? No. No, I have to go to Sligo.'

'*Sligo?* Why the fuck do you have to go to Sligo?'

I took a breath and summarized my day so far to Finn. There was silence for a long time on the other end of the line.

'Finn?' I said. 'You still there?'

'Yeah,' he answered finally. 'I'm just trying to decide if you're serious or going crazy.'

'Serious.' I rolled my eyes even though he couldn't see me. 'Obviously.'

There were another few minutes of silence, in which I could tell my best friend was wrestling with something. Eventually, he said, 'Where in Sligo?'

The bus from Galway to Sligo took almost three hours, stopping at every small town along the way. The countryside was green and grey outside the window, with the kind of sunlight that cuts through underneath the clouds, sharpens each blade of grass until the whole landscape is shining.

I took pictures of both of Mandy's letters and sent them to Finn, who was on a different bus, from Dublin, coming to meet us in Sligo. We would arrive at about the same time. He kept up a steady stream of exclamation marks to my messages as he read them, echoing my and Ida's feelings succinctly.

'I would have told on Gerald,' Ida said, as a quick pattering of light rain danced across the bus window behind her head. 'I would have hammered on the door until he came down, told his whole family.'

'You'd've ended up in jail, like she said.'

To me, Mary Ellen's revenge on Gerald made sense. She knew she couldn't hold him to account, couldn't tell his family the truth. She knew it would be her word against his, and that he held all the power. So instead she did the only thing she knew would really hurt him. She couldn't have known that by destroying his prized possession, his precious apple-tree sapling, she had cursed the lot of us – her own unborn baby included.

Ida was clearly somebody whose father had taught her from the moment she showed up on his doorstep that she deserved respect. Somebody who could speak out, speak her truth without repercussions. Somebody not accustomed to secrets, or to shame. She might look like Mandy, but there was something straightforward about her that put her in direct contrast to her mother.

Maybe *I* was more like Mandy than I thought.

'I still don't understand,' she said, 'what exactly the curse is supposed to be. You know? Like, OK, at the turn of the last century an unwed teenage girl getting pregnant and being abandoned, I get that. But I don't understand why Mandy thought something bad was going to happen to you. You seem perfectly normal to me.'

A nice, normal girl. I winced.

'I am perfectly normal,' I said. 'I just . . .' An errant raindrop raced down the bus window. 'I suppose not everybody is of the same opinion.'

'What do you mean?'

The faces of the girls in school floated past my eyes like disembodied talking heads. Then Rachel's. Our father's. 'Like . . . my dad. He's very . . . traditional. Very religious, conservative. He still believes that a woman's place is truly in the home. Which is actually backed up by our constitution, you know, so he clearly isn't alone.'

Ida rolled her eyes. 'Yeah, but nobody *actually* thinks that any more.'

'You'd be surprised.'

Ida said, 'Deena, if your family is like that, *they* sound like the bad fucking apples, not you' – and I finally heard my sister in her words.

'And yet we're the ones who are cursed.'

'Do you really believe in this curse?' There was no trace of ridicule in Ida's voice.

'I don't know,' I said. 'But Mandy would have researched all this meticulously. When it comes to finding answers, she's relentless. She said Mary Ellen heard the banshees scream. Found their grey hairs tangled round her things. Woke up with their scratches on her skin. And look what happened to her.' I tapped Mandy's letter, making it flutter.

'But she got pregnant before her seventeenth birthday,' said Ida. 'And from Mandy's story it sounds like she wanted the baby. Loved it. Kept it safe.'

'But it was illegitimate. Back then that was a huge deal. Enormous. You read what happened, how her whole family was evicted. How they just left her.'

'I know.' Ida pushed her hair behind her ears. 'But I'm just saying it sounds like *that* was the curse. Not that she got pregnant – that was before her birthday, with someone she loved – but that her lover rejected her and her family wouldn't have anything to do with her. Do you know what I mean?'

Her hair fell back across her cheeks. She looked so

like Mandy. 'I hadn't thought of it like that,' I said, a strange lump forming in my throat. 'But you're right.'

Ida touched her hair, straightened her necklace. 'What do you really think we're going to find at the end of this . . . journey, treasure hunt, whatever you want to call it?' she asked.

I watched the fields roll by, sharp and bright. 'I think we're going to find Mandy,' I said.

'But what if—'

'I think we're going to understand the curse properly. If there even is a curse.'

'But—'

'I think she's gone to break it. At the end of the world. I think the end of the world is somewhere real, and she's gone there to break the curse.'

Things were beginning to make sense, slot into place. Mandy's reaction to Dad having overheard my coming out to Rachel, so uncharacteristic, was because of the curse. She didn't think I was a bad apple because I was gay. She thought I was cursed because of how our father reacted. On the morning of my seventeenth birthday.

That was why my sister disappeared so suddenly. She left to break the curse.

She was doing it for me. Before anything terrible happened to me.

*

We arrived at the end of the market, stalls shutting down for the evening, the scent of soap and seafood still in the air. Children fished the last sweets from deep buckets set out in rows while dogs lapped fallen ice cream from the pavements. There was a match showing in one of the pubs and every so often the sound of rowdy cheers spilled out of the open doors into the street.

We stepped into the dark interior of the pub, a wash of barley and hops hitting our nostrils. There was a girl pulling pints behind the bar, chatting animatedly to some tourists. She was our age maybe, wearing a grey tweed waistcoat over a pale pink shirt. She had short, choppy brown hair, dramatic eyeliner and an electric smile that I could only look at out of the corner of my eye.

When we walked in, her eyes swung from me to Ida and back again. 'I know you two,' was the first thing she said.

'I . . . don't think so.' Ida's expression was bemused.

The girl stared at me. 'Someone who looks just like you then. Tall, red hair. The same grey eyes.'

'Oh,' I breathed. 'Mandy.'

The girl's own eyes were large and so dark I could hardly distinguish the iris from the pupil. Speaking was suddenly difficult.

'Is that her name?' the girl asked. 'Mandy? She seemed

really familiar, but maybe that was some weird sense of déjà vu. She looked like you two. Stormy eyes.'

'My sister,' I whispered to the girl. 'Ida's mother.'

The girl made an *ah* face, nodded like that somehow made sense.

'Mandy was here?' Ida twisted her head around, searching. 'When? How long ago? What did she look like? What did she say?'

'She passed by here. We can tell the ones passing by. She liked our cider.' The girl stared straight at me. 'I knew there was something about her. Some reason she stuck in my head. You're trying to find her. How come?' She tilted her head, clearly sensing a story. I couldn't explain, felt my sister's presence too keenly to talk about anything but the possibility of another letter, another clue, another step closer to her.

'Did she leave something for us?' I asked, my tongue still too heavy for my mouth.

'What would she have left?' the girl asked.

'A letter,' I said, too fast. 'No stamp or return address. It would be thick, full of pages.' *Full of secrets*, I thought.

'When was she here?' Ida asked again.

The girl's eyebrows were raised. 'About a week ago? Just passing through. Said she needed some luck, some liquid courage.' From behind the bar, she produced a bottle of pale, cloudy liquid without a label. She pushed it towards us, her mouth a small, knowing smile. 'Something tells me you'll need a little courage tonight too.'

'Are you allowed to serve us cider?' I asked, staring stupidly at the bottle.

'I'm not serving you,' the girl said, grinning. 'It's a present. Just don't tell my grandparents. They own this place.'

Ida put her hands palm down on the bar. 'About a week ago, you said? Did Mandy say anything? Did she look . . . I dunno, how did she seem?'

The girl kept her gaze fixed on me as she spoke. 'She seemed . . . like you. Like both of you. Like she was searching for something.'

'Searching for a place to hide a letter,' I whispered.

The girl leaned on the bar, her necklace – long, some kind of jagged stone wrapped in gold wire – clinking against the glasses, the bottle of cloudy cider. 'Why would she leave a letter *here* for you to find?'

'I don't know,' I said. 'But there has to be a reason.' I turned to Ida. 'The last one brought me to you.'

The girl behind the bar smiled and said, 'Maybe this one brought you to me.'

My insides were suddenly uncomfortably warm.

'You mind if we look around?' Ida asked.

'Of course,' the girl said, dark eyes still on me. 'I hope you find what you're looking for.'

Ida and I split up, moved around the bar. Outside, the evening was calm and still. The pub owners propped open the doors. A breeze sighed in like a breath and on it a church bell sounded out its call to evening mass. Several of the pub patrons paused what they were doing, crossed themselves and went on as if no interruption had taken place.

I went from table to table, muttering *excuse me*s to the people seated, looking for any trace of white, of paper, but finding only napkins, receipts, forgotten shopping lists. Ida met me back at the bar.

'Nothing,' she said.

The girl behind the bar poured us all – herself included – a glass of cloudy cider. She pushed the glasses towards us and said, 'Maybe this will help.'

It was sweet, crisp, strange. Pooled inside me like honey. I could feel the tension in my shoulders lifting. I could almost feel myself trust that we were exactly where we were meant to be.

Ida took a sip, eyed the glass suspiciously. 'What's in this besides cider?' she asked.

The girl laughed. 'Secret family recipe,' she said. 'Passed down to my grandparents from previous generations. We infuse each batch with herbs. Some for calm, some for clarity, some for finding what you seek. Some for love. Some for death even. My granda says there's nothing like fine apple cider for masking the taste of poison. But he won't teach me that recipe.'

The second sip warmed me; it rose like a small fire in my chest, tasted like courage.

'So,' the girl said, when each of us had been soothed by her cider. 'Tell me about your sister. Tell me why you've lost her and how come you thought you'd find her here.'

It took almost an entire glass of that strange cider to explain our story to this stranger and she didn't for a moment look like anything we said was difficult to believe.

Cale, we learned in turn, was seventeen, and also entirely unafraid of oversharing with strangers. Her parents were currently protesting against oil companies in the Amazon and had invited Cale to come with them, but she'd been in a relationship at the time (that had since ended, I was embarrassingly relieved to hear) and had elected instead to finish the school year living with her grandparents.

'They're just happy I want to learn the family recipes,' she said. 'Plus they pay me for working here.'

Finn walked into the bar as Cale finished speaking, breathless, shirt rumpled from the bus. The first thing he did was grab me and bundle me into a hug. 'Are you OK?' Concern swam in his brown eyes and an unexpected lump formed in my throat.

'Peachy keen,' I said around it, and moved aside to introduce him to Ida. When he saw her, his eyes went wide.

'Holy shit,' he said. 'That *is* Mandy's daughter.'

Ida raised an eyebrow and shrugged. 'Yep.'

Finn shook his head, still slightly stunned. 'Deena,' he said. 'Your life is like a soap opera.'

Rachel chose that moment to call. I watched my phone vibrate slowly across the bar in front of me, but only picked it up when it was still. The voicemail lasted a few seconds, just enough time for Rachel to hitch a sigh, change her mind, hang up, call again.

I couldn't reply. I wasn't ready to talk to her yet, and I didn't want her to ask where I was.

Her second voicemail was longer.

'Deena,' she said. 'I wanted. I just wanted to check in. After this morning. Things are tense – can be tense – at times like these and I want you to know I'm still here for you, even if I said some things I shouldn't. You were right to be angry. But— *And*, I mean. And it's OK if you need some time. I know you've got Finn, and his family.' Here her voice grew thick with the kind of vines that wrap round you, steal the air from your lungs. 'But I'm here for you if you need me. I'm not going anywhere. And I love you. OK, bye. Call me if you want. OK, bye. I'll be here when you get back. OK, bye. Bye, bye-bye, bye.'

Here, on the other side of the country, it could have been easy to forget what Rachel had said about me the week before. But, even if I'd wanted to forgive her, I knew my sister would never understand what I was doing here. It was best to leave her in the dark until I found Mandy.

Beside me, Finn was chatting to Ida and sizing up Cale, trying to figure out where this short-haired, punky witch girl fitted into our impromptu road trip.

He rested one elbow on the bar and said, 'Howya. If you don't mind me asking, who are you and can I have some of your cider?'

Finn upped his accent – and his attitude – in inverse proportion to how well he knew someone. With me, his accent was almost neutral: he could have been from any middle-class household in the country. With strangers, he slipped into the thickest Dublin accent this side of Finglas, as if to counteract their reactions to his appearance. A name like Finbarr McCormac came with certain expectations. People imagined a Celtic mountain: a great pale, bearded warrior with flaming hair and bulging muscles, dressed in denim, fresh from the tractor. What they didn't expect was a lean, queer, bespectacled black guy in a Penguin Classics T-shirt and skinny jeans.

Cale didn't even blink an eyelid, just grinned and

stuck a hand out over the bar to be shaken. 'Cale Gorman,' she said. 'Short for Michaela. No relation to the salad. Although, truth be told, my parents are total hippies.'

Finn let out a laugh that I took to mean he was warming to this strange girl almost as much as I already was. 'I would never have guessed,' he said.

She pushed a glass of cider across the bar for him.

I put my phone into my back pocket and leaned briefly against the wall. It was covered in family crests and framed photographs, ticket stubs from fifty-year-old Gaelic football matches, rusty old keys, signed pictures of Cale's grandparents with their arms round minor Irish celebrities.

There was something caught under one of them – something jammed under the frame. I pulled it out and held it between my thumb and forefinger, turning slowly so the others could see.

Cale gawped. 'I never noticed,' she said with wonder.

'What's that?' said Finn, but Ida recognized it right away.

'Where did you find it?' she breathed.

I pointed at the wall behind me, mouth still unable to form words.

'Wait, what?' said Finn.

'You were right,' said Ida, head turning, trying to take in the whole room at once, trying to see something that wasn't there. Someone. 'She was here. Like Cale said.'

I opened the envelope and the letter from Mandy slid easily into my hands. I read it aloud into the warm, sweet air of the bar.

Dear Deena,

Do you remember when you were eight years old and I brought you to that harvest festival in Galway at Halloween? How you made me buy herb bundles, incense and charms? Rachel hated those but she let you hang them up around the house anyway, just for Halloween. She said they made the place smell like a hippie commune. She wasn't wrong.

Do you remember the parade on the last night? The one that went through the village, ending in an empty field where everybody danced afterwards? You were so frightened of the costumes. Handmade from leather and feathers and bone, like the ones our ancestors would have worn in pre-Christian times, to keep the ghosts away, the banshees at bay. You said they all looked like witches. I bought you a crown of mugwort from

*one of the sellers. She said it would connect us,
keep you safe.*

I'm not sure it did a very good job.

I'm not sure I did a very good job.

*I should have told you this long ago, but here it
is. Our family history is complicated, but we both
fit into it. We're both defined by it. By the curse,
by those who came before us. By Mary Ellen,
who cast it.*

And by those who came after.

13. *Blood and herbs*

Sligo and Drumcliff, 1880

The nights were long that winter. There wasn't much to eat. The ground froze solid – sheets of ice as thick as a fist over the deep grooves of wheels on the dirt roads – and Mary Ellen could barely keep her feet. Unbalanced by her belly, she picked her way gingerly over field and fen, imploring farmers on carts drawn by skinny horses to let her sit on their hay a while to rest her weary legs some of the way.

The farmers were kind sometimes and shared scraps of food. Sometimes they were harsh, throwing her right back onto the road when they gleaned she had no husband. As if her wickedness might be catching. As if they were guilty by association; as if they'd be damned simply for having offered her a ride.

She drank from rivers and collected roadside berries. She begged for scraps from country pubs. But, even when her stomach was a gnarled and bony fist inside her, all she wanted to eat was apples.

She ended up in Sligo, a busy port town of fishers and farmers, clustered round the mouth of a river that rushed into the sea. The same ocean in which she had drowned her former lover's cherished sapling.

When she arrived, her shoes were almost worn through. She came to the town on market day. Before approaching the square, she stopped to run her cold and aching fingers through her hair, to smooth down her dress and knock as much of the mud off the hem as possible.

'I'm looking for work,' she told the first stallholder, a sullen farmer's wife who glared pointedly at Mary Ellen's protruding belly.

'You're in no condition to work,' she said.

'I'm looking for work,' she told the second stallholder, a fishmonger with a neat grey beard who barely looked at her, knowing she'd no money to buy his fish.

'The workhouse is five miles out of town,' he said. 'And good luck to you.'

The workhouse – a word guaranteed to freeze the listener with something close to panic. Great grey buildings filled to the brim with men and women, even children, too poor to live and work in the towns. They broke their bent backs over impossible labour; they slept on thin cots in endless cold rooms; they survived on the bare bones of hope.

Mary Ellen had known it might come to this. She'd known from the moment her lover had ordered the constabulary to break every window of the house she was born in. But, as long as she could, she'd resist. The workhouse was no place to birth her child.

'I'm looking for work,' she said to the third stallholder, a woman a few years older than Mary Ellen, selling speckled fruit and cloudy cider. Peeking out of the bags at the woman's side were what looked like tinctures, small glass bottles and vials nestled in among an assortment of plants and dried herbs.

The woman squinted up at Mary Ellen and her eyes were the same bright blue as the sky.

'Hmm,' she said. 'Yes. You'll do.'

The young woman's name was Ann Gorman and she lived alone in the middle of the countryside, a good hour's walk from the town, with a mangy-looking mongrel and a one-eyed cat. Ann had been cast out of her mother's house two years before for reasons she did not like to discuss. Mary Ellen found the woman to be curt and direct, but also warm and pleasant company.

It took months for Mary Ellen to grow accustomed to the quiet. Used to a family of seven children under the one thatched roof, living with only one other woman was strange to her. She filled the silence with her mother's songs, chattered both to Ann and to her belly while she worked.

Ann's daytime business was in apples, which seemed a cruel coincidence to Mary Ellen, whose downfall had been so tied to a now-destroyed apple tree. Still, she did not complain. She picked and tended the small and scraggly orchard; she helped to bottle the bitter, cloudy cider; she piled the apples too tart or rotten to use into baskets to sell to the farmers for their pigs.

Food was scarce and the cottage was tiny. She and Ann were lucky if they made nine shillings a week from the apples, but they shared what little they had. They also shared the profits from Ann's night-time business, which was something else entirely.

Ann's cottage was the only dwelling in sight. Surrounded by the scrappy orchard, it was hidden from even the narrow dirt road that led to it by tangles of hedgerows and blackberry bushes. After nightfall, Ann's skinny mongrel could hear even the softest footfall on the path outside. The creature would rise from its spot by the cottage wall and fetch Ann or Mary Ellen from the garden, or the bed, or the chair by the fire. And Ann would open the cottage door before the woman outside – for it was always a woman outside – could knock timidly on the wood.

13. Blood and herbs

Some women visited Ann and Mary Ellen monthly. They were mostly locals, faces Mary Ellen recognized from market days. The majority of the women were peasants and tenants. Some were servants. A few were the wives of millers and greengrocers, and they came to see Ann too, late at night, alone. Some came from as far as Galway town, making the six-hour journey there and back in the one night.

The women paid Ann in coin and grain, in meat and cheese, in leather and in poitín, a clear alcohol made from potatoes, distilled illegally in the darkest parts of the bog. Some women came and could not pay and Ann was forced to turn them away. Mary Ellen would see them some months later, trying to hide the shape of their slowly swelling bellies.

In the garden behind the cottage, Ann grew herbs. For the women who came monthly, she made and distilled tinctures of valerian root to ease the pain of their bleeding, or crushed monk's pepper and tansy for them to eat if they wanted to get with child. For some, she chopped fennel and hogweed for them to feed to their husbands.

For the women who came only once, the quietest ones who appeared only when the moon was dark and they were sure they could not be seen, she brewed teas of pennyroyal and mugwort, wild carrot and rue. In front of the fire with Mary Ellen learning all she could, ready to be told which herb to fetch from the garden, Ann would listen to the dazed or frenzied or sobbing women, would examine their bellies and between their legs, would ask when they had last bled. And, depending on the answer, she administered her teas.

Some of the women looked at Mary Ellen with pity; others barely saw her at all. Ann had, from the moment she took her in, let it be known to the town that Mary Ellen's husband had died of diphtheria in Donegal. The townsfolk's pity was better than their scorn, and Mary Ellen was glad of the lie.

When the time came for Mary Ellen's baby to be born, Ann laid blankets over rushes on the floor. Instead of having Mary Ellen drink laudanum and spirits, as the physicians did for the upper-class women who occasionally visited Ann, she gave Mary Ellen only water. She pushed her onto all fours and delivered her baby like a farmer would an animal's, and Mary Ellen's labour was half as long and half as painful as any of the well-to-do ladies had ever been.

When Mary Ellen's son slid out of her, bloody and gasping, Ann gave his rump a sharp smack and declared the squalling child to be named Patrick. Mary Ellen didn't dare to disagree.

14. *A weak heart*

Drumcliff, 1890–1918

Patrick Gerald Joseph Rys was a weak and sickly child. Food was scarce and, even with Ann's apples to keep her from starvation, Mary Ellen had been hungry throughout her pregnancy.

Patrick was skinny, stammered and walked with a slight limp, but he knew from a very young age that his heart was the weakest thing about him. Not a man's heart: strong, boisterous, tenacious and hardy like the hearts of the boys in school, like their fathers'. Boys with strong hearts did not cry. They hardened their feelings so that they barely knew them, didn't seem to feel fear.

Patrick, on the other hand, was indecisive, insecure and afraid. He didn't play with the other children for fear of ridicule. His teachers, the townsfolk and the parish priest declared that a boy like him was doomed from the start. Not by his limp, his skinny limbs, his trembling legs, but because of his home. No man of strong heart could be raised by two women, the men of the town insisted. No normal boy could live with witches. And deep within the ugliest part of himself Patrick believed them. From his infancy, when not in the company of his mother and Ann, he was snapped at, roughed up, smacked and beaten more than the other boys, the ones with fathers and siblings, the ones with wiry limbs and strong hearts. It wouldn't have occurred to Patrick to see the correlation. That his heart was only weak because the men of the town made it so.

Patrick only saw the rough local boys who kicked pigs' bladders around the town for lack of a real ball, who pinched the girls and punched each other, who dared themselves to jump into the river and could run around for hours on skinny, scraped legs that never trembled in the way Patrick's left leg always had.

One evening on the road home from school Patrick came across a big group of them – the limpless, strong-hearted boys – clustered tightly round some loud game. He squared himself to walk as quickly as his shaky legs could carry him right past the scrum. Patrick didn't notice until he was level with the shuffling cluster of boys that what they were circling was making noise. A heart-rending noise, a desperate noise, a noise of war and dying.

Patrick stopped despite himself. In between the boys' stick legs there was a cat. Or rather there was a creature that had once been something resembling a cat. A black and mangy thing, more sickly skin than fur, more bone than sickly skin. What hackles it had were raised and it hissed and spat as if it was five times its size and actually stood a fighting chance against six boys who had no boots on their filthy feet but managed to kick anyway.

Patrick shouted, 'Stop!' before remembering that there was one of him and six of them.

The pack of boys turned from their original prey, which seized upon their distraction and streaked away, broken tail cocked like a fish hook and bony legs working so fast they were only a black blur.

They fell on Patrick and it was like a nightmare, like the way he imagined hell when the priest talked about it on Sundays: a place where demons broke your bones and tore your skin so that your body was fire, but you deserved it because you'd been wicked, or cowardly, or wrong.

He never saw the cat again; it probably died in the bushes into which it disappeared, most likely close to death already, and Patrick's sacrifice was meaningless.

Patrick was curled on the hard dirt, kicks landing on the softest parts of him, punches beating blood into the ground. Each blow was a crunch, a crack, a wet spreading. The world was made of pain, of the taste of blood and dirt, of the smell of his own piss soaking his trousers, of the screams and screeches of the boys.

When Patrick thought that he might die, the blows suddenly stopped. Through swollen eyes he saw the boys look up as one and gasp, 'It's the witch!' and they scattered, leaving Patrick lying broken on the ground with his arms over his head.

When he parted his elbows, he saw Ann. She stared down at him for a full minute before speaking.

'Your ma has the supper ready,' was all she said. And she took him in her arms like a baby wrapped in swaddling.

When his wounds had finally healed, Ann sent Patrick out to work. Mary Ellen didn't even try to argue, although it was she who had insisted on his schooling, who harboured a secret hope of one day sending her son to the seminary. There was good money in being a priest. But both women knew there was no use in sending Patrick back to school.

As it turned out, there was also good money in farming, especially for a boy unknowingly promised to the farmer's daughter.

John O'Connor was one of the few Catholic farmers in the area. He didn't rent his house from a landowner;

he didn't work the fields for his lease. He'd built his business from his father's scrap of land and from the prize bull that was his mother's dowry.

He would never have hired a cripple like Patrick, but he had taken his wife to Ann and Mary Ellen when Patrick was still recovering from his beating. For years, John O'Connor and his wife had been waiting for a baby. They had tried everything the doctors had recommended, but doctors were expensive, and nothing had helped. So his wife had suggested they visit the witch women. Standing outside the cottage door, staring into the twisted orchard that surrounded the house, waiting for his wife to emerge from the mysterious room within, John O'Connor made himself a promise. If these women helped his wife get with child, he would owe them. It was a silent promise, a passing thought, but, once he had made it, the trees of the orchard trembled, leaves swaying although there was no wind. And when his wife emerged from the cottage, clutching a cloth bag of herbs, one of the women – the cripple boy's mother, he thought, although no one was truly sure any more which of the women was the mother – stared straight through him with her clear grey eyes and he knew his promise had been marked.

When John O'Connor's daughter was born nine months later, he sent for the witch's son.

*

On the farm, Patrick struggled. His left leg, which had always been weak, never recovered from his beating. He couldn't keep up with the other boys. The hay they hauled was heavy, the land they worked was rough and rocky, and Patrick's arms shook.

But he was good with the animals. The horses pulled the ploughs straighter when Patrick was at the whip. The chickens laid twice the amount of eggs when Patrick cleaned their coop. The cows let themselves be milked without kicking, allowed themselves to be led to slaughter without a sound.

Most importantly, Farmer O'Connor's prize bull would allow nobody but Patrick to feed him or lead him from his pen. Everybody else the bull charged at. He had gored two men already.

John O'Connor was a superstitious man. The witches had given him a daughter, and he felt that meant he owed them. Farmer O'Connor worried that if he let Patrick go, the bull would stop mating and ensuring the O'Connors' livelihood. So he kept the Rys boy on, and little by little Patrick became a man, his pay enough to bring home to Ann and Mary Ellen with a little left over to save for his own future.

Patrick's future was called Catherine. Catherine O'Connor was a plain and lonely girl who sought out as friends the girls in school who were more beautiful and more interesting than her, in an effort to somehow become – or at least to seem – more beautiful and more interesting herself. At first it would work: as a friend, Catherine was kind and attentive, and the girls would soon confide in her, study with her, invite her to tea at their houses over the summer holidays, and go over to supper at hers. But one by one the girls would leave her. It happened the same way every year: after a few shared suppers, her most recent friend would stop coming over. She would avoid Catherine at school. When invited again, the girl would turn away, telling Catherine that she had found herself a better and more suitable friend.

While Catherine's heart broke every summer, her father would secretly send his daughter's friends to see Ann and Mary Ellen in their cottage. They would come in the night, silent, the farmer's cart waiting on the road out of sight. The women's business relied on discretion, on maintaining their reputation. As they left, Ann advised them that unless they wanted to have to return for another infusion – or, even worse, to have the remedies fail and to be sent to the nearest mother-and-baby home in disgrace – they should avoid Catherine O'Connor's father's farm at all times, or, what might be more effective, find themselves a new friend.

John O'Connor, ever superstitious, felt he owed the women again. He saw their frowns, their pursed lips at the sight of him on market days. He knew they were discreet but wanted to ensure their silence. So, when Catherine finished school, her father suggested she marry the witch's son.

Catherine was quickly made to understand that she did not have much choice in the matter, so, when Patrick Rys asked for her hand in marriage, she accepted.

15. *Haunted places*

Sligo and Drumcliff, 2012

I knew what to do then, what to expect. I turned the last page over and saw an address near Drumcliff, County Sligo, scratched quickly there, a couple of lines of directions from a main road probably not far from here. Finn sat unmoving. Ida immediately took out her phone.

'It's the middle of nowhere,' she said. 'Like, literally.' She turned the phone towards me, zoomed out, then in again. 'It's not even on a road.'

But a suspicion was rising in me fast, like the tide. 'Would you say it's about an hour's walk away?' I reread the start of the letter while she checked. Mandy had described where Ann Gorman and Mary Ellen lived. *In the middle of the countryside, a good hour's walk from the town.*

'About that, yeah,' said Ida.

We smiled, bright and sudden, like two people who

have learned to see what the other is thinking in a very short amount of time.

'There's something wrong here,' Finn said. 'This doesn't make sense.'

But Ida and I weren't listening. Heads bent over her phone, we mapped out our route. Drumcliff, or close by. North again.

'We could walk it,' I said. 'It's not properly dark yet, and we have our phones for torches.'

'Have you two even stopped to consider how crazy this is?' Finn said. 'This doesn't mean Mandy is leading us to her. She could have set all this up before she died. And, either way, what kind of a fucked-up treasure hunt did she think she was playing at?'

'We were supposed to do this together,' I told him. 'As my birthday present. A road trip. She was meant to tell me all this in person. Instead, all I have are her letters. All Ida has. This is a thing we're doing, with or without you.'

Finn softened. 'I wasn't backing out,' he said. 'I just . . . Mandy's funeral was yesterday. I know you're grieving. Hurting. I can't imagine. I just want you to be careful. Because if . . . if she was here last week, like Cale said, if she left all these letters before she died . . . then at the end of this, wherever that is, she'll still be gone.'

I saved the location on my phone. 'You'll see,' I said. 'You will.'

Cale had listened throughout the reading of the letter and was standing still behind the bar, eyes on the words I had just read aloud, customers forgotten, pints left to go flat on the bar. Her grandparents, who seemed to be used to this kind of behaviour, circled round her, busily tending to the pub patrons. The sound of the last of the stallholders still chatting together after the market drifted in through the open doors.

This place was in the story I'd just read. This town was the one Mary Ellen arrived at after having walked the whole way from Donegal. The market that had been closing up outside when we arrived was the same one she'd come to 132 years ago, met Ann Gorman, carrying my great-grandfather in her belly. We were right inside the story. The past was so close we could touch it.

Cale reached across me and touched one of the pictures on the wall by the bar. Heat rose in my cheeks as her arm brushed against mine.

'Look,' she said. 'Tell me what you see.'

She pointed to the frame under which I'd found Mandy's letter. It showed a sepia print of a large group, a family perhaps, under whose feet were written the words *Sligo, 1877* in faded cursive script. Along the border of the frame a more modern hand had noted down names.

'Look,' Cale said again, with more urgency.

I read through them, stopped suddenly in the middle of the row. I trailed a fingertip up the dusty frame from the name – *Ann Gorman* – to a thin, blurry figure with light hair, blonde maybe, had the picture been in colour: a girl in her early twenties, unsmiling, flanked by an older couple, who were probably her parents.

The young woman's name was Ann Gorman, Mandy had written. *Ann had been cast out of her mother's house two years before for reasons she did not like to discuss.*

How many Ann Gormans were there in Sligo in 1877?

'You see?' said Cale.

'Ann Gorman,' I whispered. 'Ann who lived with Mary Ellen.'

'She's family,' Cale said. 'My – hang on.' She cocked her head as she worked it out. 'My great-great-great-grand-aunt.'

'What?'

Cale nodded at the photo. 'That's the oldest family picture we have. My granda found it a few years ago when he was researching our ancestry.'

'Whoa. It's the same Ann,' I said, head spinning. 'It's why Mandy sent us here.'

Cale was nodding, eyes wide. 'My granda always said there was a witch in the family. A herbalist. After she died, Granda found her recipes. They're the ones we still use now. She had a small orchard, like we do. Her parents kicked her out. Like it says in the letter.'

'Because she was a witch?' asked Ida.

'That's not what we were told,' Cale said. 'My granda always says she was kicked out because her parents found her with another girl. Which I suppose back then was just as bad as witchcraft.'

A warmth entirely unrelated to the cider I'd been drinking rose through me.

'Which means,' Cale went on, 'that if I'd been alive back then I'd've been basically screwed on both counts.' She laughed.

I studiously avoided the meaningful look I could feel Finn boring deep into the side of my head.

He cleared his throat to get my attention and when that didn't work he said, 'That's such a coincidence,' to Cale, while still staring at me.

Ida, who wouldn't have known the real meaning behind Finn's words, shook her head. 'Not a coincidence,' she said. 'Mandy knew all this. She sent us here because of it.'

'I *knew* it,' Cale said. 'I knew there was a reason you came here. And your sister, the one you're looking for.

I *knew* I recognized her. Our families' histories are tangled together.'

She shook her head in wonder, eyes dark and shining. She was so pretty it was hard to look at her for long.

Finn glanced at me, then at Cale. His mouth twisted into something that was part mischief, part innocence. 'When do you get off work?' he asked. 'Because we're going to your – what was it? – great-great-great-grand-aunt's cottage, if you're interested in coming too.'

He opened up the route on his phone and Cale tilted her head to squint at it. She gave a secret smile.

'That's the long way,' she said. 'Believe me. But I know the area better than a map. I can show you a shortcut.'

Just like that, we became four. The journey I had begun alone that morning – although it felt like several lifetimes ago already – had widened, expanded to include my best friend, the niece I never knew I had and a mysterious half-stranger, who led us off-road through fields and forests, over streams and marshes, drinking in our story like it was fine apple cider.

Twilight misted itself across the sky, changed the cloudy blue to the purple of a new bruise, streaked with scarlet. It was almost eight. Houses started to light up, windows shining in the growing dark, the people inside settling into their evenings as we walked past.

My phone buzzed in my back pocket: Rachel again. I didn't answer, couldn't face her voice, knew that the moment she realized I wasn't really at Finn's house, this journey was over. She'd be after me in a heartbeat.

My phone rang again.

'You know you should answer,' Finn said, holding aside a branch of brambles to let the rest of us pass.

I tucked my phone back into my pocket. 'I don't want to worry her,' I said.

'She'll be over at my place in minutes, checking with my mam. She'll know you've run off.'

The vibrating of my phone set my teeth on edge.

Finn gave me a stern look. 'And my mam will know I've done a runner too.'

'Fine. I'll text her.'

Got your voicemail.

I wrote quickly, the light of my phone in the darkness under the trees blinding me.

**Sorry I haven't called. Still at
Finn's. Just need to figure some**

stuff out. I'll see you tomorrow, k?
Love you too.

I let myself imagine Rachel's face when I returned home with Mandy. The shock, the awe, the disbelief. Even deep in the worst of their fights, my sisters could never seem to separate completely. Even when Rachel refused to open the door to her twin, they sent messages, they spoke on the phone. There was a mystery to their relationship, a complicated dance of affection and resentment I didn't understand.

When I found Mandy, I would ask them. Armed with the stories of our family's past, I would sit them down and make them look at what had split them, what had happened at our mother's funeral to cause their sisterhood such distress.

The evening sun started to set in earnest, and I picked up the pace, the thought of Rachel finding out I was gone spurring me on. She would not accept stilted messages and vague excuses for long. In the distance, a bird cried. A sound so like a keen, a scream.

Finn and Ida hurried to keep up, huddled together on the small and winding roads. Overhanging trees dipped their branches above us, and tangled round them, slicing through the air, glinting, were long silvery-grey hairs.

Another bird's cry broke the silence, but at this point I'm not sure any of us were certain it was a bird.

Nervously, Cale started to sing to fill the silence, old folk songs from our childhood, as if she somehow knew this was what she should do to still our fears. Her voice was clear and beautiful.

Another scream sounded, closer this time.

Finn raised his voice and sang along, full of false bravado. Ida chimed in with both a similarly feigned enthusiasm and the signature Rys tone-deaf ear. But Cale and Finn could have been a choir. High and low, bass and alto, Cale making up the harmonies like it was something she was born to do.

When another scream sounded, we all jumped, whipped round, sure it had come from close by.

'It's a deer,' Finn said quickly, too loud in the quiet. 'Or a fox. They sound like that sometimes. When they're mating.'

'That's true,' Ida breathed faintly. 'Female foxes scream.'

But I knew it wasn't a fox.

'Come on,' said Cale, touching the stone that hung around her neck. 'We're almost there.'

She motioned to us to leave the road. We hoisted our backpacks higher and hopped over a stone wall. In what was not quite a forest, we climbed hillocks and scrambled over fallen trees, tangles snatching at our clothes. Soon we were all but running.

Until Cale came to an abrupt stop. Just ahead, in a little clearing, there was a small stone cottage, long abandoned.

'You have got to be kidding me,' Finn said. 'I can see the headlines now.' He stretched his hands in front of him. '*Runaway Queer Kids Become Victims of Remote Cottage Chainsaw Killer, Surprising Absolutely No One.*'

'I'm not queer,' Ida said. 'Sorry.'

'Then chances are you'll be the only one left alive.'

It was not so much a house as an empty shell. It was not so much abandoned as reclaimed by the land. There was no roof, only a carpet of grass and three walls covered in leaves and tangles of bushes, scrambling ivy and blackberry brambles. It was hard to tell where the overgrown garden stopped and the house began.

'This is it,' I said. 'Ann Gorman's cottage.' I turned to Cale. 'Your great-great-great-grand-aunt. Where my great-great-grandmother lived too. We have to go inside.'

'No way, Deena,' Finn said, serious now, all jokes forgotten. 'It's bad enough you talking about banshees and curses and shit. If a ghost is gonna live anywhere, it's in that house right there.'

'Come on, Finn,' I said bracingly. 'It isn't even fully dark yet.'

Except it looked like midnight inside the ruins. Somehow the countryside seemed hushed suddenly. I started to wonder if maybe Finn was right.

Another scream sounded in the night. Finn's fingers were a vice-like grip on my hand, but I could barely feel the blood flowing underneath my frozen skin.

Cale set her backpack down on the remains of the stone wall around the house and from it she took a bundle of white candles and a small velvet pouch full of stones.

Finn stared, mouth agape. 'Candles?' he said, with a high-pitched edge to his voice I'd never heard before. 'Seriously? This isn't creepy enough without fucking candles?'

'Candles to see ghosts,' said Cale. She handed one to me and I held it like an altar boy about to lead a service. 'Talismans so they can't harm us.'

'Fuck,' said Finn. 'This is not good.'

'I thought you didn't believe in ghosts?' I asked him.

'Not during daylight, I don't,' Finn said. 'Not at school, like, or at home. Not when we're watching some crappy horror film.'

Cale scratched a match to flame and my candle's wick caught.

'But here?' Finn's voice went up about an octave. 'In some old ruined cottage at twilight in the middle of fucking Sligo with you looking all possessed or some shit? Yeah. Yeah, I fucking believe in ghosts.'

He continued to swear softly under his breath, but I was too preoccupied to really listen. There was something in this place. Maybe the banshees. Maybe something else. All around me, the air smelled like apples.

Cale set out her stones along the walls, as carefully as if they were glass, or eggshells. 'These ghosts are tied to us,' she said. 'To me, to Deena and Ida. This house is linked to the three of us. They're the only ghosts we should meet tonight. I don't think the banshees would come here. Their tangle of hair would snarl in the briars; their rags would rip on the thorns.'

Ida shivered. 'You talking like some kind of fairy tale isn't exactly helping.' She looked around, seemed to realize something. 'But if this is Ann and Mary Ellen's cottage,' she said, 'then Mandy must have left another letter. The next part of the story.'

I got up, holding one of Cale's candles in each hand, and I walked round the perimeter of the place. To the rear, behind the chimney, there were the gnarled skeletons of three straight lines of trees. The tops of their trunks only just showed over the epic forest of weeds.

I hadn't realized Ida was beside me until she spoke. 'An orchard,' she said.

I jumped, shoes slipping on small stones. In the shadows

of the broken stone wall, illuminated by my candles' flames, I could see what looked like symbols carved into the barks of the trees. Circles and spirals, stars and crosses. The same symbols repeated on the stones of the cottage walls, faded almost to obscurity, but still raised enough that I could feel them under the pads of my fingers.

When it happened, it was almost expected. My fingers touched paper. Impaled on the thorn of a briar, wedged into the stones of the wall, right next to the grooves of a carving that looked like an eye.

The others didn't say anything. They just waited for me to read.

Dear Deena,
Here is something you have to understand. Once
the curse comes to you, it doesn't let go. I'm a
whole lifetime from seventeen, but still the banshees
have screamed for me, sent me running. Or perhaps
I'm part of your curse.

Mary Ellen was far from seventeen when she
died, but when she did it was still the lingering
remains of the family curse haunting her. You'll see.
Once a bad apple, always a bad apple. There's no
way to climb back onto the family tree.

16. *Shared beds*

Drumcliff, 1918–1935

Sligo was a town that talked. Once it became known that John O'Connor's daughter would be marrying the local witch's son, tongues got to wagging.

'There has to be a reason,' the townsfolk said in audible whispers.

'There's only one reason it could be,' the townsfolk replied. 'The girl is already with child.'

But Catherine was a good girl, a God-fearing girl, who would remain chaste until her wedding night, and the wedding was not hasty, which meant no illegitimate child was involved in the couple's unlikely marriage. So the whispers turned again to witchcraft.

Town rumours had always held that the women who lived in the orchard down by Drumcliff were witches. It was said that the boy's mother, Mary Ellen, had the power to turn into a fox, Ann a black bat.

At the same time, Mary Ellen and Ann were afforded a certain respect. Doctors were expensive. But for a barter, a trade or a slip of coins into the hand, Ann and Mary Ellen would produce a vial or jar, a bunch of cloth-wrapped herbs that would, more often than not, cure an ailment within a week. Long gone were Mary Ellen's days of muscle strain and constant hunger. There was money to be made for midwives and abortionists with a day business in apples.

Yet the town talked. And, though it was true that Patrick wanted his own happiness, his own success, he also knew that a tenuous link to the O'Connors would not be a bad thing for his mother and Ann.

Even so, Mary Ellen worried. 'There are evil men in this world,' she told Ann after Patrick announced his engagement. 'I don't want my son to be one of them.'

'He won't be, love,' Ann said. 'There's no evil in him.'

The trees of the orchard shook their branches in the breeze. A couple of bad apples dropped to the ground.

'You're right,' Mary Ellen said softly, and she took her lover's hand. 'But still, in that house, I hope he has sons.'

Patrick and Catherine Rys had two daughters. Lizzie was as plain and blonde as their mother and Julia was as copper-haired and slight as their father, although they were both somewhat stronger of stature. Of the strength of their hearts, however, Patrick knew very little: he learned before his children could talk that his own heart lay with animals more than with humans, and his daughters were a puzzle he loved greatly but had no desire to understand.

However, Julia, like her father, was enamoured with the bull.

Patrick's father-in-law's prize bull was still going strong and when Julia was sixteen – an age when most girls, her sister Lizzie included, grew weary of animals, preferring to spend time with their friends – Julia could still be found at her father's side early each morning, small hands stroking the hide of the great grey bull.

'That girl's got her granny's witchcraft in her blood,' said John O'Connor, only half joking.

Patrick's mother still lived in the overgrown cottage with Ann Gorman. Neither had ever married. They still slept in the small bed they'd shared as young women, insisting to Patrick that this was simply for warmth. 'You know the nights are fierce cold around here, love,' Mary Ellen would tell her son, and he'd try hard to believe her, to ignore the whispers on the farm and in the town, to pretend that he didn't know the whole of Sligo spoke of his mother as the widow witch, to wish away the niggling knowledge inside of him that, in the cottage his mother shared with another woman to whom she was not related, all was not as it seemed.

So, when his father-in-law said that Julia had Mary Ellen's witchcraft in her blood, Patrick spoke gruffly. 'She's learned how to tend to the bull from me,' he said. 'That bull will outlast me, you mark my words, and, if she's not here to care for him, you can kiss the O'Connor cows goodbye.'

John huffed and shrugged, but he didn't say another word, just leaned on the wood of the fence every morning and watched Julia.

Whenever Mary Ellen visited the farm, she watched him watching. She felt his eyes on her granddaughter like a fire in the pit of her gut. She couldn't say anything – there was nothing to be said – but she added certain herbs from the garden into the cider Ann sent him, to ensure he would stay away.

Still, the fire in her gut became hotter every time she walked over to the farm and saw John O'Connor leaning on the fence, watching.

As Mary Ellen's fire grew, the rain stopped, the air became hot and dry. By July the grass was yellowing and the farmers were losing their crops. The river slowed to a muddy trickle.

'It's not natural,' the fishmonger said on market day. 'Heat like this in Sligo.'

The women at his stall stopped and shook their heads. 'It isn't everywhere,' one of them said. 'I've had a letter from my nephew in Galway – the weather's same as every year down there.'

'Unnatural,' said the fishmonger again.

At the O'Connor farm, crops wilted and animals grew thirsty. Only John O'Connor's prize bull was given the same rations of water as before, and every day the farmer sent Julia into his enclosure to sponge the creature and cool him down. It was Julia's favourite part of the day, and she would splash the water on the bull and on herself, rinsing the morning's dust from her dripping dress.

Dry-mouthed, John O'Connor watched her.

As the weeks went on, Sunday masses were a special kind of torture, the entire parish crowded into the church together. 'At least the sermons are less boring,' Julia's sister, Lizzie, said, and that much was true: the heat had inspired the priest to lecture his flock about hellfire and damnation, which was much more interesting than his usual digressions about taxes, but Julia had to admit that there was something in the sermons she found discomfiting.

Perhaps it was how they changed the after-church chatter to dark mumblings about what the people of Sligo had done to deserve such a plight. This weather, the townsfolk decided, was clearly an act of God. Why else would only Sligo be affected? Why not Ballina? Why not Carrick-on-Shannon? Why were none of the neighbouring towns and villages losing their crops to drought, their animals to starvation?

It was either an act of God or it was witchcraft.

While it is always difficult to tell where rumours are born, this one was often spread by people who had recently spoken with Farmer O'Connor. And hadn't the widow Rys been seen around the farm far more than usual? And hadn't John O'Connor had to stop drinking Ann Gorman's cider after having been awfully ill? And wasn't it strange, uncanny, two women living alone together in the middle of nowhere, with only their animals and their apples? And how were their apple trees not dying when there wasn't any rain?

Mary Ellen heard the rumours; it was impossible not to.

'Don't worry, love,' Ann told her. 'They've nattered about us before and they'll do so again. Once the rain falls, they'll come to their senses.'

But there was something dry and dangerous about these rumours. And there was a keen on the dusty air. A sound in the night that could have been screaming.

Mary Ellen went to the farm during Sunday mass time, climbed the wooden fence and called to the bull. She stroked his grey head and fed him an apple from her orchard, plucked right off the tree. She wrapped her hands round his huge curved horns and whispered in his ear.

'Protect her,' she said. 'Or I'll never let you rest.'

The bull nodded his enormous head.

When Mary Ellen had arrived in Sligo all those years ago, pregnant, starved and limping, Ann had taken her in. She'd fed her what she could, had warmed water over the fire to bathe her, had rubbed strong-smelling poultices into her blisters, had laid her in Ann's own bed. For weeks, she'd asked no questions, had only offered companionship, work and a knowledge of herbs that would serve her for years.

Later, when Mary Ellen finally spoke of how she had been betrayed by Gerald, had been evicted and shunned by her family, Ann offered her own story. Later still, she offered love.

Some loves ignite like forest fires, burn down entire towns before anybody's noticed. Ann's first love was one of those, and she didn't see the blisters from the burn until it was too late. Some loves smoulder like a turf fire, are slow to start but will then burn bright and steady through entire winters. Ann and Mary Ellen fell in love within red embers, but with those they built up a fire that lasted their lifetime.

*

It was so hot and dry that summer that a struck match burned extra bright. A group of town boys, who accidentally set an entire barn on fire after playing at camping nearby, got their hides tanned so hard they couldn't sit for a week.

So it was most likely a coincidence, what happened to Mary Ellen Rys and Ann Gorman. It was most likely the exact same thing.

Julia had heard the rumours about her grandmother – everybody had. But she never really believed them. All Julia knew was that her nanny and her good friend Ann were experts on herbs and apples, could cure a cold in a day and help birth a baby who'd turned in the womb so that its bottom was the wrong way up. Julia didn't connect the rumours to the whispers of witchcraft that ran rampant that stifling summer. It wouldn't have occurred to her.

It occurred to her father later, when his mother's little cottage in its tangles of brambles burned bright and dazzling one hot, dry night. When the fire burned out, the local doctor found the remains of the cottage's two inhabitants locked in an embrace on their shared bed, as if they had died peacefully together in their sleep.

The following morning, it started to rain.

17. *Prelude to kisses*

Drumcliff, 2012

When I finished reading, the lightest rain came down like a fine mist, a gentle touch of loving hands.

'They might have burned right in this spot,' Ida said in a whisper. 'Mary Ellen and Ann.'

'They didn't burn them for being witches,' I said, watching Cale standing, like me, in the place her ancestor died. An ancestor with more in common than just a name. 'They burned them because they were lovers.'

'I guess back then it amounted to the same thing,' said Finn.

Cale had said something similar earlier, but now her eyes were filled with tears. I felt complicated, like a sentence with too many small words, where you keep stumbling over the same ones, reading the whole thing wrong.

Mandy had known all this before she left. Had known our ancestor had been killed for whom she loved. I knew now that her reaction to my coming out wasn't intolerance but fear. It didn't matter that times had changed. In our family, so many things remained the same.

She could have told me, a traitor thought came into my head. *She knew all this; she could have told me before now. Could have said at least some of this on my birthday, before she disappeared.*

I missed Mandy like a thirst, something so vital I couldn't not think of it. I ran her letter between my fingers in the way you do a piece of velvet, rubbing it the wrong way so it almost sticks against your skin.

'It can't have been here long,' I said.

'What can't?' asked Finn.

'The letter. She had to have put it here recently. If it'd been there long, the paper would have disintegrated in the rain. It's been a week. The ink would have run. It would have fallen out, blown away. An animal would have prised it loose.'

'Deena—' Finn said, but I couldn't listen to reason. Not here, in the cottage where my ancestor died.

'I told you.' I held out the paper. 'It's a map to her. She put it here for me to find.'

'Deena.' Finn slipped his hand into mine. 'If after all this we don't – we don't find her, what then?'

I stared at Ida. My niece. Her eyes – so like Mandy's – were big.

It took me a while to form the words. 'I don't know. I don't know. But I know I need to break the curse. I need . . .' My mouth went thin, down at the edges. 'I need to get to the bottom of this. Even if Mandy is – if she did – if she isn't at the end of the map.'

'The end of the world,' Ida said softly.

Above us the sky was low, touching the tips of the branches of trees. Around us old stone settled deeper into the grooves of centuries.

'It all looks like the end of the world to me.'

It was strangely warm in the ruins of Mary Ellen's cottage, several degrees warmer than it had been on the road, as if some residual heat from the ancient fire lingered. Birds sang from the ghost orchard behind the house. The carved symbols on the walls looked down on us.

'Wait,' Ida said, grabbing the letter. 'Where's the address?'

'What?'

'You didn't read the next address.'

The last page of Mandy's letter was written on until the end. 'We must be missing a piece. A page. It must have fallen. Blown away.'

'No,' Ida said loudly. 'It has to still be here. We need to know where to go next.'

We split up, turned on the torches on our phones, lifted tree branches and brambles, shuffled through dead leaves, ran our fingers over each corner of stone.

I watched Cale hop over the back wall into the orchard, phone-torch beaming through branches. Her short hair, the waistcoat she wore over her shirt, the easy way she'd said, *If I'd been alive back then I'd've been basically screwed on both counts*, were as loud as a rainbow pin or a pair of purple plastic Venus earrings. That relationship she'd talked about back at the bar was most likely with another girl. I felt too large for my clothes, the nondescript jeans and hoodie, felt itchy and wrong behind my glasses, my mane of curls.

I swung my legs over the back wall and followed her into the overgrown orchard.

'No sign of the page so far, but these are still good,' Cale's voice called from further through the trees. 'Catch.'

An apple came out of the darkness, smacked straight into my open hands. 'Don't go too far,' I called back. The fruit crunched perfectly when I pressed it between my teeth. Its juice was sharp and sweet.

'I'm right here,' Cale said. 'Don't worry.'

She emerged from the trees like a shadow herself,

apple in hand like Eve in jeans and a waistcoat. She took a bite, licked her lips.

'Are you not afraid?' I asked her.

'Of the dark?'

The candles on the walls behind us flickered. 'Of the ghosts.'

'I think the ghosts can tell we're family,' she said.

'Do you think they can tell we're the same?'

'The same?'

I was glad of the darkness now, hiding my blush. My skin was warm, almost too warm to be comfortable. 'I mean that if we'd been alive then, we might have been kicked out of home too. Locked up. Punished. Just the same.' I could almost see embers smouldering under my feet. A sound like crackling.

Suddenly she was right in front of me. The scent of apples and smoke. She tucked a stray lock of hair behind my ear. 'Would have had to hide, you mean,' she said. 'Pretend.'

If I hadn't hidden, hadn't pretended, my father would have kicked me out already like it was 1877. I knew that. I had always known that. But was that a reason to stay silent? To sit out the protests? To let the insults of the girls in school slide? To feel sick at the thought of coming out to my sisters?

I said, 'I've been pretending my whole life.'

The heat was rising. I couldn't hear the others. My world narrowed to the trees and the sound of the flames.

'What are you looking for here?' she asked. 'Really?' She stood so close to me, the only solid thing in miles. She was so unexpected.

'I don't know.' It felt like the truest thing I'd ever said. I shook my head and the orchard spun in circles. Sparks danced when I closed my eyes.

'Hey,' she said. 'Hey. It's OK.'

Her hands were on my upper arms. Her feet next to my feet. Her eyes wide in the darkness.

'Mandy was right,' I whispered. 'I am a bad apple. Not because I'm gay. But because I'm a liar.'

Cale squeezed my arms softly. 'Everybody lies,' she said. 'If you don't feel safe coming out, you have to pretend.'

'I couldn't even say it to Ida.'

'You only just met her.'

'I only just met you.'

She pressed her palm against the side of my cheek, stroked my skin with her thumb. 'Yeah. But we'd've both burned,' she said.

The burning. I felt it in my belly, in my bones. As though somebody else was lighting up inside me. I'd been feeling it this whole time. Somebody with rough skin and calloused hands, chapped lips, salt-stained hair. She was as hot as a flame tip you flick your fingers through, a magic trick. She stared out of my eyes.

The girl looking back at me wasn't Cale, not exactly. Her hair was fairer, her skin lighter, her eyes blue instead of black in the darkness.

We stood in the quiet dark of the orchard and her hands were in my hair, mine round her waist. I wondered how much of this moment wasn't ours at all. The taste of apple in my mouth. Since the first bite, I'd felt the burning. We had only just met but this was an old love. This was a love that ended in flames. I pressed closer to her, knowing that this wasn't really me, it wasn't really her, but it also *was*, like the kind of knowledge that comes in dreams.

She tilted her head to kiss me, but before our lips could touch a shout rang out in the night.

'I found it!' Ida's voice came as if from far away, but in reality she was just there, behind the tumbledown wall of the cottage. 'The next address! We only read half the letter. The rest was hidden here in the doorway.'

Cale and I sprang apart. The spell was broken. Cold returned, blanketed me in goosebumps; I hugged my arms to my chest to warm myself. The thing that was in me had left, but it also felt as if something that hadn't been there before had now appeared.

Cale shook her head, took a shaky breath.

'Maybe we shouldn't stay here too much longer,' she said.

'Yeah.' I wanted to sit with this new thing, examine it up against the light. 'Let's go see what the rest of the letter says.'

18. *The bull's promise*

Drumcliff, 1935

When Mary Ellen and Ann died, everything changed.

The whole town felt it. They felt it in the rain. Julia Rys felt it in the animals.

The cows' milk was thinner. The chickens were skittish, more so than usual. A week after the fire burned down Ann and Mary Ellen's house, a fox got into the chickens' enclosure for the first time in Julia's almost-seventeen years. It ate half her father's best hens.

Julia's grandfather's prize bull grew stroppy and strange, as if he was gearing up for a fight. Patrick told her that before he'd married her mother the bull was always like that. Wide-eyed and angry. He told her that only he had been able to tame the beast.

It was undeniable that Julia had the same way with his prize bull as her father did. More than that, she was genuinely fond of the creature. So she started singing to him from her perch on the fence: songs she learned at school, songs she'd heard on the wireless, songs from church. The rain that had waited to fall until Mary Ellen burned was like a curtain between Julia and the bull and the rest of the outside world.

Julia was a dreamy slip of a girl who knew she wanted for nothing yet dreamed of wanting constantly. She spoke all her yearning into the silent, twitching ears of the bull: a new dress, a cardigan that hadn't first been worn by her older sister, shoes with buttons on the sides like Maggie O'Leary's. A kiss from the son of the grocer, a seat at the table with the village's prettiest girls.

The bull was impassive, didn't much hold with frivolities like dresses and buttons, cared very little for grocers' sons and popular girls. But he loved Julia, in his own way, and so he listened, and said nothing, until the day the village gathered to celebrate St John's Eve.

It was the morning of Julia's seventeenth birthday and the girl was all chatter. She told the bull every tiny detail of the evening's plans after having tired of repeating them to her mother and sister. She'd be going to town with her sister and her parents in her grandfather's car. They would attend the party together, then later their parents would return home with their neighbours, allowing their teenage daughters to attend the evening dance for the first time. Their grandfather would stay on as chaperone, and would bring them home before midnight.

Julia felt like a girl in a fairy tale, and she chattered to the bull about how she and her sister had been practising their steps for the ceilidh, had curled their hair in rags all night, how their Sunday shoes were sitting, shined and waiting, by the door for them to dance in.

The grocer's son would be there, and the pretty village girls. There would be no chores that night, no muck or chickens or – no offence intended, friend – bulls, and it would surely be the best night of young Julia's life.

But the bull knew better. Showing under the sleeves of Julia's new dress and just above the tops of her stockings as she clambered onto the fence, unnoticed by her as of yet, there were long, raised red lines, as though she had scratched herself in her sleep.

It was Julia's seventeenth birthday. The bull knew this too.

Julia's sister called out from the house, wanting help tying the ribbon in her hair.

'Coming, Lizzie!' Julia called, and she climbed carefully off the fence, not wanting to dirty her beautiful body, pale and freckled, stockings white and cheeks flushed. She was a picture.

The bull came up to the fence, pressed his head against her back to make her turn. When she did, there was a fleeting trace of fear in her expression, watching the great beast right before her, his eyes wide, his horns thick, the ring in his nose bright and gleaming.

The bull spoke. He said, 'Stay.'

But Julia only heard the word as a grunt and a sigh, an animal sound, something that could never have been a warning.

'I'll be back to feed you in the morning,' she told him, and she pressed a palm against his warm, bristled cheek. 'Wish me luck!'

In the morning, the farmhands would marvel at the state of the fence, how the bull had reduced it to splinters, how he had knocked down half the stone wall at the edge of the farm in an effort to break through before collapsing, as though from exhaustion, or pain.

At the feast there was lamb stew and carrots, potatoes roast and buttery, bread baked fresh that morning and berries picked straight from the vine. There was beer and stout aplenty, and the best poitín brought up from Mayo to wet the whistles of anyone who wouldn't tell. Julia and Lizzie were allowed to drink half a small glass of stout each, and both agreed that the bitter, iron taste was barely worth the treat.

They sat on the benches that lined the hall beside their classmates, the grocer's son and the prettiest village girls, and they felt pretty themselves, with their rag-curled hair, their berry-stained lips.

Later, when their parents left for home, they were all clapping hands and stamping feet, turning round and hand in hand as the dance took up the whole barn, everybody stepping in time to the fiddles and flutes, their feet kicking over hay and dried rushes, sending up sparks.

The sisters' hair came loose; their cheeks were flushed. They hung onto each other for dear life, skipped back to their tables to drink long draughts of water and returned, vibrating with energy and filmed in perspiration, to the best dance they'd been to in their lives.

The dance was fast. The barn was hot. The hay was trampled underfoot. Julia spoke to the pretty girls from the village, danced with the grocer's son. They stepped outside for some air and her grandfather was there, looking out for her, keeping an eye on her for her father, he said. Julia's head spun from the heat and the dancing. Dizzy, she drank more water to cool herself.

The water didn't taste like water any more. It stung her mouth, made her cough. Her grandfather gave her another gulp to wash it down, but it tasted the same. Less like water and more like strong liquor, not that she'd ever had any before.

A hand wrapped round a glass bottle of that same

something clear that wasn't water, but she was so thirsty. Her throat was a desert. Her throat was a storm. Fires and flames. Going down her throat, the liquid was like burning and her sister was nowhere to be seen. She slid down the wall outside the barn. Her grandfather held her hair as she retched into the hay. She wanted to go back in, enjoy the dance, but her legs just wouldn't hold her.

A voice said, 'Here,' as a hand held out a bottle.

'Try some,' the voice said. 'G'wan. Try some.'

It hit her mouth like an icy wind at the cliffside. Slid down her throat like a scream.

'Good stuff, this, eh?'

His body was so close to hers.

'I'm . . . tired.' She didn't know what made her say it, but once the words were out she realized they were true. Her eyelids drooped. She was so tired.

She heard a *Heh*. Heard an *Is she all right?* Heard a *Poor child, too much excitement, she isn't used to all this dancing, to staying up so late.*

She heard a *Don't worry, I'll take her right on home.*

The wheels of the car ran over rubble and puddles. Her eyelids twitched in not-quite-sleep. When the car stopped, she half wondered that they weren't home yet, could see no welcoming lights in the windows. A car door opened and shut, opened and shut again. Her eyes were too heavy to keep open. She drifted, uneasily, into sleep on the back seat.

She thought she felt something – a light breeze perhaps, a cat's back arching against her – touching up under the hem of her skirt.

Good stuff, this.

In the morning, when she woke up in her own bed, there was blood on the sheets.

19. *Ghosts and other night terrors*

Drumcliff and Donegal, 2012

When I read the last sentence, I was so full of adrenaline I had to stand, pacing the ruined cottage, wall to carved stone wall, back and forth. Ida was pale, her mouth wide open. Finn frowned as if he hadn't yet understood. Cale sat tense and still.

'That's . . .' Finn said finally. 'That's fucked up.' His voice sounded as raw as I felt.

Mandy knew how to tell a story, Ida had said as much that morning, but this was something else. I could see her – see Julia up on the wooden fence, stroking the grey hide of a bull. I could smell the sweat and the hay of the barn, could feel my own legs shake with the thrill of the dance. I could taste the spirits sliding down my throat.

I swallowed once, twice, three times, then turned and vomited over the broken stones of the missing wall.

'Let's just go, OK?' Ida said. Tears slid slowly down her cheeks. 'This isn't like before. Finn's right – I don't know what Mandy's playing at. Finding clues, reading letters. Let's just go.'

'No,' I said. 'This isn't supposed to be some wild goose chase. We have to follow. We have to honour the story.'

I turned over the last page of the letter and there was an address written there, hastily, in thick black ink. Just outside Donegal town.

Ida hadn't stopped crying. 'I *know* that,' she said. 'I know that. It's just getting to be a little much right now.'

Finn moved carefully, slowly put his arm round her, as if waiting for her to push him away. Instead, she leaned into him, taking comfort. Friendship comes fast in trying times.

But I wasn't listening to anything except the feeling in me that said we needed to keep going. 'One step ahead maybe,' I breathed. 'What if she's only a couple of steps ahead?' I started to gather our bags and jackets in the candlelight with quick determination. 'We can't stop now,' I said. 'We need to catch up. We need to find her.'

'Whoa, wait a sec.' Finn held up his hands to stop me. 'It's the middle of the fucking night. Where do you expect us to go?'

'South of Donegal town,' I said, reading out the address.

Ida tapped the details into her phone. 'It looks like a factory,' she said. 'There's no name for it on the map, but it's on that road. This must be it.'

Finn kept his hands up, shook his head in disbelief. 'That's *hours* away, Deena. We can't walk it. There's no bus. How the hell do you expect us to get there?'

'She might *be there*, Finn. Mary Ellen was from somewhere in Donegal. This might be it. The end of the world. The place where the curse began. This might be where we find her.'

'I mean –' he shook his head again – 'I agree that fucking Donegal is pretty close to the end of the world, but that doesn't change the fact that we can't get there tonight, Deena. We'd be walking all night and we still wouldn't be there.'

The trees of the orchard rustled, listening in. Long silver hairs glinted in the light of our candles, tangled round old stone. Far away, again, came a sound like a scream.

Cale and Ida jumped. Finn took me by the elbow, his grip kind but firm. 'Let's just head back to the town,' he said. 'Get a room for the night. Call our goddamn families. We can take a bus to Donegal in the morning.'

Behind me, the cottage glowed.

'What if the morning is too late?'

'Deena,' Finn said, his hands pressing. 'Mandy isn't there.'

The heat of the ground started to rise up through the soles of my feet, a strange knowledge, a deep need.

'We have to follow,' I said. 'We keep hearing the screams.'

Ida was giving me a long and considering look when I turned towards her, tears drying on her cheeks. 'I think Finn's right,' she said finally. 'I think a night's sleep will do us all good. We can keep going in the morning.'

'Cale,' I said, imploring. She had felt the same thing as me, back there in the orchard. The same presence taking over. She had brought her candles, her stones in their velvet pouch, had talked so much about family ghosts. She had to believe.

'I don't know,' she said. She wouldn't meet my eyes. 'But Finn's right about the journey.' She showed her phone, the glow of the map too bright in the darkness. 'It's a full day's walk and there won't be any buses now. We have no choice but to wait for morning.'

Finn gave a perceptible sigh of relief and led us away from Mary Ellen and Ann's cottage, back through the briars and brambles, back towards the road.

My phone dipped in and out of signal, but every time I checked it I had several new messages. All Rachel calling, texting. She may not yet have known where I was but she knew something wasn't right.

Rachel had trouble sleeping – she always had. Some nights were 2 a.m. showers or 4 a.m. baking, the clattering of pots and pans finding their way into my dreams. She'd play the radio low so as not to wake me, but sometimes when I got up to go to the toilet in the night I'd hear it, quiet notes of classical music on Lyric FM and often, just underneath the music, the sound of crying. The next morning there would be fresh bread for breakfast, raisin-filled scones packed in my school-bag for lunch. After Mandy's funeral, there were so many cakes we couldn't eat them all. The house smelled like yeast and hot butter and cooked apples, all salted with my sister's tears.

It occurred to me that, at this moment, Rachel was probably cooking, lights blazing in the kitchen, curtains closed to the street lamps outside, eyes on her phone as she chopped apples and rhubarb, waiting for me to call.

We stumbled in the darkness, our fingers stuck in cobwebs that looked like they were made of shining silver hairs. We were breathless, tired, rushing towards the road. I tripped over a tangle of grey hairs and couldn't catch my breath, couldn't keep the panic from rising in my chest.

I signalled to the others to stop, fumbled in my bag and pulled out my inhaler, took two long puffs.

'Sorry,' said Finn. 'We can slow down a little.'

Ida shifted her bag on her shoulders. 'Let's give it a minute. It's OK.'

I breathed deep, lungs fighting against the feeling I was drowning.

'There are places,' Cale said, as if to distract me, hand pressed against the trunk of an ancient tree gnarled over the road. 'Places where you kind of almost remember how it used to be. Before us, I mean. When there were no roads or people or telephone poles.'

We shone our phones round the scraggly field, the grassy wilderness, the tumbledown wall. Piles of rocks in a weedy grave.

Ida said, 'It's because, in places like this, nothing's really changed.' She shifted her weight, her shoes crunching brittle twigs underfoot, laces shining in the moonlight.

'We've changed,' I said, watching her.

Maybe Cale was right. In some places, it was easier to remember that you were standing on ground your ancestors once walked. There were places where you could touch the past. Press your fingertip into the bullet hole on an angel's breast, brush up against a tree that was only a sapling when your road was built, walk paths that ancient armies once travelled on horseback. There were places where, if you listened closely, you could still hear the rhythm of long-ago hoofbeats.

When we reached the road, I knelt in the middle of it as if I was about to pray and pressed my ear to the potholed tarmac. Faintly, from far away, I was sure I could hear wheels turning, wooden carts creaking, the clump of horseshoes denting the ground.

'Deena?' Ida said, panic creeping into her voice.

Finn touched her arm gently. 'She's OK.'

Cale stepped out onto the tarmac and joined me, listening.

The others clustered round us. Ida crouched and touched the surface of the road. 'Maybe that's why Mandy wanted us to follow the map,' she said. 'Maybe she wanted us to feel the past, smell it, taste it. Not just read a list of dead names off our family tree.'

I raised my head to meet my niece's gaze, said in wonder, 'That's exactly what I was just thinking.'

The cartwheel rumbling beneath the road became a vibration that set small stones skidding. Before I could properly form the sudden fear that the past was about to run us over on this tiny country road, a car appeared from round the bend and stopped suddenly in front of us.

I stood. The car was an alien thing: old, large, once

red, now dotted with rust and fallen petals from last spring that had never been washed off. For hours, we had felt so far from civilization that the car looked wrong, like it had come from another time. Or perhaps *we* had.

Behind the wheel was a broad, lined woman in her sixties, maybe older, with coarse grey hair escaping from a bun, wearing a shirt rolled up at the sleeves. She stared at us, unsmiling, and stuck her head out of the window like a dog. A real dog – large and black, the kind of Labrador that might have been crossed with a bear – bounded up from the back into the passenger seat and stared at us, tongue lolling.

'It's late,' said the woman. Her voice was harsh, loud. 'What are ye four doing out here?'

'We were out walking,' Finn said quickly. 'Lost track of time.'

'We weren't drinking or anything,' said Ida, immediately making it sound like we had been.

'We're just heading home,' said Cale.

'We were looking for a lift,' I said.

The others gaped at me in disbelief.

'Were you now,' the woman said in a way that was more a statement than a question. 'I'm driving up to Donegal – be there in forty-five minutes. There's room in the car if that's where you're headed.'

'No thank you,' said Ida, as I said, 'Yes please.' I added, 'That's exactly where we're going actually,' for good measure.

Ida's eyes widened. She shook her head.

'We could be at the next place in less than an hour,' I whispered. My phone vibrated in my pocket again. Whatever the others thought, I knew we were running out of time. I knew that the faster we got to Donegal, the sooner we'd find Mandy. If we went back to Sligo, Rachel would be on to me by morning.

'This is crazy,' Ida hissed back. 'We can't just get in a car with a stranger.'

'People hitch-hike all the time.'

Finn puffed out his cheeks. I could almost see the point at which he accepted the perfect serendipity of the moment, the point at which he convinced himself that this was just a story, a treasure hunt, an adventure, a way for me and Ida to grieve. 'What the hell,' he said. 'Let's just go.'

'Back, Lucky!' the woman barked at the dog, who loped over the back seat to settle in the boot. Finn got in the front and I sat at the window behind him, Cale in the middle and Ida behind the old woman, who grabbed the gearstick like it was the neck of a chicken she was killing, wrestled the car back into gear, and sped on.

*

Less than an hour later, the woman stopped unceremoniously just off the main road and told us we'd arrived. We tumbled out of the car and she gave a brisk nod, then shot out of sight.

'Well,' said Ida, when the roar of the car had faded into the distance, 'that was weird.'

'That *was* weird,' I agreed. 'And this is not what I expected either.'

This was our destination: a big grey building that looked like it might have once been a factory, and a dilapidated red-brick section next to it that looked somewhat more like an old boarding school. It was surrounded by a tall iron fence, the gates unlocked. The windows were high, only holes in the stone, the ones at ground level boarded up with thick sheets of metal. But the front door was open: a great black mouth.

The street lamps on the road opposite shone eerily. It was past midnight. The roads were deserted. Only the wind whistling through the empty windows, small rustlings in the grass and weeds of a garden that seemed too scared to grow inside the old factory. Or maybe they'd been burned away. It looked like there were building works going on during the daytime. As if they planned to tear the place down or build it up, start anew.

'OK. This is it.' I creaked open the heavy gates and walked towards the derelict building in the darkness.

'That sister of yours sure liked her creepy, abandoned places,' Finn remarked.

'Yeah.' Ida twisted her mouth around. 'What's with that?'

But I just walked across the garden. I didn't hear the others follow me. When I finally turned round, Cale was biting her lip and Finn was frowning. Ida hung back.

'It's just a building,' Cale said as if to reassure herself. 'There's nobody here but us.'

'And if you're wrong?' said Finn. 'I mean, this place *really* reeks of ghosts. And not the quiet family kind.'

Cale and I exchanged a look. She took a box of sea salt out of the front pocket of her bag and shook it. 'We just pour a ring of it around us and make sure it doesn't break.'

'Fuck,' Ida muttered. 'Don't let the salt circle break. Fuck fuckidy fuck.'

There was no sign that my sister had been there. The place was empty, dust-carpeted, with high ceilings and thick walls. We walked through two huge rooms, our footfalls echoing so that it sounded like there were more than four of us. Forty shoes maybe, tapping on stone.

There was a hallway at the end of the second wide room, the remains of heavy wooden doors propped open. Darkness spilled out. Between the two rooms was a crumbling staircase, leading up.

'She isn't here,' Ida said with certainty and a strain in her voice. My skin crawled.

'No,' I said. 'She isn't.' My resolve faded; whatever force had driven me to reach this place tonight was gone. In its absence was a kind of fear. I knew what I had felt in Ann and Mary Ellen's cottage. I knew now the power of old ghosts. I did not want that to happen here.

Unanimously, we decided to wait until morning to look for Mandy's letter. Exploring this place in the dark seemed unwise. Without really discussing it, we settled ourselves in the first room, close to the doorway that led outside. Around the walls were the rusted carcasses of empty bedframes, as though they had been pushed aside to make room to move things through the middle. Other objects were stacked round them: boxes and bags, wire hangers, rickety metal shelves. We stayed away from the shadows they cast, from the way the beds seemed to creak in the corners, as though invisible bodies were sinking down upon them, watching us.

Cale drew a circle of salt round us. I thought of Mandy, of the bull skull she put into a salt circle with me, of the bull I saw, of the bull who spoke to Julia, tried to get her to stay, tried to protect her like he'd promised Mary Ellen he would. I fell asleep with the ghost of a feeling of rough hide on the palms of my hands.

Something woke me with a start. A subtle switch in temperature, a different sound from the night air whispering in through the empty building. Almost empty. I opened my eyes, expecting to see sunlight. But inside the room everything was grey.

We'd settled ourselves a few feet from the doorway, hoping that the ghosts, if there were any, were hiding furthest from the door. From time to time, a car had driven by, its headlights splashing like paint on the walls behind us, half waking us before the darkness lulled us under again.

I hadn't expected to sleep at all that night, in that place. It was like we were under a spell.

We'd slept in a pile like puppies, Cale and Ida, Finn and me. We'd stacked our bags and things around us as protection, reinforcing the thick circle of salt. Finn hadn't let us light Cale's candles again. 'This is creepy enough as it is,' he'd said, and he'd hidden her matches in his pocket. We trained our phone-torch beams on the high ceiling.

It felt awfully real, that circle of salt in the darkness. Like it was the only thing keeping the true darkness out.

Cale mumbled something in her sleep. Ida shifted closer to her. Finn threw one arm up over his head, cushioned by his backpack, our hoodies and jackets blanketing us all. I slid my hand carefully into his trouser pocket and took out Cale's matches.

My phone had gone dark and Ida was using my portable charger. I flicked a match alight and touched it to one of Cale's candles. When I stood up, I took the box of salt with me.

The others awoke when I stepped over the circle.

'Where are you going?' Ida asked, at the same time as Finn said, 'What the fuck are you doing, Deena?'

I whispered, even though we were all awake. 'I didn't want to take the phone for light,' I said. 'But I really need to pee. I'll be back in a minute.'

'Goddamn.' Finn shuffled himself up. 'Give me that.' He unplugged Ida's phone and exchanged it for my candle. 'It's only slightly less creepy if we're the ones with the candle. It'll just blow out on you out there.'

I kissed my best friend's cheek as thanks and hurried out into the garden.

I peed in the bushes behind the front wall, not wanting to go any further into the overgrown garden, and when I came back inside I walked quickly, stared straight ahead.

But I could feel it. Something. I knew that if I took my eyes off the flickering candlelight lapping round the shapes of my friends I'd see it. I'd see her. A girl with a shawl and a candle at the bottom of the staircase, beckoning me on.

I think I whispered, 'No.' I think I said, 'I can't come with you.' I think I moved towards her anyway.

'Deena!' came Finn's voice. 'What are you doing?'

This had to be a dream. That's why I was carefully placing one foot in front of the other, walking through the second room, towards the stairs instead of back to my friends, protected by their circle of salt.

A sound from the stairs like fifty footsteps. A sound like children's laughter and screams.

'DEENA!' Finn bellowed, but it was Ida who ran out of the circle of salt, scuffing it with the toe of her shoe.

'I have to follow,' I said, and I climbed the stairs.

'*Stop, stop, stop!*' my friends shouted from behind me.

The shawl-girl's light rounded the corner of the landing. I could hear Finn and Ida's footsteps on the stairs, see the dance of their candles in the shadows, but I was at the top, already turning into a room, a long room like the one downstairs, with a big open space in the wall where the window used to be.

That's where the girl was. Her candle blew out in the night breeze. Mine was the only flame in the room. The girl stood up on the ledge of the window as if she was about to jump and, right when Finn, Cale and Ida came clattering into the room, she disappeared.

Ida gave a small, low cry. I could hear Finn's teeth clacking as he shivered.

Cale said, 'Did you see – did you – see—'

There was a letter on the windowsill. A letter addressed to me. It was weighted down by the girl's brass candleholder.

My own candle's flame flickered. But I wasn't carrying a candle, was I? Wasn't I just holding a phone?

'This is . . .' Ida was pale, eyes bright and wide. 'This is some mass hallucination or something. This is some mass hysteria. This isn't real. This can't be real. We're all just imagining together.'

Cale had her eyes closed. She was muttering, 'I can't see you, I can't see you, I can't see you,' over and over again. Finn's hands were clenched and he was shaking.

I stood in the middle of the room and spoke in a clear, loud voice that even my own ears didn't recognize. 'We see you. We hear you. We feel you. What do you want?'

Follow, came the whisper. *Follow us.*

'Why are you doing this?'

There are tears in the landscape. Pinpricks in the map. Pain stays on in places like this.

'What do you want us to do?'

You won't see us in the photographs. The history books. But the landscape remembers.

By then I was crying. Huge tears blinding. 'What do you want me to do?'

The only thing you can do.

Tears ran like rivers down my cheeks, dripping onto the dry floor, salting the earth. 'I can't find my sister. I can't break the curse. I can't do anything. I can't help you. I'm just a bad fucking apple. Just like her.'

So were we. Don't let us be. Tell the story.

The tears were choking me, stealing my voice. 'What story?'

Break the curse, Deena.

'Shit.' My voice broke first.

I sank down to the dusty floor and wept.

Dear Deena,
None of this is easy. This isn't a simple story to tell.
True stories often aren't, especially those that have
been hidden for so long. This is where you come
from. The history of this country is tied to the roots
of our family tree. I need you to know this. She
needs you to know this. They all do.

  This is what a curse does: it takes a truth and
twists it. It punishes those who don't conform. It
sets parameters of conformity so narrow that few

*can actually stick to them. Ask Rachel, she knows.
We're more alike than she wants to admit. We are
all bad apples, Deena, plucked before we were ripe
and ready, right off the family tree.*

Here, read this, you'll see.

20. *When a home is not a home*

Drumcliff and Donegal, 1936

It took almost six months for anyone to notice that Julia was pregnant. She had only had her monthly blood once or twice before and her mother assured her it was normal for it to come and go during the first year. It was also normal, she said, for Julia's breasts to be tender, her joints stiff and sore.

'Growing pains,' her mother said fondly, brushing her daughter's long red hair. She never imagined that Julia could be pregnant. Not even Julia imagined that.

She wasn't sick the first few months, just tired. (*Growing pains*, her mother said again.) She didn't start to show until Christmas, and even then it was easy for her to tell herself she was simply changing, becoming a woman. (*Growing pains*, her mother kept saying, and certainly her words were true, but it wasn't only herself that Julia was growing.) The swell of her belly was well hidden under her skirts, and only her sister ever saw her undressed in the room they shared.

It was Lizzie who exposed her, although she could never have imagined what would happen when she did.

It was a shock and a shame on the family. That's what Julia's parents both said. It was a curse and a burden. It was all her own doing. It was a great sin.

It was a smacked face. It was a dress torn away from a swelling belly. It was hair pulled to drag her over to the fire, press her hand against the burning stove until she told whom she had been with, whom she'd sullied herself for, whom she'd let turn her into a fallen woman, someone beyond repair.

Lizzie listened outside the kitchen door and her tears were salt and shock and sudden guilt. She was the one who'd told her mother, who'd spied Julia's round abdomen when she got changed for bed and hadn't known what to do, had done what any child does with a problem she can't solve: she'd found an adult to help. Except these adults weren't helping.

The following morning, Julia nursed her burnt hand and cried while her parents went to speak to the priest. They returned with a solution.

'A home,' Patrick called it. 'For mothers and babies. A place for you to rest. To repent. To make things right.'

But nothing would ever be right again.

Patrick remembered the herbs his mother had used. The hot baths she'd prescribed, the teas and ointments. But he also remembered how she'd died, burned to death in her bed. It was difficult not to attribute it to an act of God. It was difficult not to see Julia's current condition as a form of penance.

Julia never said who the father was. Said she couldn't remember. Said she must have drank poitín at the St John's Eve dance, which made her mother smack her all the more, but didn't answer the question. Not even when Catherine had pressed her daughter's hand to the hot stove.

'Cast her out,' Catherine hissed that night, hair askew and face wild. 'Let her find her own way in this life, the little slut.'

But Patrick calmed her, stroked her blonde hair until it lay flat again, told her that everything was not yet lost for Julia, that Father Hannigan was right, that since this was Julia's first offence she could be spirited away to the home before anybody else noticed, could come back to the farm right after and none of the rest of the parish need know.

'She made a mistake,' said Patrick.

'A mistake is a kiss,' Catherine insisted. 'A mistake is an indecent word at a dance. A mistake is drinking a few too many glasses of Guinness. *This* was not a mistake. *This* was a sin.'

Within a day, Julia's bags were packed, excuses concocted about staying with family up in Donegal, helping out an elderly relative, what a kind, good, selfless girl, a credit to her parents.

Early the following morning, John O'Connor drove his pregnant granddaughter up to Donegal. He whistled as he drove. Julia would not know it, but, when John O'Connor returned home, let himself into the bull's field to feed him, the creature would charge him, putting him in hospital for three weeks with a broken collarbone. For the rest of the year, the bull would have to be chained and sedated so he wouldn't attack or escape.

The Sisters of the Blessed Virgin Mother and Baby Home was an imposing block of a building built alongside the main road. Tall iron railings surrounded the property and, when a nun emerged to unlock the gates so the car could pass through, Julia caught sight of a small courtyard and a garden before the car stopped and she was led inside. Once a workhouse, the home and orphanage had high ceilings and long rooms well suited to dormitories. Corridors stretched through the home to the laundries that extended from the original building.

In the Mother Superior's office, Julia's clothes were taken away. She was given two brown tunics that looked more like sacks for potatoes than clothes for a girl. She was given one floor-length nightdress made of the same material as the day clothes and a bed in a room with nine others. All of the girls were unmarried, all of them pregnant or recently mothers, and they had come from all over the province.

They lived on the west side of the building, adjacent to the laundry, where the girls worked. On the east side of the home was the orphanage, and the nuns.

Work in the laundry began at 8 a.m., after breakfast and bed-making, after morning prayers. They broke for lunch at midday and again for supper at four. At six o'clock they were given tea or hot powdered cocoa and sent to wash for bed. The only days they didn't work were Sunday, Good Friday and Christmas Day. They finished work at midday on Christmas Eve, for a treat.

The washing machines were huge beasts of gnarled metal, and the presses were heavy rolls that needed to be turned by hand. The worst stains they scrubbed out on grating washboards. The irons and the presses were so hot that to simply brush your sleeve against them in passing would raise blisters. Girls got scalded by the steam itself.

With salt and steam, with bleach and lye and boiling water, the girls washed the blood off their own clothes, washed the stains off hotel bed linen, washed food they'd never be served off tablecloths so long it took four girls to fold them. They got blisters from grating the laundry over the washing racks, rashes from spilled bleach, burns from the steam irons, eye infections from the washing chemicals, fungal infections from standing up to their ankles in dirty water for eight hours a day over two weeks before the leaks in the machines were fixed. Some of the girls left with hacking coughs that never got better. Everyone's skin took on an ashen-grey hue.

In the darkness, it was hard to tell if the screams they heard were wailing ghosts or the others' night terrors.

The days were all the same in the home. Every morning they woke early and ate their porridge. They went to work. They worked in silence. They were not encouraged to make friends. Every afternoon they ate the same supper, they knitted until lights out and nothing ever changed until one of the girls, round and fit to burst, was brought into the small ward at the back of the building to give birth.

There was a maternity ward in the nearest hospital – in almost every hospital in fact – but none of the girls in the home were wanted there.

At night sometimes, they heard the cries. Or in the daytime, from the corridors, holding their sweeping brushes. The pregnant girls knew from the ones who were already mothers that they would not be offered pain relief. They would not be offered glasses of water or soothing words. The pregnant girls knew that it would hurt, for however interminably long it lasted. They knew this was their penance.

The pregnant girls didn't cry often, however much they felt like it. They learned not to. They learned to hold it in. They knew they'd cry plenty enough when their baby was born. That no matter how uncomfortable and shameful they felt, no matter how painful and lengthy their labour would be, they'd feel a thousand times worse when it was over.

21. *Washing the clothes*

Donegal, 1936

The girls of the home were not encouraged to make friends, but you cannot spend every waking hour with nine other people without beginning to know each other's stories. Without learning each other's ways. Without recognizing each other's moods.

The girl in the bed to the left of Julia's was called Cecilia; the girl to the right was called Nellie.

Nellie was fourteen, one of the youngest girls in the home. She had been there a year and a half. Usually, the girls stayed for one year after the birth of their child, working in the laundry to pay the nuns back for their maternity care. But Nellie's family had not yet come to collect her.

When they learned that she was pregnant, they showed her the door. None of her family would take her in. So she walked from her home in Letterkenny – thirteen years old, six months pregnant and alone – to the home in Donegal town. Almost thirty miles. Over twelve hours. A whole day. When she arrived, she was starving and her feet were so bloody her brown boots had turned red.

Cecilia had been in the home for six months. Her daughter was called Daisy. Cecilia was engaged to be married, and had been even before she became pregnant.

'I didn't know,' Cecilia whispered to the other girls one evening after work, her words hushed under the clack of knitting needles, the crackle of burning wood in the fireplace, the prayers of the nuns. 'I didn't know what was going to happen. How could I have?'

The other girls softly shuffled their chairs closer to her, didn't look up from their knitting for fear of giving away the fact that they were talking.

'I have no older sisters,' Cecilia went on. 'My mam surely wasn't going to tell me. I asked her what happens on your wedding night and do you know what she told me?'

'What did she tell you?' Nellie breathed.

'She said to have a glass of sherry and close my eyes.'

Nellie and Cecilia laughed quietly at that, heads bent to their knitting, but Julia suddenly felt as though there was no air in her lungs. No air in the big echoing room with its high ceilings and hard floors, no air in the world at all. She didn't understand how her friends could be laughing when their lungs must have been as empty as hers.

Julia had two thoughts before she fainted. The first was that Nellie and Cecilia were clearly town girls; anyone who had grown up on a farm knew exactly how a baby was made, even if their mothers rapped their knuckles for looking, even if their fathers tried to steer them from the fields during mating season, even if it took years of surreptitious curiosity to properly figure out what went where when a bull mounted a cow. Julia's family farm relied on her grandfather's bull making calves with fine dairy cows; it was natural that she should know how that happened.

The second thought she had – and it was a thought that had not yet occurred to her, despite having known of her condition for a couple of months now – was that somebody must have done to her what the bull did to the cows. Mounting and rutting. A base and animal act. No wonder they wanted to lock her up.

When Julia came to, she found herself in the home's sickbay, a cool, damp cloth on her forehead.

'A little overheated,' said the matron nun. 'It's normal, in your condition.'

Julia raised herself slowly, muttered a *Thank you, Sister* before returning to her room.

She could not speak to her friends again for a full

week, and then it was only because of what happened
with Nellie's baby.

After Julia fainted, she became obsessed with washing
clothes. In her dreams, she could not find the dress she
had worn to the St John's Eve dance, the one she wanted
to wash above all others. Each night her dreams were
endless labyrinthine terrors in which she searched
through every room of every house she'd ever known,
armed with salt and soap and water, armed with bleach
and lye, but she could never find the clothes she needed
to wash the blood out of.

But it wasn't just that dress – she needed all her clothes
to be clean. Her sheets. Her friends' nightgowns. She
begged the nuns to be allowed to wash her spare dress
daily, often stayed in the laundry all through lunch. She
spent her days scrubbing fabric, wringing it dry, hanging
it up on the line, mending its rips and tears. Cleaning
and mending clothes in the way she could never clean
and mend herself.

Everything was dirty. The girls bled after having their
babies; they bled when they were beaten. She washed
the children's clothes as well, and they bled too. Scraped
knees, bloody noses, fights and scuffles, canings when
they were bad. There was blood everywhere and she
needed to wash it all off.

Sometimes the children died. They fell down the stairs; they became sick; they didn't eat enough; they coughed up blood that Julia cleaned out of tiny clothes. The babies died even more often. One every couple of weeks. Sometimes their mothers were gone already – back home, or on to one of the industrial schools. Those mothers were never even told their babies had died. Sometimes the mothers were still in the home. Sometimes they knew it was coming – their baby was weak or sickly; there had been signs, symptoms. It didn't come as a surprise.

For Nellie, it was sudden.

She'd followed the other mothers into the nursery for the one hour a day she was allowed to spend with her child. Her son, Henry, who was over a year old, would light up when she came into the room, would babble nonsense at her while she tickled and hugged him, played peekaboo from behind the curtains.

He wasn't a healthy child – none of them were. All a bit thin, all a little grey, like they were reflecting the walls around them. Maybe the day before he'd been more sullen than usual, but Nellie chalked that down to him having had a row with another baby or having been scolded by the nuns. There was nothing Nellie could do about it anyway. There was nothing she could have done.

The other mothers filed in before her, picking up their

babies and toddlers, finally smiling for the first time that day. Nellie came through the door and looked around for Henry. Thought it strange that he wasn't there.

Her first thought – filled with horror – was that he had been adopted out and she hadn't been told. That he was now on his way to live with a family, to have a life outside these tall grey walls and away from the fourteen-year-old mother he only saw for sixty minutes of every day.

Her tears had already begun to fall when the nursery nun saw her. 'So you've been told then,' she said to the crying girl.

'When did it happen?' Nellie choked out.

'Last night,' the nun said. 'It was fast and painless. He's with the angels in heaven now.'

The words sank like stones.

Nellie was led out of the nursery because her screaming was upsetting the babies. The Mother Superior wanted to send her back to work, but she threw herself on the floor of the laundry and wouldn't move. Her howls were heard all the way through the home, echoed round the empty dormitories, screamed through the kitchens, screeched over the noise of the laundry machines.

'I want him buried!' she cried. 'Beside my baby sisters in the angels plot in the cemetery. I want to put flowers on his grave. That's all. That's all I want.'

Cecilia and Julia averted their eyes from their friend. They knew the baby wouldn't be buried in the angels plot for unbaptized babies. This child, born of sin, wouldn't lie in consecrated ground at all. He would lie with the other home babies in the mass grave at the bottom of the big garden.

It took a few days for Nellie to realize where the nuns had buried her baby. No priest, no funeral. Just a few prayers, like when a family pet dies. Illegitimate children were not buried in consecrated ground.

Neither were suicides.

When Nellie disappeared, her friends assumed she had finally been sent home. The nuns believed they were protecting the other girls by not telling them, and the girls didn't think anything of the extra prayers the nuns required of them that evening. They didn't think to wonder why the bishop had been called over from the town.

And they didn't wonder why the big window on the main landing had been boarded up, the ground below scrubbed clean.

22. Penance

Donegal, 1936–1937

After Nellie left, Julia and Cecilia grew closer. They worked side by side, exchanging whispers when they could. They tried to slip out to the bathroom together, to take a few minutes outside the heat and the steam and the noise of the laundry, to talk and to breathe.

In the laundry, the girls washed the nuns' habits. Julia was fascinated by those black robes, so like witches' cloaks. You couldn't even see a body underneath them. It was like they were floating across the floor. Except for the clacking of the heels of their black shoes. When you heard that, you knew that if you were doing something you weren't supposed to, you'd best stop at once.

The girls' tunics were like the robes, Julia thought. Designed in such a way that any sign of there being a female body underneath was entirely masked by the heavy drop of the fabric that flattened even the largest of breasts, that erased even the widest of hips. Julia's baby was due within the month, but in those dresses even the swell of her belly was lessened.

It was so hot in the laundry that girls often fainted for want of fresh air, for want of lighter clothing, for want of a ten-minute break. Julia's own sweat pooled into her scratchy underwear, seeped into the fibres of her dress, ran down the space between her breasts. She kept looking down to see if it was showing through. But nothing showed through those dresses. Nothing except blood.

Julia's arms were deep inside the sink, soap suds to her scalded elbows. Cecilia joined her with a fresh load of dirty laundry, leaned close so she could whisper without the nun in charge that day hearing.

'Am I bleeding?' Cecilia asked.

Julia started, afraid that her friend had injured herself, but Cecilia turned slightly to show the back of her dress.

'I've my . . . monthlies,' she whispered. 'They've only just come back after the baby. And it's been too busy to change my rags in the bathroom.'

'There's nothing,' Julia assured her.

Cecilia bit her lip. 'I can feel it, though.'

Timidly, Julia managed to beg the supervising nun, Sister Theresa, to let her and Cecilia run to the bathroom.

22. Penance

While Cecilia changed her bloody rags as best she could (there were no pads and belts in the laundry, only thick wads of fabric that got cleaned at the same time as everything else), Julia stood a moment in front of the bathroom mirror, breathing in the air that, while it smelled of piss and poor plumbing, was easier to breathe than the steam of the laundry.

She was so warm. She ran the tap, splashed cool water on her face. She pulled up her heavy dress and cupped more water in her hands to run it down the front of her overheated body, to wash off some of the day's sweat.

'Oh, that's an idea,' Cecilia said when she opened the toilet door, and she joined Julia at the sink, pulling up her own dress and splashing herself with water. They shivered and giggled at the cold against their skin.

'Oh look!' Julia laughed, delighted. 'The baby likes it.' The skin just beside her belly button pulsed out with one of the baby's limbs.

'Hello, baby.' Cecilia touched Julia's stomach, feeling the baby kick under her palm.

That was how Sister Theresa found them. Dresses pulled up in front of the mirror, water running down their stomachs in shining droplets, Cecilia's hand on Julia's skin. She grabbed them both and marched them to the Mother Superior's office, gripping their arms so hard they were both bruised for days.

'We were only warm,' Cecilia cried when Sister Theresa told the Mother Superior what she had walked in on. 'We were only trying to cool off from the heat.'

'We didn't do anything wrong,' Julia whispered. 'The baby was kicking. The baby was kicking, that's all.'

The Mother Superior looked grave, nodded towards Sister Theresa who reached over into a drawer and took out a pair of scissors.

Julia felt the blood drain from her face. She didn't even struggle when the Mother Superior grabbed her by the hair and forced her into a seat. Cecilia gasped.

The nun took Julia's thick red ponytail in one fist and with five decisive snips cut it off just under her ears.

She pushed Julia, sobbing and shaking, out of the chair and pointed at Cecilia, who came over without a word.

Sister Theresa gathered up the fallen hair, damp and dirty now, lifeless, red mingled with brown, and threw it all in the bin.

'You must never touch each other's bodies,' she said to Julia and Cecilia. 'Do you understand? It's unclean. It's unholy. You must never, never do anything like this again.'

As the Mother Superior watched them leave her office, Julia could have sworn she heard the old nun say, 'Or your hair's not the only thing you'll have cut.'

*

After that, Julia and Cecilia's beds were separated. They barely spoke. Instead, Julia cleaned with more fervour than before, scrubbing the blood off clothes and sheets, and as she worked she prayed. She prayed when she folded the linen; she prayed when she fed cotton sheets through the rollers, when she brushed the steam-sweaty hair out of her eyes; she prayed when she felt her baby kick as she knitted in the evening with the balls of scratchy wool that was the only kind the nuns allowed. She was not sure to whom she prayed, but she knew for whom she was praying. Small spark of life fluttering and growing. Small love in her belly making her soft and round.

Love wasn't something Julia had thought of before with great seriousness. She'd loved her parents and her sister, Lizzie, that much she knew. She'd loved the animals on the farm – especially the bull. She knew she didn't love the grocer's son or the pretty village girls. She knew she didn't love in the way the priest described each Sunday: all bored responsibility and weekly devotion that sounded like a sermon more than an emotion.

Instead, Julia discovered that she loved fiercely. She loved desperately. She loved blindly. She could not see who it was she loved apart from the push of a limb against the skin of her belly, the tossing and turning at night, and something undefinable that somehow touched her heart.

*

In the evening, Julia wrote letters with hands bandaged over steam scalds from the laundry. To her parents. To her sister. She didn't put anything in about the hair cutting, about the hard work for no pay, about the fact that she hadn't been to school in months, that doctors only visited when the girls were dying, that she hadn't been outside the high barbed-wire walls once, that it was like she imagined prison would be. She didn't write these things because she knew that the nuns read every letter that left the laundry. Instead, she wrote about her knitting and her prayers, about the daydreams of the future she had, and how excited she was to see her family again. She asked, in every letter, when she would be allowed to come home. But the answer never came.

What she didn't know was that, while the nuns read the letters, they rarely if ever sent them. They also rarely gave the girls letters from their families back home. Once, in secret, worried that her letters were getting no replies, Lizzie called the laundry's office, asking for news of her sister. The Mother Superior answered, told her not to be wasting her daddy's money on phone calls like that and put down the telephone.

Julia had been in the home three months when she felt the first contractions in the middle of the night. She ignored them in the way she'd ignored the cramps, the heartburn, the discomfort. She rose and washed and cleaned. She had no stomach for her porridge. Halfway through the morning, there was a tightening belt of fire around her. It started in her lower back and wrapped round her whole body, sent her shuddering on all fours to the floor of the laundry, convinced she was going to die.

The nuns, who were trained midwives, brought her onto the ward. They were stern, but kinder than she'd expected. They laid her down and mopped her brow and moved out of the way when she retched out what little porridge she'd eaten onto the floor from the pain.

She wanted to move, get off the bed, but the nuns held her down. She wanted to roll over, to get some relief from the great weight pressing in on her abdomen, but the nuns told her to lie still on her back.

'This is your penance,' they said. 'The pain is your punishment.' They did not say this to be cruel, just so that she would understand. 'You're not the first girl to come through these doors,' they told her, 'and you won't be the last. Now. Chin up, trust in God. It'll all be over soon.'

It was not over soon. Julia's labour lasted for thirty long and excruciating hours. At some point around hour twelve, the nuns called in a doctor from the town who came with his bag and his instruments, who asked the nuns to brace Julia's feet up, who stuck things inside her and pressed so hard on the cage of her pubic bone that she could almost feel it breaking.

And even that wasn't the worst of it. The worst was after. Like the other girls had said. The worst was when it was over.

Her baby's head crowned close to two in the morning. Julia was so exhausted she could barely bring herself to push. The doctor held her baby's head in his gloved hands. Suddenly, in a wet, sucking squelch, Julia's baby was born.

She heard the baby crying, heard the doctor tell the nurses that he was a boy. She could hear her own voice croak that she wanted to see him. She knew what she wanted to name him. William. But they wrapped him up and took him away.

Julia slept, and the following day she went back to work – with blood spilling into her skirt, milk leaking into her apron from her breasts, her belly still round, still contracting, the skin mottled like a sponge, just like the other mothers who stood beside her.

Four times a day, and twice at night, they filed into the nursery to feed their newborn babies at their breasts. Precious stolen moments to coo and cuddle, to smell the spicy milk scent of the crown of their heads, to stroke their tiny fingers. Four times a day, and twice at night, they were sent back to the laundry, to their rooms, to their penance.

22. Penance

One year. That was how long they were forced to stay in the home after their babies were born, to pay for their birth and their care by working six days of every week for the nuns. Seeing their children for one hour a day only, after their early infancy. Just enough time for a cuddle, a song, a story. Just enough time for the tiny child to recognize his mother. Just enough time for her heart to break again, and again, and again.

William was all Julia thought about. When she made her bed in the morning. When she ate her porridge at breakfast. When she worked through the noise and steam. She dreamed of the day they would be together, without whitewashed walls and rows and rows of identical cribs, without nuns watching their every move.

She dreamed of him all night, lying alone in a crib on the other side of this enormous building, separated by stairs and doors and nuns.

On the day of William's first birthday, Julia's father came to fetch her. He folded her into his arms and said, 'It's over now, it's over. You're coming home.'

Julia ran to the nursery to get her baby. The nuns stopped her at the door. They shook their heads.

'We'll take care of him, Julia,' they said. 'Go home now, and be with your family. Go home and take your second chance for a proper life.'

Inside the nursery, the babies were crying. The toddlers stared at her with round, open eyes. They understood nothing. Julia understood nothing.

The nuns took her hands, took her elbows, took her under her arms when she started crying, started screaming, started trying to run back to the nursery, pleading, 'I'll stay, I'll stay, I'll work here forever, just let me keep my baby.'

They kept walking; they held her up; they wouldn't let her fall; her – fallen woman already. They led her to her father, who bundled her into her old coat, pinning her arms to her sides. She had screamed all there was in her to scream.

As her father pushed her gently into the car, one of the nuns said, 'You'll see, Julia. You're one of the lucky ones. From a good family. You can still have a good life, find a husband. Nobody in your parish needs to know.'

The other nun patted Julia's shoulder and said, 'Now you can put all this behind you.'

Julia still believed somehow, in the depths of her heart, that her family would send for her baby when he had finished his nap. That she would raise her beautiful baby to love the animals on her family farm, to become a bustling and loud darling little boy. To see him off to school in the morning. To mend his clothes and kiss his knees when he skinned them. To tell him stories and sing him songs and let him fall asleep in her arms.

Her father would allow her to fetch him. She'd tell him – she'd explain the all-encompassing love she felt. She'd explain that none of this was her son's fault. That he shouldn't have to suffer for his mother's sins.

The nuns shut the car door and Julia finally managed to speak, croaked the words out of the open window: one last plea.

'I didn't even say goodbye.'

Her father started the engine. The nuns waved as the car pulled away. Before they left, Julia heard one say, 'You see, it's a kindness. It's a good thing we didn't let you get too attached.'

23. *The fallen and the forgotten*

Donegal, 2012

The morning was something unexpected, as if not a single one of us thought we'd wake up to see the dawn. And yet eventually, as it did every morning, then like now, pale white light shone through the high empty windows, painted the stone walls a lighter grey. After a virtually sleepless night, our faces had taken on the same hue.

Outside our salt circle, darkness retreated, slightly, to the corners of the room, pooled in the shadows of the old bedframes. Or perhaps we had grown accustomed to the gloom. We turned away from the stairs that led up to where we'd seen the girl the night before, and instead walked deeper into the building. The doorway at the far end of the hall had once been bricked up, but had since been broken open, stones stacked neatly to either side. Beyond it, time was strange – simultaneously paused and speeded up, stark and startling.

23. *The fallen and the forgotten*

This room was even larger than the one we had slept in. Long tables filled the space, covered in dirt and creaky Singer sewing machines under faded dust covers. Measuring tapes, rusted scissors and needles littered the floor. Over each door, a large crucifix and a framed photograph of an old pope.

Weak sunlight filtered through windows set high in the walls, illuminating the long fluorescent lights that swung on rusted chains from the ceiling. Pipes ran underneath the windows, over the exposed walls, disappeared into other rooms like worms inside a dead animal. Only our footprints disturbed the dust.

As we walked, the sound of our steps echoed off the ironing boards and steam presses, the pumps and hydraulics of the boiler, the giant vats for bleaching, the industrial-sized washing machines twice as tall as the tallest of us (Finn, whose face was the same stone-grey as the walls underneath the ancient peeling paint).

Through a far door was an office, its walls covered in cardboard boxes on metal shelving, interspersed with ceramic statues of Mary (the Virgin, naturally, not the Magdalene). Inside the boxes were folders, files, stacks of metal hangers, the same detergent and fabric softener that Rachel used at home.

In a corner stood a large fridge-freezer, empty now, door yawning open. On the countertop beside it, an electric kettle, a radio – a cluster of reminders that this place was open not so long ago.

'This looks . . .' Ida spoke suddenly, broke the silence. 'This looks newer. I mean, more modern than I thought it would.'

I realized I had been picturing everything happening in the early 1900s, unconsciously filing excuses for the very existence of such a place because of the time period. But Julia's time here was only seventy-six years ago, and now the past seemed suddenly even closer.

Ida flicked through some of the files. '1993,' she said heavily. 'This place was still operating in 1993.'

Silence fell like a weighted press.

We opened the boxes, flicked through the files. They were invoices, accounts, details of the hotels, companies and hospitals that used the laundry for their businesses. There was nothing about the women the laundry used as unpaid labour. Nothing about the children stolen from the women. No names, no details, no death notices.

Ida, her phone glowing, read with a heavy voice from the screen. 'They didn't keep records, and those they did were destroyed when the first investigations into abuse were called for. They didn't want people knowing what went on here. They didn't want the numbers getting out. The babies sold to rich couples in America. The illegal adoptions. The deaths.'

23. *The fallen and the forgotten*

Finn whispered, 'How many babies were buried in that garden since Nellie's?'

I grabbed hold of the nearest hand without thinking and squeezed it. Somebody squeezed back quickly, before letting go.

Shock made my face sting. Tears pattered into the dust at Ida's feet.

'Can we go now?' someone said. It could have been any of the four of us: me or Ida, Finn or Cale. It could have been somebody else.

'Yes. Yes. It's over. It's finished now. We can go.'

Retracing our steps through the building, between the imposing walls, Finn whispered, 'Fuckers, fuckers, fuckers,' under his breath over and over.

'I was born in 1996. If I'd come along a few years earlier, this is where I could've ended up,' Ida said. 'Unmarried mother, barely eighteen. They'd've taken Mandy in and then pushed her back out again. I'd've been raised by nuns and then shipped off to America with a new name.'

'Things were different back then,' Cale said, touching Ida's shoulder gently, but I gave a hard, dry laugh.

'The more things change, the more they stay the same.'

A seventeen-year-old girl in 1936 was still a seventeen-year-old girl, was still a whole person, regardless of her time. Her baby was a whole person too.

When I took a moment to consider the timeline of my family history, realization rose like steam. Dates shuffled in my mind. Julia gave birth to her son in 1936. The same year my father was born. Julia was my grandmother. My father was born in this place.

There's a lot you don't know about your sister, he had said, but clearly there was a lot we hadn't known about him as well.

We walked to the nearest bus stop silently, and people appeared around us: old ladies off to hairdressing appointments, mums with babies in buggies, old men with dogs on leads. The world had kept turning somehow. Did they know what'd happened in the old crumbling building that stood, silently overlooking the town? Perhaps, if some people had known, they'd forgotten. Maybe even women who once were in there had forgotten. We do whatever we can to survive.

Ida held Mandy's letter like she was afraid to lose it. The next address, as always, scratched hastily onto the last page, led us on, west, closer to the ocean.

'This was going on for so long,' Ida said, her voice strained. 'Some of the girls who went through this place could still be alive today. Women. How do you live a normal life after something like that?'

Finn kicked a loose stone on the pavement, sent it

scudding angrily across the road. 'It's all fucked up. All of it.'

'That Mandy sent us here?'

Finn looked up at me, surprised. 'No. No. I understand it now, I think. Why she'd do this. Like Ida said, sometimes you have to feel the past to believe it.'

'It needs to be told like a story in order to be heard,' I said.

'Right. Exactly.' He shoved his hands into his pockets, shrugged. 'It's the story itself that's fucked.'

I took my phone from my pocket, swiped away the three missed calls from Rachel, then called her back.

'Deena!' she said, relief in her voice. 'Where were you? Why weren't you answering my calls?'

Ida was typing on her phone, probably messaging her dad, who believed her to be staying over at her best friend's. Cale called her grandparents. Finn was already talking to his parents, fast and somewhat frantic, offering love and reassurance that he was at my house with me, that we were both OK.

'Deena?' Rachel's voice said in my ear.

'Sorry. Hi. Yeah. I'm fine. I'm sorry I didn't call you back. I'm in Finn's house and just sort of couldn't face talking to anyone else.'

'Deena,' my sister said again. She took a minute, sniffed softly. 'It's OK. It is. I'm glad to hear from you.'

My eyes prickled suddenly, my throat thick. 'Me too,' I whispered. I turned my back to the broken hulk of the laundry building, took a deep breath. 'Me too.'

Tears ran down Ida's cheeks as she put her phone back in her bag. Cale's lip trembled as she talked. Finn's eyes were watery when he hung up.

There was so much I wanted to ask my sister. About Mandy, about our father. But if I talked too long she'd hear the sounds of the town around me through the phone. Suspect that I wasn't three doors down from her, playing video games with my best friend. I was running out of time.

'I have to go,' I said finally. 'I'm sorry.'

'OK,' said Rachel, then her voice changed very slightly, perceptible only to somebody who had lived with her forever, who knew her better than anyone. She had somehow guessed that something was up. 'Call me later. And come home for dinner. I know you're having a hard time. I understand. But we need each other right now. And you need to be home.'

'Rachel, I—'

'There's loads of leftovers from the wake, plenty of veggie options. You have to keep up your strength. I've changed the sheets on your bed and hoovered your room so you'll be nice and comfortable. There's that programme you like on the telly tonight, the singing one, what's it called? Doesn't matter. We can have dinner on the couch, just this once. You can even have a glass of wine.'

'But, Rachel—'

'This is not a discussion, Deena. I'll see you at six. OK, I love you, bye. Bye-bye. Bye.'

I stared at my phone for a minute after she hung up, then turned it off completely. I shook away my worry. Rachel would understand. When I came home tomorrow with Mandy, she'd have to understand.

On the bus, I sat beside my niece. 'Are you OK?' I asked her.

'Yeah. I mean, no. But yeah.'

The sun outside the bus windows strained to break through low rainclouds.

The next address on Mandy's letter – a disused industrial school in a small town west of here – was only a brief drive to the Slieve League mountain, whose cliffs ended, with a steep and brutal two-thousand-foot fall, in the wild Atlantic Ocean.

It was at these cliffs that my sister's car had been found.

24. *Kisses*

Killybegs, 2012

Outside the window, the fields alternated cows and sheep, splashes of colour on their coats to mark them. I let my eyes skim past them, barely registering, until I realized that I kept seeing the same thing. It started as a quick blur as we drove by, but once I'd noticed it was unmistakable. It was in the sheep fields and the horse paddocks. It was in among the cattle. Huge hulk of a thing, great white horns.

In every field, the same grey bull.

'I keep seeing a bull,' I told Ida.

'A bull?' She leaned round me, looked out of the windows on both sides of the bus, frowning. 'Where? I haven't seen so much as a cow for miles.'

I turned my head from the window, ill at ease.

Cale knelt backwards on her seat in the row ahead of us, faced me across the rough fabric of the seat back.

Her eyes were lined with the grey smudges of yesterday's make-up, her hair sticking up slightly at the back from the way she'd slept.

'You OK?' she asked.

I hated that I blushed at a simple two-word question. I hated how hard it was to look her in the eye.

'Fine,' I lied, casting about for something else to say. The first thing that came to mind was: 'So what's your alibi?'

'My alibi?' Cale asked.

'For being here. Ida's supposed to be sleeping over with a friend. I'm meant to be at Finn's. Finn's parents think he's at mine.'

'Ooh!' Cale laughed. 'That's a risky one.'

Finn's head appeared over the seat back beside Cale's. 'She's right, you know,' he told me. 'One call from my mam or Rachel and our cover's blown.'

'I had to think fast,' I said. 'It's not exactly like I had another choice.'

'I don't really have an alibi.' Cale shrugged. 'I just told them the truth.'

'The truth.' Ida looked about as incredulous as I felt.

'Yeah.'

'Let me get this straight,' said Finn. 'You told your grandparents that you were following three complete strangers to an unknown location given by a woman who everyone else believes to be dead?'

'Pretty much,' Cale said.

I tried to pick my jaw up off the floor. 'What did they say?'

'I dunno, like, *Have fun, be safe, let us know where you are?*'

I was glad to see that Finn and Ida were both staring wide-eyed at Cale; it wasn't just me whose mind reeled at the thought of being able to tell a family member the actual truth.

'Your grandparents sound ... kind of unreal,' I told her.

'They trust that I know how to handle myself,' she said. Her eyes stared straight into mine, her mouth half a smile. 'And I told them I'm with good people. Important people. People I have a connection with.'

My face lit up like a beacon at how much I wanted to connect with this strange, pretty girl who seemed to live her life with an authenticity I could only dream of. Instead, I let Ida lead the conversation to talk of childhood and grandparents, music and TV, as if to keep us all from memories of the laundry, of Mandy's letters, of old ghosts. As if to keep me on the bus with them, instead of deep inside my head, staring out of the window at the same bull in every field: a sight that apparently only I could see.

*

A little after midday we arrived at the next address. The bus left us on a windswept road in a small village, in a sprinkling rain. The north-west of Ireland felt more remote than any place I'd been before. These were not destinations you chanced upon, took a wandering road towards. To get to these far-flung places, at least from Dublin, you needed to really mean it.

Our destination was a large red-brick building with arched doorways. Skips stood half full on the street in front of it and a large sign announced the site as the new vocational college, opening next September. The concept art on the sign showed the imposing structure modernized with glass-fronted conference rooms, wheelchair ramps, tech labs. But today the place was closed, empty, looking more like the bleak industrial school it was decades before.

We stopped on the street, Finn and Cale circling the building to find a way in. Somewhere in the village, car brakes screamed. A sense of foreboding washed over me. I reached into my bag for my inhaler and, when my sleeves hitched up, I caught sight of scrapes on my arms. Raised red lines like I'd been scratched.

A cat, I told myself, closing my bag with shaking hands. A stray cat who'd crept through the old laundry last night. Brambles, from climbing through the thickets. Branches in the orchard at Ann and Mary Ellen's cottage. Somehow I just hadn't noticed. That's all.

I rolled my sleeves over my hands, bit holes in the seams to poke my thumbs through. If you can't see something, it may as well not exist.

Cale and Finn returned, pointed to the far side of the building where a door had, inexplicably, been left open.

'Time's almost up,' I whispered without really meaning to. Ida shot me a strange look.

Finn came closer, touched the back of my hand. 'You know we'll have to go home soon,' he told me. 'It's been twenty-four hours already. They're going to notice we're gone. If they haven't already.'

My phone sat heavy in my pocket. 'I know.'

'Deena, if Mandy isn't out here—'

'I know.'

'OK. OK.' He squeezed my hand.

Inside, the school was as black as night, one long beam of grey daylight stretching from the open door. The windows were boarded over with hammered iron sheets, and the thick walls kept in an unnatural cold. We clustered in the doorway, shone our phone torches at the high ceilings, the stark blocks of the stairs, the folded tables and workbenches the builders had set up. Everything was dust and rubble, coils of electrical wire and stacks of bricks, uncut sheets of glass.

'Let's get this over with quickly,' said Ida. 'Find the letter and get back outside.'

24. Kisses

We dumped our bags and jackets in a pile by the door and split up, moving slowly through the hallway, torchlight seeking out a white envelope amid all that dust and greyness.

On the ceiling there was a flaky stain where the paint had peeled and it looked like the shadow of a bull's head, grey and horned. It winked.

'I'm going upstairs,' I said.

'Deena, wait—'

On the bottom step, my footsteps crunched. I shone my phone light at my feet. There were bits of bone comb smashed under the staircase, silver hairs tangled round the banisters. From upstairs there came a short, sharp scream.

Somebody grabbed my arm and I jumped so hard my phone fell from my fingers.

'Don't go up there,' Cale whispered, panicked, beside me.

Follow, follow.

The banshees were getting closer, getting stronger. It was so hard to resist the pull.

I turned my face back towards the light shining weakly from the open door and let out all my breath in a sharp gasp of fear. Tangled round our bags and jackets were more shining silvery-grey hairs.

They were here. They were close. I think I knew where they wanted me to go. The cliffs that Mandy jumped from were about twelve miles away. I could feel their pull from where I stood. Could hear the scream of the wind. A scream that sounded a lot like it came from the open mouth of a banshee. A scream that sounded like it was coming from a room at the top of the stairs. Before I even realized I'd moved, I took three quick steps towards the sound.

A pressure on my shoulder; the pinch of long nails on the top of my arm. I turned, expecting a ghost. Someone with tangled hair and grey skin wanting to lead me away. I think I might have followed.

'Don't go.'

It wasn't a banshee. It wasn't a ghost. It was only a girl with smudged black-cat eyeliner and choppy hair, shivering through her waistcoat.

'I would have followed.' I closed my eyes. 'They're calling me.'

Cale looked nervously towards the stairs. 'Stay here,' she said. 'Stay with me.'

'I think there's only so far left to go,' I said – Mandy's next letter was in my hoodie pocket. I crinkled the paper between my fingers like a dried leaf. Crumbling.

'Do you think we carry them with us?' I asked. 'All the stories of the past?'

Cale touched her fingertips to the spot above her belly button that mirrored the place on my own body where

I had first felt the burning back at Mary Ellen and Ann's cottage. 'For a while maybe.'

That spot still burned. The cliffs still called. There was still a screaming on the wind. Panic froze me like a shock of cold water, the same sensation as falling, hard, into the sea.

I voiced something I was too afraid to say to Finn, who knew me, or to Ida, who was my sister's daughter. 'What if that's the only place Mandy is?'

'Hey,' said Cale, and she put her arms round me. 'Hey. It's OK.'

When she kissed me, I didn't expect it, and I'm not sure she did either. Her lips were soft and tasted of Burt's Bees. She touched the side of my face and her hand was soft too, and cold. The kiss started slow and deepened so fast I didn't even realize what I was doing until her hand was halfway up my shirt and I was pulling her hips towards mine as if we could fuse together, grow into each other like trees over wooden fences, meld muscle and bone.

If pain stayed on in places like this, maybe love did too. Maybe Ann and Mary Ellen had followed, recognized us as their own. Maybe their lips guided ours – how else would I have known how to hold another girl's hips, how to touch my tongue to hers, how to press, press, press myself against her while her hands lit up the skin under my clothes? How else would I have actually let myself?

My first kiss was interrupted by my friends, who tumbled back into the entrance hall from another room. Cale and I didn't manage to break apart fast enough for Finn and Ida not to notice. Their eyes widened; their mouths moved to make silent Os.

'Right,' said Ida, a drawn-out vowel cut off by a *t*. She touched her hair, straightened her long, thick plait. 'OK. Wow. Sorry.'

'Sorry.' Cale looked sheepish but not ashamed. 'Got a bit carried away there.' She bumped her hip gently with mine as if kissing me had been the easiest thing in the world, simple and spur of the moment.

My breath was short, my head spinning. My return to earth was a crash-landing.

Behind Ida's back, Finn gave me a sly thumbs-up, a wink. I must have still looked terrified because I definitely felt it. I cast about the room for something to say, hands in my pockets, then out of them, as if I didn't know how to control my own body – which didn't seem unlikely given what had just happened.

'What's that?' I said, pointing.

'What's what?'

'Under the workbench there.'

'Under here?'

Ida crouched to peer under the wooden bench by the

boarded-up window. She surfaced with a frown on her face and a letter in her hand.

I couldn't help but let a small sigh of relief escape me. 'Here,' I said. 'Give it here. Let me read.'

Dear Deena,
You're almost there. Only a few more branches
left to climb before we get to you. Before we get
to me.

I want to tell you I'm sorry. I want you to know
this was the only way for me to share this story.
I would have brought you with me if the curse
hadn't come to you too. Instead, I left to break it.

Help me break it, Deena. We're almost there.

25. *Things that hold you*

Donegal, 1936–1947, Killybegs, 1947–1953,
and Dublin, 1953–1978

They had a name for William Rys and it wasn't the one
he was born with.

Home Baby, they called him. As if he was still suckling
at his mother's breast. As if he even knew what a home was.

He left through the front door of the home with the
other children every morning at half past eight and they
walked, silent and in single file, to school. They sat at
the back of the classroom.

They didn't speak to the town children, the ones with
mothers and fathers. They hardly spoke to each other.
They saved all of that for the home, and when they
spoke in their rooms or in the gardens, with the nuns
turning a blind eye, it was all in shouts and insults, and
the desperate, lonely language of fists and kicks.

There were only three ways out of the home for the

home babies. Some were adopted as infants, usually to wealthy Catholic Americans, usually without the consent or knowledge of the babies' mothers. The rest were sent to industrial schools after the age of ten, and the industrial schools were almost identical to the home except that they were run by the Christian Brothers, not the nuns, and there were a lot more beatings. The third option was the unmarked grave at the back of the garden, behind the perfectly tilled rows of cabbage and lettuce, behind the greenhouse, behind the septic tank that treated the home's waste after it was flushed away.

Nobody wanted to go to the bottom of the garden. If a ball rolled past the cabbages, it was never recovered. The bravest, oldest children dared each other to run down there at dusk, to touch the back wall of the home's land, to feel under their feet the earth that was turned over once every few weeks when a fresh tiny body was buried.

There were no headstones, no names, no markers. Most of the time, the mothers were never even told.

William Rys didn't remember his mother. He didn't even know what she was called. She was gone before he'd learned to speak.

William didn't miss what he'd never had, but he held closely to the one thing his mother had ever given him. His name: William Patrick Rys.

*

There are things in life you hold, and there are things that hold you. William's name was his power, his strength, the secret he wrapped round himself like the warm woollen coats the town kids had. The ones that weren't handed down from ten other older orphans. The ones that didn't have holes in the armpits, too-short sleeves. The ones that hadn't faded to a homogeneous brown-grey from decades of washing.

He knew Home Baby was not his name. His name was William Patrick Rys. There was great power in a name like that. He held it like a fist.

The things that held him were passed on by the nuns and had their grip tightened by the Christian Brothers when he left the home in Donegal town at the age of eleven to live in St Brendan's Industrial School in Killybegs.

In the industrial school, there were no town kids with their fancy black coats, their new shoes, their penny sweets and magazines. In the industrial schools, there were only boys like him. Bastards and thieves, vagrants and orphans. All they had were fists and spit, cocked heads and cheek.

William found that, strangely, the boys in the school fought more seldom than the children in the home. He soon realized that this was because the home babies were neglected, while the boys in the industrial schools were never for a moment left alone.

William had grown up with the strict and disciplinarian nuns, but never had he known so many rules as this.

Everything moved fast in the school. If you were last to make your bed in the morning, you were clouted about the ears. If you had the misfortune to wet your bed, you could expect a beating. If you were last out of the classroom at break time, you'd get a wallop on the back. If you were last to the latrines, you'd get a kick up the arse. If you were last to finish your sums, you'd get a ruler across the knuckles. The smacks and slaps became a metronome by which to measure your days. Sleep, food, smacks, class, chores, slaps.

William missed the nuns. The ones who'd shush them, knit in silence. The ones who hummed hymns. The ones who'd shout that they were dim. The ones who'd tell them about the sins of their mothers.

The brothers called their mothers sluts and whores, but this was hardly news to most of the boys. The brothers who shushed and shouted weren't the ones to look out for. The ones who smacked and slapped, who hit with rulers or leather straps, those weren't the ones to look out for either.

The ones to look out for were the ones with tempers. Like Brother Jack who beat a boy unconscious for sniffing all through class because he had a cold and no handkerchief. Like Brother Francis who broke a boy's arm for laughing at the crumbs in his beard one morning. Like Brother Carl who gave a boy a black eye for doodling a cartoon picture of him farting.

But knowing whom to look out for didn't mean you wouldn't get hurt. In William's six years at the school, the local doctor was only called once, and that was when Daniel O'Callaghan fell from the second-floor stairwell running away from Brother Jack's beating and cracked his head on the bottom step. He died in hospital three days later. The police never came.

Knowing whom to look out for didn't mean you could avoid a night-time beating, after you knew you'd angered a brother that morning and had hoped he'd let it go, until he swooped into the dormitory, black cloak billowing like some kind of demon bird, woke you up and threw you into the nearest wall.

Knowing whom to look out for didn't mean you could keep a brother from forbidding you to go to the toilet during football training, didn't mean you could help pissing yourself where you stood and getting caned for the smell on your shorts. It didn't mean you could avoid following the summons of a brother into his office, where he stood with his robes all askew, didn't mean you could run when he brought you inside and shut the door. Didn't mean you could move your eyes from the statue of Mother Mary the Blessed Virgin hanging above the brother's door, halo all shiny and golden, blue dress like a summer sky, arms outstretched.

These were the things that William held. His name, and the angels and saints. The Blessed Virgin on her pedestal, St Brigid celebrated in woven rushes, St Agnes the virgin martyr, Mary Magdalene who renounced a life of sin to serve at the right hand of the Lord. All of these glorious women, pure and virtuous, arms outstretched to save him.

When he left school at seventeen, William walked out of St Brendan's with the clothes on his back and he hitch-hiked all the way to Dublin. He arrived on O'Connell Street with no idea where he would spend the night. He looked up at the statue of Daniel O'Connell (whoever he was; William's history was patchier than Brother Francis's temper) and was awestruck by the giant bronze angels supporting the base of the statue of the man.

There were four of them, all stern and stunning, with long, straight noses, crowns of laurels in their metal hair, and huge wings like those of great black birds, taller than William twice over.

William wanted to curl up on the cold laps of these giant winged women and fall asleep. Instead, he followed the stony gaze of the bullet-wounded angel holding a snake, walking away from O'Connell Bridge, past the shops and offices across the busy road, then down side streets and along alleyways until he found himself in front of a St Brigid's cross. Below it was the door of a bakery. Inside was a small iron statue of the Virgin Mary, the same colour as the angels on O'Connell Street.

Also inside was a little girl with her mother, folding down the pastry edges of a row of apple pies.

There is no doubt that William loved our mother. That he cared for and idolized her, placed her on a pedestal like the statue of an angel. He thought of her as his angel, his saviour, his bright blonde chance at redemption.

He was ten years older than her – the little girl in the window whose father employed him the very day he walked in the bakery door. William was seventeen, had only the clothes on his back and his name, but the baker, Seamus MacLachlan, our grandfather, felt a strange kinship with the young man. Perhaps because the boy was pure and damaged, or perhaps because he knew he could vastly underpay him. And, as time went by, because of William's devotion and his unwavering morals, which echoed then, as they do now, those of the baker's family. William fitted into the MacLachlan family like he'd always belonged.

Which is why it came as no surprise to Seamus, when his daughter came of age, that William should ask him for her hand.

25. *Things that hold you*

Until they were married, William refused to give his sweetheart more than a chaste kiss on closed lips. There are things that you hold, and there are things that hold you. What held William was the conviction that sex was a sin outside a marriage sanctioned by God.

Our mother lost six babies in the next ten years: some so quickly she only knew it by the unusual length of her bleeding the next month; some well after she had started to show.

When the two sisters were born, the doctors told our mother she would not be able to birth twins herself – each child pushing over seven pounds and almost full term – but Mandy came out feet first and screaming before the doctors could schedule a Caesarean. Twenty-four hours later, Rachel got tangled up in her umbilical cord on the way out, had to be cut from her mother's womb on the operating table. William would have liked a son but, after the girls, the doctors told our mother she would most likely never bear children again.

You, Deena, came later.

William grew up with a seventeen-year hole in his past. He was married many years before he told his wife about his origins, about where and how he was raised, and he only did that because his mother's family had been determined to find him, whether he liked it or not.

26. *On the back of a bull*

Killybegs and Fintra, 2012

When I turned over the page, we all saw the next address, written so hastily it was almost illegible: *Fintra beach, Glencolmcille, County Donegal*.

Closer, again, to the cliffs Mandy jumped from. We were almost there.

My phone vibrated in my pocket, made a sound like bees.

'We need to go,' I said, breathless. 'We need to go now. Find a bus. Get a lift. Walk it if we have to.' I ran out of the building.

Outside, the rain had started to fall. The others, their bags half falling off their arms and shoulders as they grabbed them to follow me, surrounded me, slowed me down.

'Come *on*,' I said, head spinning, breath catching, wheezing. 'We need to go *now*.'

26. On the back of a bull

'Stop, Deena, *stop*.' Ida held out her arms in front of me, palms up, a brick wall. I swayed when I hit it.

Cale's voice was worried, came from beyond my narrowing peripheral vision. 'She looks awfully pale . . .'

'Deena.' Finn's face appeared in front of mine. My vision yellowed at the edges.

'We've hardly slept,' said Ida. 'We haven't eaten. She needs to sit down.'

Finn pressed my inhaler into my hand. 'Breathe,' he said. 'We're going to find you something to eat.'

I puffed once, coughed, said, 'No, we have to go,' puffed again.

My friends frogmarched me to a nearby coffee shop right across the road from the school, beside the bus stop. 'We can go after a cup of tea and a sandwich,' said Finn, and I laughed faintly because of how much he reminded me of Rachel.

I didn't expect to miss Rachel, a day and only a few hours' drive away. Miss her ceaseless bustling round the kitchen, the kettle boiling, a pan on the hob simmering, her fond complaints about my vegetarianism mixing with the clattering of the dishes she needed to have clean before sitting down to any meal.

I wasn't just doing this for Mandy or for me. I was doing this for all of us.

While the others ordered food and tea in the stuffy,

overheated coffee shop, I pulled off my dusty hoodie, threw it on my chair, and went into the bathroom to try to calm down.

I stared at my face in the mirror the way madwomen do in films. My cheeks were still flushed from the heat of Cale's kiss, the blush of it still on my lips.

My lips had been kissed like in my wildest dreams in the middle of a wild goose chase. It didn't fit; the timing was all wrong. I couldn't fathom what should happen next. What if she had only kissed me because of the ghosts? Why else would she have? Still, a small involuntary smile quirked at the edges of my blurry, mirrored lips – I was on the path to Mandy with my oldest friend, and had gained her daughter and a girl with cat eyes and wild kisses along the way.

I splashed water on my face, swept the splashed droplets from the mirror with the palm of my hand, and in my clear reflection could suddenly see my shoulders, my chest, my neck. Raised red lines ran over the length of them, as though I'd been pulled through briars or scratched by three pairs of hands with long, sharp nails. All the way up my neck, like somebody had tried to choke me.

My breath stuck in my throat like a scream.

When I came out of the bathroom, Finn and Cale were at the table, their expressions grave, Finn holding a piece of paper like a summons. Ida had just arrived with our food.

'What is it?' asked Ida. 'What's happened?'

Cale and Finn exchanged a look. I couldn't read it.

'What's going on?' I said.

Cale reached forward and put the piece of paper on the table. A letter. Another letter from Mandy.

'This fell out of the pocket of Deena's hoodie.'

'No.' I tried to grab the letter, but Ida was faster.

'What is this?' Her eyes darted between paragraphs, narrowing as she understood. This letter contained the next part of the story.

'It's all there,' said Finn. 'The rest of Julia's life after she left the home. How she found William. Her grandfather's death. We just weren't supposed to have found it yet.'

Ida looked round the coffee shop, through the open door at the quiet road outside. She raised her eyebrows questioningly. She still wanted to let herself believe.

Finn shook his head. 'Mandy isn't here,' he told her. 'She was never here.'

My heart beat so hard it choked me.

For a moment, Ida looked like she was about to cry, but when she turned to me her face hardened. 'She hasn't been leaving these notes for us to find. Has she.' It wasn't a question so nobody answered. 'Mandy didn't put the notes anywhere.' Ida's voice was loud; people around us paused to listen with teacups raised part-way to their mouths. 'Deena's the one who's been leaving them. Leading us around. Mysteriously finding pristine letters in bizarre places – how were we so stupid?' She threw the letter across the table and it fluttered on top of our plates, our uneaten sandwiches, our cups of tea.

'I knew it was impossible,' Finn whispered, mostly to himself. The three of them faced me with deep hurt in their eyes.

Cale shook her head very slowly. 'Why didn't you just tell us, Deena? I was honestly starting to think it was magic. All this talk of ghosts . . . You could have told us. You know we'd have followed you anyway.'

'I didn't put them there,' I said, my voice a tiny vanishing thing.

'How can you expect us to believe that?' Ida cried. 'For all we know, you wrote these. For all we know, it was never Mandy at all. Whose handwriting is this really? Is it yours?'

'It could be,' said Finn. 'It's similar. Like she's disguised it.'

My voice was going. My voice was half gone. 'It's Mandy's handwriting. It was Mandy all along.'

'But—' said Cale.

Ida cut her off. 'Why are we here, Deena? Really?

To walk back through your family tree? You know all this already. Obviously.'

'I don't.' My words were strangled. I didn't know anything. 'I don't know. I just know that I have to break the curse. Find Mandy.'

'None of this is even *real*, Deena,' Ida said.

'OK,' said Finn with a single clap of his hands, all business. 'Maybe it's time to bring this road trip to a close.'

'But we're not there yet!' I cried. 'We haven't found Mandy. We haven't broken the curse. The banshees are still following us. Look at my arms, my neck. Look! You've felt them. You've all heard them. You know what that means.'

Right then all I could feel was our ragtag group unravelling at the seams.

Finn pulled gently at my sleeve. 'Time to go, Deena.'

'No.'

'Deena,' Cale said.

'*No*.' I couldn't leave. 'I don't have time for this bullshit. I have to go. You can come with me or you can leave. That's your choice. This is my journey.'

The letter was sprinkled with crumbs when I grabbed it and shoved it back into my hoodie pocket with the others. What did it matter who left them where? All that mattered was that this was my family tree, branch by fragile branch, reaching back through a weathered trunk to the very beginning, to the casting of the curse, to the key to being free of the banshees forever. To finding my eldest sister, if I still had a sister to be found.

'We've come all this way,' I said.

Finn's voice was gentle, in contrast to the fire in Ida's eyes. 'And now it's time to go home.'

'I didn't ask you to follow me.' I only realized I'd shouted when the coffee shop fell silent. 'I never said I needed any of you. You just latched on, came along. You did the cider and haunted houses bit, gold stars for you. This is serious. For me. For my family. I never asked any of you to follow me.'

Quiet settled on the room.

'OK,' said Finn. 'OK, Deena. We'll stop following. We'll leave you alone if that's what you want.'

'But really,' Ida continued his sentence as if it'd been hers all along, 'you should probably just go home. Your sister's obviously worried about you. And honestly I think she should be.'

'I called her,' said Finn slowly. 'I told her where you are. She's on her way. It's over, Deena.'

My head shook, spun me dizzy. He'd called my sister. My so-called friends were abandoning me, safe in the knowledge that Rachel was coming to fetch me. They'd seen me safely here so now they were free to leave.

They'd promised to look out for me, but now they were disappearing too.

Finn took Ida's bags and her hand and they walked away without turning once. At the door, Cale looked back and gave me a strange, sad smile. She half waved and walked out.

I didn't follow.

It didn't matter that my friends were right. That I didn't tell them about the letters. There was enough to tell already. They were enough, I thought: Mandy's words written by my hand. Mandy's work, pulled together, pieced together, dropped like breadcrumbs across the country. Everything in those letters was true.

Mandy believed there was a curse on our family, but for the longest time she didn't think to break it. The first she heard of it was rumours. Whispers at infrequent family events. Our mother's family, the MacLachlans, were a tight but judgemental clan, more concerned with appearances than affection. In families like that, gossip is like air: constant, intangible. Impossible to know where each rumour came from or if it was true.

Family rumour spoke of the Rys bad apples, a tree full of them, rotten almost to the core. (Our father, obviously, had avoided being given that particular label.) Family tattle said that at seventeen bad things happened to Rys women who deviated from the family tree. Family gossip said they always deserved what they got.

'It's a curse,' Mandy said to Rachel.

'Nonsense,' her sister replied.

But Mandy's interest was piqued. She poked and pried, finally got out of our extended family members that there was a connection with the Ryses and Sligo. She spent three weeks travelling round the county, following town gossip and local history, until a tenuous lead brought her to a long-abandoned cottage in an overgrown orchard.

In the middle of the burnt-out ruins was the huge gleaming skull of a bull. Inside its jaws was Mary Ellen's story.

Maybe Mandy had found Lizzie's diary, where she wrote every story her sister had told her about the home, where she had pieced together the details of Mary Ellen's life from letters her grandmother had hidden in the barn with the bull. Maybe that's where Lizzie left her diary after Julia died: safe and hidden in the skeleton jaws of her sister's prize bull.

Or maybe the bull came back to life, opened his mouth and spoke.

Mandy had a name now, an idea of where our family history began. She took the bull skull for protection and kept researching, digging through our family's past, reconstructing its history, drawing the roots of its scraggly tree. Piece by piece she put it together, but it wasn't until the day she left, the day of my seventeenth birthday, when she'd put the final branches in place, that she had a hunch: had suddenly considered that there might be a way to break the curse.

To do that, she thought, she had to go back to the very beginning. To the apple-tree sapling. To the end of the world.

She left her notes behind. The papers and books and diaries that had been stacked in folders on her desk. A decade of research.

I found them, the morning after my birthday, in Mandy's room with her note. I brought them home.

I wrote the letters. It took days, while Rachel spoke to the Gardaí, while they searched Mandy's flat, while her car was found, while they interviewed the witness who'd seen my sister falling to her death.

While Rachel sobbed and stared into space, organized the funeral, fended off our family's meddling and backhanded insults to the memory of our sister, I locked myself in my room and wrote.

I scratched down the story as though I was possessed, and the words came out of my pen in Mandy's handwriting. It felt like she was talking to me. It was the closest I could get to her. Maybe it was her working through me. It was all so much like a dream.

Follow, follow.

I knew I had to follow, suspected that once Ida had heard my story she would want to join this pilgrimage, recognizing the desperate need to understand where you came from. I kept the stack of letters in my backpack – later, my pockets – and placed each one when nobody was looking, and every time it was as if Mandy's hand left them, not mine.

Belief was a fraying rope bridge over a stormy sea. Strand by silver strand, I unravelled.

When I stepped outside, there was a bull.

Maybe it wasn't a white horse that carried the warrior Oisín on its back to the fairy land of Tír na nÓg. Maybe it was never a horse. Maybe it was a bull. I climbed onto his back.

Bulls travel fast. You wouldn't think it, great beasts that they are. Especially this one. This huge grey mountain of a monster, horns twice as big as my forearms, hair coarse and legs long, loping across the countryside like an animal on a mission. But then I suppose we both were.

The journey would have taken an hour and a half on two human feet, but on this enormous creature the trek was halved. We crested the coast then veered inland, across fields and boglands that nobody was allowed to cut any more to make turf for the fires in the way they used to.

I don't know how I knew he was the same bull as the one in the story, as the one who'd been haunting my steps since I left Dublin, the same as the one whose skull I'd been blessed with protection by Mandy years ago. But I knew, deep in the bones of my own skull. Mary Ellen had cursed him never to rest if he failed to protect her granddaughter. Maybe Mandy had called him back to protect me. Maybe my ancestors worked through her the way they did through me.

I wasn't afraid. I knew where I was going.

I could tell we were close to the shore by the wind, wild and restless. This coastline kept its own climate and right now it was mirroring all the storms I'd ever known. It stole my breath. It tangled my hair. It chilled my skin to a dull grey. It screamed.

The bull took me down, down, down the steep steps and the dunes until his hooves sank into sand. I slid off his back and my muscles hurt as if it had been me running across the landscape. What was it the ghosts in the laundry had said? Julia and Cecilia's voices in whispers; Nellie at the window, candle lit, ready to jump. *The landscape remembers. Pain stays on in places like this.*

On the beach, the bull left me like everybody else had

left me. He turned and walked away. I wanted to call out to him, ask him to stay, to hold my hand through all this, but he didn't have any hands, and at this point I couldn't feel mine either. I was numb to the bone. No hands, no arms, no feet, no heart. My voice was just a scream on the wind.

Listen, said the ghosts. *Listen.*

There were big black crows flying out over the sea and I knew that was where I needed to go somehow, the knowledge clear and immediate. I took off my shoes and left my bag on the shore.

In this country, everything happened in the water. I had seen the banshee in the sea and Ida thought she'd seen Mandy in the rain, watched over by stone angels. Iron and bronze. I wondered how they decided who to make statues of. Daniel O'Connell and all the angels, Jesus on everything, all these Marys, but only the virgins, not the Magdalenes. Our Lady, Star of the Sea, who watched over Dollymount Strand and Bull Island. Who watched over the ferries to England. She should have been the Magdalene, not the Virgin. Crying over the baby at her breast.

'Our Lady, Star of the Sea,' I said to the water. 'Different sea. This one's an ocean. Goes all the way to America, like a bunch of babies with different names on boats and planes. Never to be seen again.'

26. On the back of a bull

A voice came from the top of the dunes, called down to me on the wind. 'Deena, stop, you don't have to do this!'

But I did. I didn't have a choice. None of us did, all the bad apples.

Follow, follow.

I thought the shock of the first wave would bring all my blood to the surface, fill in my skin like a watercolour painting. But I could barely feel the water. So I went in deeper.

Numb feet, numb knees. Numb belly when I got in that far. I might not have been in water at all. Rising, rising, rising numb where my breasts used to be. The rolls of my waist, the swell of my belly over tight jeans, an extra hole in the belt I borrowed from Rachel. Thighs that rubbed together when I ran. All that, gone. The skin pale and prone to flushing. The freckles like grains of sand that got stuck and decided to stay. Stray hairs everywhere that I plucked and shaved. Spots and pimples. Nerve endings. Endings.

My neck barely felt the tug of the ocean. My lips barely felt the water's kiss. If my lungs were this numb already, how would I know that I was drowning? If I was this close to dying, how could I tell I wasn't already drowned?

When I went under, I tasted apples.

Dear Deena,
It's almost finished. I don't have much time. I'm
leaving but I amn't leaving you. I wouldn't do that.
The story is almost done and after this you'll find
me. I believe with all my heart you will.

27. Happy families, part II

Sligo, 1938–1995

It took Julia Rys almost sixty years to find her son.

Julia never married. Never wanted to. She never had children after William, her only son. After she returned to her parents, she set herself to work.

She still felt a compulsion to clean, to scrub and bleach each piece of fabric in the house. Her clothes, the towels and bed sheets were always worn and soft from so many washes. But in the laundry she had hated the heat and steam, the thick grey walls of the building closing in around her, so she was happy to be out in the fields. Little by little, she took over the farm, getting in good dairy cows to mate with her favourite bull and selling their milk all over the country. She would travel herself to shops and pubs, to schools and hospitals, saying, 'Just wait, just taste. I know you think the bigger dairies' milk tastes better, but just wait till you taste mine.'

And it was true that there was something different to the milk from the O'Connor cows – for John O'Connor, Julia's grandfather, whom I'm sure you remember, still owned and oversaw the farm. Still watched his granddaughter from afar as she fitted the cows with the metal teats and patted their hides with her small freckled hands.

There was a certain sweetness to the milk that Julia brought. A certain crispness to the cheese. A strange tart taste to the cream. It tasted almost like apples.

By the time Julia was twenty-one, when she had been home for around three years, she was all but running the farm. Her parents left the entire dairy in her care and although her mother often asked when she would find a husband, form a family, her father always shushed his wife.

'We've Lizzie for that,' he told her. 'And without Julia this farm would be near its end.'

What Julia never said to her mother, but always wanted to, was always on the brink of blurting out, was that she did have a family. She had a son. A baby who had her whole heart, kept it with him wherever he was, which, she hoped with whatever heart she had left, was with a good and happy adoptive family. She had no way of knowing what had happened to William – even if she had asked the nuns, they never would have told her.

Julia inherited the farm when her grandfather died. It was strange, the town thought, that John O'Connor should bypass Catherine, his own daughter, and his son-in-law, Patrick, who had run it for years, and leave the farm to Julia in his will.

It was almost as strange as the circumstances of his death.

John O'Connor died on St John's Eve four years after the night he brought Julia home from the dance on her seventeenth birthday. That particular year, the night Julia turned twenty-one, the dance was held in an unused field of the O'Connor farm. A makeshift barn was rigged up, an echoey dance hall with creaking wooden floorboards. The farmhands carried long tables from the house, unloaded chairs stacked in lorries from all over the parish. A generator hummed, lending light to the shortest night.

The morning of the dance, Julia, in freshly scrubbed clothes, let herself into the bull's enclosure and led him, palm on his grey hide, into the neighbouring field. Then she stood a moment on the fence beside the bull, reached over to stroke his horns, then climbed carefully off the fence, not wanting to dirty her freshly pressed dress, her white stockings.

'I'll be back to bring you home in the morning,' she

told him, and she pressed a palm against his warm, bristled cheek.

The morning after the St John's Eve dance, John O'Connor was found dead in the neighbouring field, his prize bull watching impassively from the furthest fence. Drank too much poitín, the people said sadly. An accident. A tragedy. Such a shame. Pillar of the community.

For weeks afterwards, the whole of Julia Rys's farm smelled of sweet, fresh apples. The bull's horns gleamed.

After that, Julia owned the farm. When her parents grew older and moved to a smaller house closer to town, she, Lizzie and Lizzie's husband and their three children lived there happily and manned the dairy.

It was only many years later that Julia could bring herself to speak to her sister about her time in the home, her work in the laundry, her baby. Julia let her words fall like a flood of tears. Lizzie clung to her sister and shared, wretched, in her grief.

When the mother-and-baby home Julia had given birth in closed in 1993, when Julia was well into her seventies, she wrote to the council to try – not for the first time – to find her only son. It took two years of calls and visits, letters, threats and tears, but finally the council gave her a name. She expected them to have changed it – the nuns, the records, his adoptive parents. She had spent most of her life clinging to the hope that her son had been part of a loving family, in America hopefully, where times seemed kinder than they did in Ireland, where he could grow up with opportunities and family, be whoever he wanted to be.

She cried for three weeks when she learned that he had spent his childhood in the home, his adolescence in the industrial school. Her sister held her in a way she had not been able to do as a teenager, years of wounds wrapped up in each other's arms. And, as Julia mourned her son's imagined childhood, Lizzie and her children went about contacting the man he had become.

Three days after they had sent a letter to William Rys's address, Julia collapsed. She'd been feeding the bull when she'd felt a sharp pain, had fallen right beside the beast, who'd made such a noise her sister ran out of the house at once. At the hospital, Julia was diagnosed with lung cancer, fast-spreading and serious.

Her family didn't wait for William to answer their letter before finding his number in the phone book and calling him at home.

William didn't want to know his mother. He never had. The words of the nuns, of the Christian Brothers still rang in his mind. He'd had no other guardians, no other teachers. Their word was stone-written law for him, and always would be. To William, his mother had abandoned him – her, a fallen woman, unclean sinner. She'd sentenced him to a childhood with the nuns and the brothers. Why should he want her? Why would he bother?

'I've no desire to meet the woman,' he said when Lizzie had explained who she was, had detailed his mother's history through barely suppressed tears.

'She's in the hospice,' Lizzie told our father. 'She only has a year at most. Don't you want to say goodbye? Don't you want to see her one last time?'

'She's all yours,' our father told her. 'And after that she's in the hands of God. He forgives sinners. You'd better hope He forgives her.'

Julia died before he could change his mind.

Dear Deena,
Come find me. Come find me at the end of the world.
    All my love,
    Mandy

28. The house at the end of the world

Slieve League cliffs, 2012

When I was pulled out of the sea, all that was left were parts of me. As if I had crumbled half to dust on the shores of the real world. As if I really had made it to the otherworld, to Tír na nÓg, to the land of eternal youth.

I came back in pieces, one leg stuck in the sand. Pressure on my chest, then nothing. There were metal bars where my shoulders used to be. A vice-like grip holding me down. Water everywhere.

If you are the branches of your family tree, what are the roots? Who are the worms burrowing in underneath? What land holds you up?

Something turned me over on the sand. My mouth spat salt water. Rivers of it, waves, convulsions. I coughed, I spluttered. My throat felt scraped raw.

I heard an *Is she OK?* The voice was strangled, frantic, familiar.

I heard a *Give her space, child*. A strange trick of my hearing made the words sound like they were coming from three voices at once.

Something lifted me up. I stared into the grey face of a banshee, tangle of hair and wild eyes. Her grin was full of teeth. I wanted to scream but my throat was salt crystals, crow claws.

A warm hand slipped into mine. Squeezed. I hardly had the strength to feel her touch but still she held me.

Mandy. She'd come back for me.

The world swam away.

I came to in a cottage with a thatched roof and whitewashed walls. In the corner there was a clunky old television set with wonky reception playing one of my favourite reality-TV singing shows. From somewhere inside the house, three voices sang along.

I struggled to sit up. A rough, thick blanket covered me, stuck with coarse grey hair that was probably a horse's, but also maybe a bull's. The room spun.

My clothes were not my own: a tunic and long jumper I vaguely recognized but could not tell from where.

Outside the wind screamed and the storm battered at the rattling, single-glazed windows, whistled through the cracks and left small pools of rain on the chipped white paint of the sills.

Beside the front door, lying with his eyes closed, his sides heaving with breath, was a bull. The bull. The bull whose skull I sat with inside a salt circle while Mandy chanted words to the waves. The bull whose eyes stared at me through the window of a bus on a busy street in Dublin. The bull I'd seen, impossibly, in a series of connecting fields. The bull who had brought me down to the shore.

'Are you really Julia's bull?' I whispered.

The creature opened his eyes and looked at me. Slowly, he nodded his huge head.

I wanted to ask *Where am I?* but it seemed like a stupid question. The answer was right outside the window. Windswept cliff face, rain slanting sideways on the gale. Waves crashing in the darkness.

Obviously, the end of the world.

There came the sound of footsteps from further inside the house. I clutched the rough blanket against my legs. Into the small living room drifted three women. They moved with eerie synchronicity to circle me. Three grey ghosts: hags with matted hair and wide mouths.

I wondered if they would push me down the cliff. Tear out my salty throat with their teeth, leave scratches like red lines all up and down my skin.

Their skin was so pale it had a grey hue. Their hair was silver and tangled. Their nails were long. They surrounded me.

'C'mere,' the banshees cackled. 'C'mere and we'll tell you a story. Come closer while we tell you our tale.'

The tea was strong in front of me, stirred thrice about the pot. Not much of a weapon if it came to it. The bull blocked the only exit.

'A good cup of tea is a witch's brew,' the old women said together with wicked grins. 'Heals all ills.'

'I'm not ill,' I said, voice almost choked with terror. I made to stand, run away, but they held out their hands to stop me.

'Listen to us, Deena,' said the three banshees. 'We know your story. We are of your kin.'

'My family?' The salt still scratched my throat.

'That's right. Quiet now and listen. Hear how we've been looking out for you all this time. Hear how well we know your quest.'

'*You* cursed us.' Behind my voice spoke Mary Ellen, spoke Julia. 'You've ruined so many lives.'

'Oh, pet,' they said. 'Oh, love.' Their voices hit each syllable at the same moment, created an uncanny chorus. 'We never cursed you. We only ever wanted to keep you safe.'

'Bullshit.'

The bull himself raised his head, huffed warm air through his ringed nostrils. It sounded a lot like the word *stay*.

28. The house at the end of the world

'You like stories, don't you?' the old women said. Beside the teapot sat a stack of letters. Mandy's letters. Mine.

'Yes,' I whispered.

'Have a cuppa.' One of them pushed the tea towards me. 'Have a bikky. We'll turn down the telly and have a little chat.'

'Where's my sister?'

'Your sister?'

'Yes. Yes. My sister. I came here to find her. Where is she?'

The banshees looked at each other, looked at the bull, nodded in unison. 'She'll be along shortly. Don't you worry about that.'

My head swam with the strangeness of it all.

'When?' I demanded. 'When will she be along? Where is she?'

A sudden loud knock on the door answered me.

'There she is now,' the witches said.

The door opened to reveal Ida, rain-drenched and windswept.

'Oh, Deena, thank God,' she breathed, and she rushed into the house to embrace me. Behind her came Finn and Cale, followed swiftly by Rachel.

Rachel grabbed me so hard by the shoulders I thought they would be shaken clean off.

'What were you thinking?' my sister shrieked. 'What

in the goddamn world were you thinking? You could have drowned. You could've been joining Mandy in her fucking grave and I would have had to bury both of you. Oh God—'

Rachel collapsed in a heap at my feet and great shuddering sobs shook her body, came out in a keen that sounded like an endless scream. The others stood in stunned silence.

The three banshees disappeared into the kitchen to boil the kettle for more tea. Finn helped Rachel up and she sank onto the couch beside me, head in her hands.

'They called us,' Ida explained softly, perching on an armchair by the fire. 'Those women. They found you on the shore and got Finn's number from your phone. We'd already told Rachel you were here. She was already on her way.'

Rachel's breath was ragged from her wailing, her sobs now as short and harsh as a cough. She kept her face hidden behind her hands.

I didn't know what to do. I had been so sure it would be Mandy at the cottage door.

'Did you see Mandy?' I asked. 'Is she here?'

Three faces stared at me in silence and sympathy. Maybe they were no longer angry. Maybe they thought I was going crazy.

28. The house at the end of the world

'She's not here,' Finn said finally. 'Deena. You knew she wasn't going to be here.'

My fingers traced the raised patterns of the jumper I was wearing, the stretchy floral tunic underneath. 'Then how come I'm wearing her clothes?'

'Did you take them?' Rachel's voice came from between her fingers. 'From the boxes of her things.'

'*No.*'

Ida said, 'How do you expect us to believe anything you say any more?'

'You *saw* her!' I cried. 'You said so. After the funeral, in the rain. You saw her on the bridge at the feet of the angels. You recognized her. You know she isn't dead, you *know* it.'

Ida shook her head.

'Sisters,' said the three banshees suddenly, re-emerging from the kitchen with a fresh pot of tea. 'You can always tell sisters. The trick is in the eyes.'

They opened theirs wide and each had stormy irises, as grey as the sky. They laughed as one as the others looked unsettled.

The banshees poured us all tea, sat on the second couch opposite Rachel and me.

'Not to be rude,' Ida said carefully, 'but why is there a bull in the living room?'

'He frightens the cows,' the banshee in the middle told her.

'We can't put him in the barn with them,' the one on the right explained.

The banshee on the left just cackled and dunked a digestive in her tea.

'Thank you,' Rachel said, rather stiffly. 'For taking care of Deena. I'll bring her home once it's safe to drive, after the storm.'

'Oh, there's more storm to come yet, loveen,' said the banshees.

The wind howled through the cottage. The waves broke on the rocks. Sitting beside the sister who raised me, I felt my heart shatter inside my chest, my emotions sparring, colliding, a battle inside me. The love I held for my ever-practical sister – head of the household, her own love as reliable as the newspaper in our letterbox every morning – and the deep betrayal I felt at realizing, by the ways she had reacted after the funeral, that Rachel had known about Mandy's daughter all along.

'Have you been formally introduced,' I asked icily, 'to Ida Nolan, Mandy's daughter?'

Rachel swallowed hard, met Ida's eyes, nodded once. 'Finn told me everything,' she said.

My broken heart was a landslide of pieces, small stones sticking in my throat. 'You told me nothing.'

28. The house at the end of the world

'Deena—'

'NOTHING!' I could have out-screamed the wind. The way she'd dismissed me when I said we needed to find her. The way she hadn't even seemed surprised when she learned about Ida. The way she had always kept Mandy at arm's reach from me. 'You *knew*. You always knew. I wondered why you weren't shocked to read that part of Mandy's note. Why you didn't want to look for her immediately. Find her. Mandy's daughter. Why it wasn't this big mystery for you like it was for me. Because you knew already.'

'There's a lot you don't know about our sister,' Rachel said heavily.

'Yeah. I'll bet. And there's a lot you don't know about me.'

A twist in my heart, in my head. I'd heard these words before, the day after the funeral, yesterday, Rachel's words in our father's mouth. Or vice versa. We said the same things over and over. History just kept on repeating itself forever.

'You're just like him,' I said. 'You try so hard to be just like him. But *you're* the bad apples, the two of you. Not us. Not us.'

Rivers of tears ran down my sister's face.

'You keep on following his lead, but if he knew about me he'd do the same thing to me that he did to Julia. His own *mother*. He wouldn't even *know* her. You think you're so much better, but you're still just his puppet. Just as full of fear as he is of hate. You drove Mandy away with it. Thinking she was so messed up and you were so superior. And you wanted me to be just like you, just so you could be the perfect daughter to prove to dear old fucking daddy that we're good apples, that we're worthy of his rotten family tree. But he doesn't deserve me. And neither do you.'

Rachel gulped, gasped for air like a fish on the shore. I couldn't stop my words from coming, hardly knew what I was saying through my bright-burning fire of anger and tears, didn't think I meant the words; I just wanted them to hurt. Hurt like I was hurt because she had kept all this from me.

'I'd've been better off with Mandy,' I said, voice shaking, loud and terrible. 'She would have made a better mother than you.'

'Oh,' said Rachel. 'Oh.'

I grabbed my sister by the shoulders. I shook her like she shook me the minute she'd come in and, when she did nothing, I threw myself into her arms and cried.

29. Best-laid plans

Slieve League cliffs, 2012, and Dublin, 1995

Rachel's arms were an ocean around me. For the first time since Mandy had left, I felt something close to safe. Washed out and weary, rid of all my words, as though my sister's arms were taking all my anger, my fear, my grief, leaching them out of me and throwing them through the cottage windows back into the sea.

Slowly, softly, into the silence left by the storm of me, Rachel told a story. Tea grew cold in mismatched mugs. Biscuits went untouched. By the door, the bull sighed in his sleep. The three banshees leaned bony elbows on their knees. The world was listening.

This is what she told us.

Before the age of seventeen, Rachel Rys had her life all figured out.

At the end of the school year she would pass her Leaving Cert. exam with all As, which would enable her to go to Trinity College to study journalism. She would break up with her current boyfriend somewhere in the middle of Freshers' Week and would spend the next year having sexual adventures with exciting undergrads. After three years, she'd graduate with first-class honours and go on to do a master's in investigative journalism, which would land her an internship with the *Irish Times*.

It was there that she would meet her future husband, a current-affairs correspondent. They would both make their careers in the broadsheets, where her position would be slightly higher and slightly better paid than her husband's – something he would always secretly resent her for. They would have two children – after the age of thirty, when her career was established enough for her to afford to take maternity leave – and she would then make millions ghost-writing the autobiographies of famous politicians.

She expected she would divorce her husband eventually. He would probably have an affair with a much younger woman when their children were in their early twenties (owing in no small way to his resentment of his wife's great talent and success), finally allowing Rachel to live out her days in a penthouse apartment in Brooklyn, writing for the *New York Times*.

29. Best-laid plans

At seventeen, Rachel had very little room for manoeuvre in her life plan. There was room for her study, her folders of newspaper cut-outs, and there was also a certain amount of room for keeping her boyfriend happy by going to see inane films and letting him feel up her breasts in the back-row cinema seats. Rachel tolerated a certain amount of cliché as necessary.

One such cliché was her virginity, which was not something she wanted to carry with her into university, nor was it something she wanted to have to worry about during her exams, when it was crucial that she shouldn't be distracted. So she decided that on her seventeenth birthday she and her boyfriend would have sex.

She planned it all out meticulously. She researched the best brand of condoms; she carefully considered the position that would cause her the least pain; she talked to her more experienced female friends about what to expect.

She had seen her boyfriend's penis already; they may not have had penetrative intercourse yet, but they had fooled around more than a few times. It was longish, with a small circumference; somewhat snake-like: even erect it veered ever so slightly to the left.

Rachel found it entirely underwhelming. She found the sex underwhelming too, but she'd expected that.

When it was done, she took a shower and brought

the bathroom bin with the used condom in it out to the bins outside. Her parents were away that weekend and wouldn't be home until the following day to celebrate her birthday, but she knew that if they came across a premarital condom in the bin her father might well cast her out. He would probably have assumed it was Mandy's before ever suspecting her, but Rachel's sister had run away (not for the first time) several weeks beforehand. ('More trouble than she's worth,' our father spat, while our mother said peaceably, 'She'll have to resit her exams next year. Just don't tell the family, OK, Rachel love?')

The night air cooled her skin as she closed the lid of the bin. A scream sounded, sudden and frightening, through the night. Rachel jumped, then laughed at herself, smoothed down her hair self-consciously, although there was no one but her around. *Kids messing about in the park*, she thought. *Or cats fighting.*

In the jamb of the front door as she closed it were caught a few strands of long grey hair. *Bloody cats*, she thought, swatting the hairs away.

When Rachel came back into the bedroom, her boyfriend was asleep, happily snoring. She read a little, rubbed moisturizing cream on the long red scratches on her skin that her boyfriend had clearly given her in the throes of his brief but obvious passion, and then fell asleep beside him, content in the knowledge that everything was going perfectly to plan.

Having a baby at seventeen was not part of Rachel's life plan.

It took a while for her to figure it out. She had always had regular, perfectly timed periods that lasted four days for every twenty-eight and gave her virtually no premenstrual symptoms. The first one wasn't even late. By the time she had understood that the second wouldn't show up, she was puking three times a day and couldn't stand behind a man wearing aftershave on a bus without gagging. By the time she figured it out, she was almost eight weeks pregnant.

The first person she told was not her boyfriend. It was an anonymous voice on the other end of a telephone line. One of the crisis pregnancy call centres advertised on the back of every public toilet door, the ones you never in a million years think you'll ever have to call.

The agency Rachel called promised to 'allow women to explore all options, at home and abroad'. Rachel was a smart girl. She knew that 'at home and abroad' was a veiled reference to abortion. Terminating a pregnancy was illegal in Ireland. Even taking pills was punishable by up to fourteen years in prison. Going to prison until she was thirty-one was not part of Rachel's life plan either.

The only way to end a pregnancy legally was to get out of Ireland. To travel to a clinic in the UK. Rachel had some money saved up for college, hoping that she could move out of her family home and live with friends in a dingy flat-share, which was clearly a large part of what college was all about. She figured that with a bit of financial help from her boyfriend she could afford the flights and medical costs. But she wanted to make sure, figure out what to do. Did she need a referral? Was that even legal? She wanted the agency to tell her. Help her. Send her on her way.

When she called the centre, she didn't dither. She told the woman on the other end of the line that she was pregnant and didn't want to be. Couldn't afford to be. Was far too young to be. She used the euphemism everybody knew. She said: 'I want to know how to, you know, take the boat to England.'

The woman said, 'You'll have to come in for a consultation. I can't give you that information over the phone.'

What Rachel got could hardly be construed as a consultation.

30. *The boat to England*

Dublin and London, 1995

The appointment was for evening. Creeping ink splashes in a darkening sky. The crisis pregnancy agency was down a lane a few side roads across from O'Connell Street. The statues by the bridge – giant stern angels, iron or bronze; *grumpy-looking things*, Rachel thought, *so haughty* – stared blankly in the other direction. They wouldn't be watching out for her tonight.

Rachel followed the phone woman's directions to a small plain door with a laminated sign beside a vacant shop that might once have been a bakery. A ghost of the smell of apple pie still floated on the air.

In the waiting room, she sat in a blue plastic chair, ignoring the adoption services leaflets with smiling, dimpled babies on the front. A crying older woman was the only other person there.

The counsellor was friendly, shook Rachel's hand

warmly. 'Rachel, isn't it?' she asked. When Rachel nodded, nervously taking a seat, the woman said, 'My name is Joyce. It's lovely to meet you. Please don't be nervous – I'm here to help.'

Rachel tried to relax, crossed and recrossed her legs as Joyce asked how far along she was, if the baby's father knew.

'I, um,' Rachel said. 'I'm going to tell him tonight. Ask him to lend me some money for the procedure if he can. It's a lot, with the flights and all. I think I might be OK to come home the same day, not need to pay for a hotel room or . . .' She ran out of steam, waited for Joyce to pick up the thread of the conversation, to tell her what to do and how to go about it. *I'm here to help.*

'Well, I definitely think it's important to tell him.' Joyce smiled. 'To give him all your options. How long did you say you've been together?'

'Almost two years. But I don't see it lasting. I'm going to college next year and—'

'Two years is a long relationship, for your age,' said Joyce, still smiling. 'Shows true commitment. Real maturity.' The woman smiled some more.

'Um. I suppose.'

Joyce reached into a drawer and pulled out a leaflet like the ones in the waiting room. 'I think you'll agree,' she said, 'that being armed with all of your options, all the relevant information, is the most important thing when it comes to making choices like this one. Life-changing choices.'

'Sure,' Rachel said. 'Of course.' She took the leaflet. It unfolded like an accordion when she stretched out her arms.

Joyce leaned over the desk and pointed to one of the accordion's panels. 'Nine weeks, is that right?' Under her painted fingernail was a picture of a tiny palm-sized baby with its thumb in its mouth.

'But no,' Rachel said, her tongue suddenly too big, blocking the air behind her teeth. 'I've done this in biology class. At nine weeks, it's just a blob. It doesn't have hands or a face.'

'If you're certain you want to go through with this,' Joyce went on, 'you should be aware of the side effects.' She turned the leaflet over for Rachel.

Increases the risk of breast cancer by 78%, a list of bullet points said. *Increases the risk of future miscarriage by 62%. Increases the risk of sterility by 67%. Studies have shown that women who have terminated pregnancies are five times more likely to show abusive behaviour towards children, including their own future children.*

'But this can't be— Is it true?' Rachel asked.

'These are some of the risks involved,' Joyce told her.

275

'Not all of these might happen to you, maybe even none of them will. But it's important to be aware of the risks. Would you like to have children someday in the future?'

Rachel nodded. 'Someday, yeah,' she said. 'But I'm seventeen. I'm still in secondary school. I've my Leaving Cert. in June. I want to get the points for Trinity. Study journalism.'

'That sounds very exciting.' Joyce smiled. 'I can tell you're a very intelligent person. I'm sure you'll make a wonderful mum.'

'Someday,' Rachel repeated.

Joyce smiled once more, rummaged around in a drawer again. 'Have you picked out names yet? For your future children, I mean. I knew what I wanted to call my children since I was just a child myself.'

'Um,' said Rachel.

Joyce came out of the drawer with a TV remote. 'Here we are,' she said. 'I want you to watch this video, to prepare you for the procedure. They don't always show this at the clinic, but it's important you realize what you're going to put your body through. Just so you're prepared.'

'Um,' Rachel said again. 'OK. Um. Are you, um, affiliated with a particular clinic in the UK or . . . ?'

Joyce pressed play. On the television on a shelf in

front of Rachel, a woman in a hospital-issue paper gown screamed in pain.

'We just want to give you all your options,' said Joyce, smiling again.

Rachel came out of the counselling agency with screams stuck in her head. The video was graphic. Terrifying. It didn't matter that Rachel knew, logically, that what she'd been made to watch wasn't what was going to happen to her. That at nine weeks all there was in her womb was a small blob. That there was no way abortions led to child abuse. Or breast cancer, sterility or miscarriage, like the pamphlet had said. That she'd been tricked. But it didn't matter. The seeds of doubt had been sown. That was probably their plan all along.

She let herself be led by muscle memory down O'Connell Street, past the shiny big windows of Clerys department store, but something made her look up. Made her keep walking towards the bridge, towards the angels sitting stony on their pedestals. The angel that Rachel was sure had been staring straight across the River Liffey when she'd gone to her appointment was now staring straight at Rachel.

That couldn't be right.

Very slowly, almost unnoticeably, the angel inclined her head.

Rachel turned and ran for her bus like she was about to miss it, like the number 130 from Abbey Street didn't leave every eight minutes, like her life depended on her making that very bus. It was the stress. It had to be the stress. The hormones. The emotions. It had to be something like that.

Rachel watched the coast go by from the top deck of the bus. Cranes and ferries, the wooden bridge leading out towards another statue, Our Lady, Star of the Sea. Rachel was glad she couldn't see the statue's face, couldn't see where she was staring. Probably the same place she always stared, following the boats across the Irish Sea. The boats to England. But Rachel could feel a strange and faraway gaze on her all the way home. A nod of the head. A benediction.

The following morning, Rachel booked a round trip to London.

The clinic sent a taxi to collect her from the airport. They suggested she book a room in a hotel if she could, rather than travel straight home, but Rachel didn't want to spend any more money than she had to.

After she'd contacted the clinic, she'd told her boyfriend, who had agreed that they shouldn't have a baby together at seventeen. But, when she asked if he could spare some money to put towards the cost of the procedure, he suddenly had a lot less to say.

'Donal,' Rachel said. 'This is your problem too. Nobody gets pregnant by herself.'

'Yeah,' said Donal, wincing. 'But abortion? Really? Like, my mam'll want to know what I used the money for.'

'So tell her we're going on holiday. One night in London. Nice romantic break before the exams.'

Donal's face fell. 'You want me to come with you?'

'Well, yeah,' Rachel said in disbelief. 'I sure as hell don't want to go through that alone.'

He said he'd think about it. He said he'd see how much money he had saved up in his account. He said he'd get back to her. The day before her appointment, she hadn't heard a word.

She took out all her savings. She went alone.

Rachel's abortion was nothing like the video the crisis-pregnancy agency had shown.

There was no hospital gown, no screaming, no legs in stirrups, no surgical instruments that looked like medieval torture devices. Instead, she swallowed a small pill in the morning and came back in the afternoon to be given another set of tablets.

Her flight home was later that night. She spent the hours in between at the cinema, staring blankly at a film she'd forgotten before it was halfway through. The nurses had given her pills to take for the pain and pads for the bleeding, and before the film's credits rolled she was starting to feel the need for both.

Rachel was supposed to fly home that evening, but the flight got cancelled. The pain was still blurring the edges of her vision, so she was glad. She called her best friend Sorcha from the phone in the hotel room she'd booked from the airport.

'Oh my God, Rachel,' was the first thing Sorcha said. 'Donal's mam's after telling everyone.'

'Telling everyone what?'

'About your—' Sorcha lowered her voice. 'Abortion.'

The pain in Rachel's abdomen came in waves, rocked her like a boat. 'Everyone who?'

Rachel could hear her best friend's hesitation.

'Everyone *who*, Sorcha?'

Finally, Sorcha said in a rush, 'Mrs Cleary had us praying for your soul in homeroom. I'm sorry. She told everyone.'

'I'm going to kill him.'

'He swears he begged her not to tell anyone. I cornered him the second I heard. He says she went spare when he told her, kept saying she would've raised the kid or whatever, like that was even the point. So then when he said you were already on your way to England she went and told the school.'

'I'm going to kill *her*.'

'Want me to do it for you?'

Rachel gave a hollow laugh. 'Thanks, but one of us breaking Irish law is enough.'

There was silence on the other end for a moment. 'You know you didn't do anything wrong, right?' Sorcha said softly.

Rachel sighed. 'I know.'

'Aisling O'Donnell out of Ms Simmons's class had one last year. And Gary's older sister.' Gary was Sorcha's boyfriend. 'And I'm pretty sure Sarah's Aunt Jenny did too.'

'But Mrs Cleary's praying for my soul.'

'And the baby's.'

'Fuck.'

'Yeah.'

Rachel watched the city settle into evening outside her hotel-room window. She wrapped her arms round her legs, drawn up to her aching abdomen. She wrapped her arms round the bones of her life plan. Virginity, exams, university, break-up, studies, journalism, career, marriage, eventual babies. She could still do this. She could keep to the plan. So what if the whole class was praying for her soul? In a few short months, the exams would be over and she'd be on her way to the rest of her life.

'You still there?' Sorcha's voice came through the phone, over the Irish Sea, under the aeroplanes, over the ferries.

'Yeah,' said Rachel. 'Yeah. Can you do me a favour, before I come back?'

'Anything,' said Sorcha.

'Just make sure my dad never finds out.'

31. *The funeral that felled the family tree*

Dublin, 1995

Sorcha was true to her word. She threatened Donal until he told everybody it had all been a big misunderstanding, that Rachel had been studying with her best friend all weekend. He somehow even managed to convince his mother because, sure, wouldn't Dr Jones, the local GP, who was his mother's uncle, know if Rachel had been pregnant? It couldn't possibly have been true. Not studious, hard-working Rachel. Good girls didn't get abortions after all.

At Monday morning assembly, Rachel led her fellow prefects in a prayer for the unborn. She held her head high and her hands clasped: a carbon copy of her father. She talked about the constitutional right to life of the unborn and about the sanctity of motherhood, and she hated herself every second, but knew this was the best way to protect herself. She was extremely convincing.

Only Rachel knew how much she bled and how long the cramping lasted, how the exhaustion became a large rock inside her ocean, holding her down.

She still kept hold of her plan. She was no longer pregnant. Her exams were coming up. If she could get through this, she could get through anything. She could have the life she'd always wanted. If she just focused on sticking to the plan.

But all this was leading to a funeral: the funeral that felled our family tree, that sent our father running, that broke the two sisters apart, that changed everything. There was no plan in place for this.

Our mother had had a small stroke the week before, had recovered in hospital before coming home, had insisted our father not tell their children how bad it was. That was who our mother was, to Rachel. The peacemaker, the mediator, the quiet force that balanced the family (just about) and that above all didn't ever want to worry anybody. Worry wasn't worth it, and besides what would the family think?

'I'm fine,' she told her husband. 'Stop fussing.'

But the only reason our father stopped fussing was because Mandy showed up suddenly after four months away, the day their mother came home from hospital.

'The Mandy drama-wagon,' Rachel told her friend Sorcha. 'Every time she comes home, I could parade round the living room naked and nobody'd ever notice.'

There was always a lot of shouting and slammed doors when Mandy was home, so Rachel made herself scarce the moment she heard the telltale sounds of a fight, before even seeing her sister. She stayed over at Sorcha's house where she could study in peace. Her mother would still be resting, and Rachel didn't particularly want to see Mandy.

The day after Mandy returned, Rachel came home just to get a book and a change of underwear, presuming her parents would hardly notice her absence when Mandy's presence filled the house with all its might.

When she walked past the kitchen, her father called her in. He was sitting at the table in his flannel dressing gown and slippers, drinking a tall glass of whiskey.

He said, 'Your mother's had a baby.'

Rachel was sure she'd misheard. 'A what?'

'A baby.'

'A *baby*?'

'Yes. A baby. A baby, I said. Are you deaf?'

'I'm not deaf – I just don't understand. How could Mum have had a baby?'

He chugged his whiskey. 'The feckin' stork came,' he said gruffly. 'And now your mother's had a baby.'

'But how could Mum have had a baby? She wasn't pregnant. She's almost fifty. That's not possible.'

Our father placed his whiskey glass down carefully on the table. 'Now you listen here, lass,' he said slowly, enunciating every word. 'Your mam is after having a baby. A baby girl. A little sister for you. She's tired after the labour and you'll have to mind her, and mind the baby. You hear me?'

Rachel shook her head. 'I hear you,' she said helplessly. 'I just don't understand.'

'You don't have to understand. You just have to do as I say. Now come upstairs and kiss your new sister.'

Rachel's new sister was small and red with a wrinkled, alien face that wouldn't stop crying.

'Colic,' said our mother fondly. 'I remember you were just the same.'

'How is this possible?' Rachel asked.

Her question was met with a smile. 'Bodies are miracles, Rachel,' our mother replied. 'I didn't think I'd ever have another child. It had been so long since I'd been pregnant my body mustn't have known how to react. I thought it was the change – you know, the menopause. It hadn't come yet. I was always a late bloomer. But then I went to the hospital last week and – surprise! Here is little Deena.'

Rachel touched the baby's cheek and said, 'Hello, little Deena.'

Little Deena cried and cried.

The house was loud suddenly, louder than it had ever been. Those were weeks of baby cries and adult tears, doors slammed and plates smashed and harsh words shouted up stairs. Those were weeks of bottles and bibs, dirty nappies and sleepless nights.

Rachel spent entire days in the library, studying after school, and most weekends at Sorcha's. Her exams were six months away. Her entire future depended on her study, her results, her constant focused determination. She wouldn't let herself be distracted now.

But on top of the noise of her parents fighting with Mandy and of the baby's constant crying, her mother's parents and siblings and aunts and uncles and cousins and nieces and nephews came in droves to see and congratulate the new mother on this unexpected miracle – and to chastise her husband on the state of their eldest (so rude, so unruly, and there had been rumours she'd run away, and were there drugs involved, and what kind of a teenage girl dressed like that these days, and what was our father going to do about it; that girl brought shame on the family).

As for Mandy, she loved the baby. Because her mother

was so tired, it was often Mandy who woke in the night to feed her, who got up early in the morning to take her for walks, along the blustery seafront, across the wooden bridge and all the way to the Dollymount Strand, down to the statue of Mary at the edge of it, staring out across the water.

The only time the baby stopped crying was when she was being rocked, or when she was submerged to the chin in the warm water of the bath.

'That kid certainly hates staying still,' Rachel observed one morning to her sister. 'Must take after you.'

Mandy stared at Rachel for a full minute before answering.

'Yes,' she said. 'I guess she does.'

Two months after Deena was born, when the family had just about become used to her presence, their mother suffered another stroke. A cerebral aneurysm, like the one before. She slipped into a coma and stayed that way for almost eight weeks.

It was January, bitterly cold. For weeks, the wind had screamed in under the rafters, echoed round the attic. Nobody could sleep.

Mandy, who had been so attentive to the child until that point, disappeared the moment their mother fell ill. Their father was just as absent, splitting his time between the pub and the church, as if one cancelled out the other.

There are things that hold you, and there are things that you hold. The father held onto pints and prayers, one after the other in rapid succession. Mandy held onto the hands and lips and wallets of any man who'd take her. And Rachel held onto the plan for her future as best she could while caring for the baby.

After almost two months, their mother slipped away. There was no plan in place for this.

The day of the funeral was crisp, uncompromising, so dry and cold the ground snapped mourners' heels off their shoes and sent them skidding.

Our father shook hands with our family, nodded, stalwart, at their tears. Beside him, poised and graceful in her black pencil skirt, Rachel held her baby sister, rocked her so she wouldn't cry.

Mandy was almost late, slipped into the church after most of the mourners, skulked up the far wall to the family pew, slumped down beside her sister.

'What the hell happened to you?' Rachel snarled as the congregation settled. Mandy's hair was lank and tangled, her black shirt wrinkled, her face a pale grey marked with red like she'd been scratching at her skin.

'What do you mean what the hell happened to me?' she snapped back. 'My mother's just died. We can't all become Polly Perfect at times like these.'

Rachel's mouth grew thin. She sat as straight as a statue, rocked the baby. Halfway through the service, Rachel's arms began to shake. She was glad of Mandy then; how she knew without asking to take the baby gently, to make the exchange from one sister to the other without disturbing the rhythm of the rocking.

In the pub for the wake after the burial, the baby finally slept. Rachel slipped into the toilets to once more attempt to dry her tears, splash water on her face. The door to the bathrooms slammed open and Mandy stalked in.

'Fucking family,' she said when she saw Rachel was the only occupant. 'Fucking nightmare family won't leave us the fuck alone at our own mother's funeral.'

'Yeah.' Rachel ran the cold tap over her wrists to wake herself up, set herself straight. 'I wasn't expecting a liturgy on sitting like a lady today of all days.'

In reply, Mandy threw up in the toilet.

'Whoa,' said Rachel. 'Mandy. Are you OK?'

Mandy took deep breaths. 'Yeah. I mean, no, but you know. That helped.'

Rachel felt an unexpected surge of warmth towards her sister. They had never really seen eye to eye, but neither had they fought much. Besides, Rachel told herself, with the father and extended family they had to contend with, they only had each other now.

'Where were you,' Rachel asked, leaning back against a sink, 'over last summer? Where were you these past few months, for that matter?'

Mandy spat into the toilet, made a face. 'Don't you start,' she said.

'I wasn't. That's not what I meant. I was just curious.'

Mandy searched her sister's face for signs of judgement and must have decided Rachel was sincere because she answered truthfully. 'Outside London,' she said. 'Got a job for the summer working in this orchard.'

'You were *apple-picking.*' Rachel couldn't hide the incredulity in her voice.

'What, you were expecting jail? Ibiza? Fucking, I dunno, month-long raves in some punk commune?'

'Something like that, yeah.'

'Nope. Picking apples. Good, wholesome work, fresh air, decent pay.'

Rachel shook her head. 'You'll never cease to surprise me.'

'Yeah,' said Mandy. 'About that.'

But Rachel had spoken at the same time. 'So where have you been since Mum went into hospital? A sanctuary for baby seals or something?'

Mandy rinsed her mouth out. 'With a guy.'

'Right. See, now *that* I would have expected.'

'Yeah,' said Mandy. 'And now I'm pregnant.'

There was a certain scent in the air when our family was gearing up for drama. We all knew it. I'd smelled it myself at ten when Mandy brought me back from our road trip. Both sisters smelled it when they walked out of the pub toilets at our mother's wake. It was a sharp and bitter smell, like metal or unripe apples.

When they came into the room, the air was rife with it. Electric. The family huddled round their small tables, their well-poured pints of Guinness (for the men) or glasses of Chardonnay (for the ladies). Our father stood in the middle.

What my sisters didn't know but were about to discover was that the walls between the ladies' and the gents' stalls were thin. That, without the taps running or the toilets flushing or the hand driers humming, voices carried. That, as my sisters were talking, our father had taken a moment in the gents alone to compose himself, blink away his tears, ball up and release his cramping fists. That, in the silence of his suffering, our father had overheard everything.

'Get out,' he said to Mandy. The family was still

and silent, hanging on every word. 'Get your filthy, disrespectful self out of this place.'

Rachel reached for her sister's hand. 'Dad—'

'No. No. She's no daughter of mine. Not after this. Not any more.'

Mandy looked as though she might faint.

'How could you do this to me?' our father cried. 'To your own mother? How could you do this to yourself again?'

He was haggard and worn, eyes bruised from holding back tears, face lined from grief, breath reeking of whiskey.

'I'm a cursed man!' he bellowed. 'This whole fucking family is cursed. Sluts and whores, the lot of them. It's cursed. I'm cursed. It's a curse.'

'Again?' said Rachel softly.

Mandy shook her off. '*Fine!*' she yelled at her father. 'That's *fine*. I'm leaving – I hope you're happy. I'm not gonna be your bad fucking apple any more.'

'Ha!' roared our father. 'Ha!'

'*Stop that*,' said Rachel, trying to stand between them. 'This is not the time or the place for a fight.'

Behind her, the family began to murmur. The sharp tang of gossip was so strong she could taste it. Rachel took Mandy and our father by the elbow and led them outside, and in the pub car park, surrounded by the big black cars with funeral-home logos on the sides, out of earshot of the family trying surreptitiously to peer through the windows, our father faced his daughters with fire in his eyes.

'What kind of a stupid slut gets knocked up twice in the same damn year?' he said to Mandy, low and dangerous.

Rachel took two small steps back, stared at Mandy. Of course, she had suspected. She must have unconsciously known. Sometimes we only see the things we want to see.

Mandy's face was flooded with tears. She held herself and sobbed. She said, 'I can't do this. I can't do this. I'm sorry.'

She walked out of the car park and onto a bus and Rachel didn't see her for another five years.

Two weeks later, in the middle of the night, our father packed his bags and left Rachel in the house alone to raise the baby. To raise me.

After that, Rachel's best-laid plans fell like a branch of rotten apples from a gnarled and dying tree. She didn't get the points she needed. She didn't have the money to go to college. She had to work.

With only an occasional phone call from Mandy, Rachel's bitterness grew fruit. She tried not to pick them, ripe resentment straight from the tree. She tried to stay steady. She made a new plan. She would work hard; she'd raise her baby sister; she'd ensure I had every chance she'd never got.

She would make sure we were respectable, good apples, worthy of our family tree. Without Mandy.

Without my mother.

32. Sisters and mothers

The end of the world, 2012

Rachel's hand was a rock on my knee, so heavy, keeping me in my place.

'Deena,' she said. 'I'm sorry. I'm so sorry. Deena. Look at me.'

There was nothing but a void inside me. I hadn't come here for this.

'I can't do this. I can't do this. I'm sorry.' The past was the present and those were my mother's words. The words she said when she knew she couldn't keep me. Everything kept looping round, unravelling.

I stood. 'I just need a minute. Just need a minute to myself.'

I walked woodenly on bare feet through the little cottage in Mandy's old clothes (did I take them? I must have taken them. I wrote the letters after all, couldn't be trusted with the truth, bad apple that I was).

32. Sisters and mothers

I lifted the latch of the back door and ran out into the storm.

At the cliffside, the rocks were sharp, the mud slippery, the ground uneven. The wind was a wild thing, pulling, pulling. The rain fell in glass shards. Everything was so cold. Everything was screaming.

Everything became this haunted darkness, this sharp cliff's edge, there, right there, my bare feet toeing the line between ground and sky. Steep fall to the ocean below, tempest-tossed and foamy. The wind was fierce. Pushing, pushing. One more step and I'd be falling.

One more step, one more push and I'd be on the back of a bull on my way to Tír na nÓg. Wasn't that what was out here? Wasn't that why Mandy came? Isn't that what everybody else thought? Not that she'd made her way here to break a family curse, but that she'd come to escape it?

The storm took a deep breath. The wind screamed. Only it wasn't the wind – it was me. I screamed my mother's name to the crashing waves, the cliff face hard and fatal beneath me. I screamed my mother's name to the sea.

I didn't believe it. Couldn't believe it. Mandy was my mother. She wouldn't leave me like that. She had to be here still. She had to be here, somewhere, at the end of the world.

A figure appeared on the rocks behind me, grey of skin and tangle-haired. I could barely see with the dark and the rain. But I saw her. Not a batty old lady dunking digestive biscuits in her tea and watching reality TV. This was a real ghost. A real banshee. Her mouth was a wide ruin. She opened it to scream for me.

I turned to run, to search the cliffside in the dark, to climb down if I had to, to find Mandy. To find my mother. Before the banshee could get me. But the banshee's voice stopped me. Not a scream. Not a whisper. Just a voice on the wind.

'Deena,' she said. 'Deena. I see you. Step back. Come here.'

The rain clawed my skin.

'Deena,' said the ghost. 'Come away. Come to me.'

Like Mary Ellen so many years before me, I stepped back from the edge of the cliff and I walked towards the banshee. The rain was a curtain blurring the world. I couldn't see.

The barest, lightest touch of a hand. 'Follow, follow,' said the ghost. Tangle of curls and apple cheeks. 'Follow, follow me.'

There was nothing to do but let her lead.

The grey ghost – or was she so grey? Did her hair not have a hint of red in the rainy darkness? – gestured at me to come. I stepped away from the cliff. I followed. I followed her round the back of the banshees' cottage to an ancient, crumbling hovel, the ruins of which the three old sisters' house had been built around a century ago. The cottage and the ruins still shared a wall, the one closest to the edge of the cliff, practically falling into the sea. The rest of the ruin had tumbled down, was only held up by a large, gnarled hawthorn tree that grew right over it, roofed it, provided shelter from the storm. The wind whistled through its branches. I knew at once what this place must be.

The end of the world. The ruins of the cottage in which Gerald and Mary Ellen met in secret, in which Patrick, Julia's father, was conceived. The cottage near where Mary Ellen tossed the magic sapling to the crashing waves below. The cottage in which the curse began.

My eyes took some time to adjust to the low light. To the impossible sight. At first I thought my sanity might have cracked completely.

But then I threw myself into Mandy's waiting arms.

Instead of giving me an explanation, Mandy told me a story. I shouldn't have been surprised, I suppose; the apple, after all, does not fall far from the tree. I stilled the sudden anger that was in me. The confusion and relief, the grief and fear. It was my turn to listen. The storm came close to hear it too.

Here is what she told me.

Mandy was a restless child with bright eyes and wild hair she had to be caught to brush. Catching Mandy wasn't easy. Her father tried it – tried grabbing at her hair and smacking her bottom, locking her in her room. Her mother tried it – tried cries and bribes and empty threats. The teachers tried it with punishments, prayers and failed tests. The parish priest tried it with tales of temptation, damnation. The local boys tried it with kisses. None of it ever worked for long.

Had her parents been any other parents, they would have understood Mandy to be a wandering soul, fast-acting and quick-thinking. Would have known she had a precociousness that should have been nurtured, not scorned. But, as it was, Mandy came of age in a family so focused on what others would think, they didn't stop to think of what was best for her.

The first time Mandy ran away, she was eleven. She made it halfway to Galway before the Gardaí caught up with her at the bus stop, told her to get off the coach and come with them. The second time she was thirteen and there were four friends with her. They lasted two days on a beach in Wexford before their money ran out and they came home, filthy and triumphant.

For years, all Mandy heard were variations on *Why can't you be more like your sister?* Mandy's sister was studious. Mandy's sister was still. Mandy's sister stayed silent in the face of emotional manipulation. Mandy thought her sister was the worse off for it. So Mandy kept on running away.

She didn't know which boy it was, the one who got her pregnant the first time. She and a few friends had planned to spend that summer hulling corn in rural France, but by chance one of them had a relative who worked in an orchard close to London. They set off for England without saying much to their families and spent three magical months bunking one on top of the other, climbing ladders, picking apples from the sun-drenched trees and taking the train to London on the weekends to party their wages away.

There were deer in nearby forests that screamed in the night, woke her up, heart racing, hands clutching her chest. There were strange silver foxes that no one ever saw, but that left long grey hairs caught on her windowsill in the morning.

There was something strange about the orchard, Mandy thought, something magical. She listened to the tales told by the owners' grandparents about a mysterious sapling that had grown up overnight to feed the cravings of a starving pregnant woman, a witch perhaps, or some kind of mythic queen. Mandy took it all in, wide-eyed and full-stomached, crunching on apples she knew were not magic, but that she craved deliriously nonetheless.

It was there that Mandy realized she was pregnant. Six months gone, according to the doctor. She'd just thought she was getting fat. She had no idea who the father was and she didn't care.

She came home with a daughter. A small, squalling, milk-drunk secret, a few months after her seventeenth birthday. A wonderful secret. A beloved secret. An impossible secret that belonged only to her which she took into her family home and shared, joyously, with her parents.

Mandy's parents did not agree with her opinion.

It didn't take them long to wear her down. To employ every trick in their arsenal they'd ever tried before. Denying and threatening, screaming and smacking, crying and bribing and locking her in.

'You've no money to your name to raise her,' they said. 'You'll get no charity from us.'

'She'll grow up knowing her ma's a little slut,' they said. 'Never worked a hard day in her life, doesn't even know the father. She'll be shunned, you mark my words.'

32. Sisters and mothers

'You've no business raising a baby,' they said. 'You're barely more than a baby yourself. No schooling, won't graduate, what kind of a life d'you think you can give a child, you selfish, ungrateful wretch?'

There was nothing to do but follow their lead. For the first time in her life, Mandy listened to her parents, let them make her decisions, let them claim her child as their own.

'It's in her best interests,' they said. 'It's for the baby. We're only doing this for the baby.'

'Her name is Deena,' Mandy said.

It was too much. Too much for Mandy. The screaming and sleepless nights, and days, the coos and sickly smiles of the neighbours, the extended family, the exclamations over this miracle, this baby girl, Mandy's *little sister*. She slept fitfully, woke even when the baby slept to discover that she had clearly been scratching at her skin in her sleep. Soon her body was covered in raised red lines running up and down her arms and legs, her torso, her chest, even her neck. Some mornings she awoke to find them on her face. So when her mother fell ill, was hospitalized, slipped into a coma, Mandy did the only thing she knew to do.

Running away had always been how Mandy faced her problems.

She was drinking in a bar in Galway when she met him. Jeremy Nolan. He believed her lies (they all did) but he, unlike most of the others, was kind. He listened. He cared. She lost herself in him for a time. Then her mother died and she ran away all over again, with raised red scratches all over her pale, freckled skin, and her belly slowly swelling for the second time.

In the next nine months, Mandy's belief in the curse became something real. A pip inside her that grew into a spindly skeleton tree. *What else*, thought Mandy, *could this hellish year have been? How else could so much be stacked on top of the one person, the one family?*

My father was right, Mandy decided. *The Rys family name is cursed. My daughter will be better off without it. Better off without* me.

When her second daughter was born, she nursed her for a month, then wrapped her warmly in her car seat and left her on her father's front porch. This one she was sure of. This one had a family outside hers. It was the right thing, Mandy told herself, over and over throughout the years. Ida was a Nolan, not a Rys. She was good. She was safe. The curse could never come to her.

But as for the first one, the first baby, Mandy was forever torn.

*

32. Sisters and mothers

Mandy showed up at Rachel's door on a Wednesday morning early, straight from the airport, tired and haggard, her clothes wrinkled and musty, with only a backpack and fifty quid to her name. She hadn't seen her sister in five years.

She stood on the front step and listened to the sounds coming from inside: the doors opening, wardrobe drawers closing, five-year-old feet clattering about in tiny shoes. Rachel's voice came through the closed door, firing off instructions and reminders, brisk and practical, telling the child off when she was too slow, saying they were going to be late: *Hurry up now, Deena, get your coat on, quick as you can.*

Rachel opened the door to leave the house before Mandy could ring the bell.

She stopped on the threshold, Deena – me – ahead of her, the tiny coat of my school uniform hanging by one sleeve, Rachel still wrestling with the zip of my oversized schoolbag. The zip shut with a sound like a tear.

Mandy tried a smile, sank down onto her hunkers and stared into the face of her younger sister – *sister*, she told herself again and again, *sister* – and said, in a voice made faint by love and guilt, regret and exhaustion, sorrow and relief, 'Hi, Deena.'

I had never, to my knowledge, seen Mandy but I recognized her. Rachel had made sure of that. Whatever resentment she had for her sister she'd tried to put to one side. She told me stories of her childhood with her twin sister, the wild one, the one off on wonderful adventures. The walls of our house were covered in pictures of the lot of us: Rachel and me, Mandy, our dead mother, our absent father. I recognized them all.

I shoved my arm into the remaining sleeve of my coat, shrugged, said, 'Hi, Mandy, are you coming to stay?'

Mandy's eyes met Rachel's. Her sister's mouth was a thin line.

'We're going to be late for school,' she told me. 'Give your big sister a hug and hurry up and get in the car.'

Mandy only let go of me when I pulled away, waved cheerfully at her, skipped over to the car and threw my schoolbag in. Mandy stood.

'So,' she said to Rachel. 'I'm home.'

Rachel locked the front door behind her, readjusted her handbag on her shoulder. 'It's been five years,' she said, face impassive. The slightest warmth came through the stiffness of her words. 'It's good to see you.'

'Sorry I didn't call to say I was coming.'

Rachel looked towards the car, to Deena – to me – fastening my seat belt in the back seat. 'How long will you stay?'

Mandy took a breath. 'I'm home,' she said again. 'I'm home for good.'

They both watched the small child in the car open her schoolbag and sneak a snack from her lunchbox. Watched me.

Mandy could tell that her sister was also surreptitiously watching her, taking in her unkempt clothes, her tangled hair, the one backpack she'd brought with her. Mandy knew she didn't look like someone who was home for good.

Still, she asked, 'Can I've a key?'

Rachel took a breath. 'You know you can't stay in the house.'

'Rachel—'

'Dad won't have it. And, besides, Deena and I have our routine. I can't let you disrupt that if you're just going to disappear again for half a decade. I have Deena to think of. Her home, her stability.'

Mandy felt as though she had been kicked, hard, in the stomach. 'Rachel, Deena is my—'

Rachel cut her off. 'I know,' she said. 'She's your sister too. Which is why I know you're going to do what's best for her.'

There was so little left of Mandy. She was raw, ragged, a cursed thing.

'You can stay a couple of nights,' said Rachel, unlocking the door for Mandy. 'There are towels in the spare room; the bed is made. There's a lasagne in the freezer or leftover spaghetti in the fridge. I don't think Deena ate all the scones – there should be a couple in the bread bin. Take a shower, eat something – you look like you need a decent meal. I'll pick up a paper to find you a flat-share if you're set on staying in Dublin. I'll get some money out to help you set up. But you can't stay here, Mandy.'

'I don't need your money,' Mandy said, temper hot, words like bullets. 'And I don't need your charity either. But I *will* see my daughter.'

Rachel shushed her, looked with panic again towards me. Her shoulders slumped; her voice grew weary. 'I'm not a wicked witch, Mandy, keeping the child locked in a tower. But I have been raising her – alone – for the past five years. *Alone*, Mandy.'

Mandy looked deflated. Rachel took out her car keys, made a move to leave.

'It's good to see you,' she said again, touching the handle of the car door. 'It's good for Deena to see you too. But show me that you can stay. Prove that you can be still. And then we'll see.'

But being still was never something Mandy was good at, and wavering from her rules was something Rachel could not do.

33. *Sisters and mothers, part II*

The end of the world, 2012

So Mandy remained as my sister, my fairy godmother, my flighty but loving kin. And at the same time Mandy dug deep and muddy, got her hands dirty, asked for favours and uncovered secrets. Mandy researched our family curse without knowing that she could one day break it. That she could one day make sure her daughters never had to change their true selves, damp down, pretend. Never had to live in fear.

Mandy did her research, coaxed rumours from our family. With what she found, she was able to speak to Lizzie, who knew Julia's story, to old classmates of William's, who knew his. She was able to trace the family tree to an old burnt-out cottage, found its history in the skull of the bull. There were letters, things Mary Ellen had left for her granddaughters, so they would know where they came from. A journal that Lizzie left to lie with the bull. And there was Mary Ellen's magic, the memories she spoke to the bull made manifest for when her ancestors would need them.

But for all the beauty and sadness, all the wisdom in Mary Ellen's story, Mandy couldn't find anything concrete about the woman; didn't know where she'd come from; couldn't find a record for a Rys man who had died of diphtheria in Donegal, which is what was still widely believed had happened to her husband. But in Mandy's travels somebody gave her a phone number for three sisters by the name of Boyle, said they might know, had lived in the area Mary Ellen had said she was from for years. *Three old sisters*, they said, *might be relatives, might be family, you never know.*

When she spoke to the old Boyle sisters, Mandy understood. She pieced together their talk of local history that said that many years ago the Big House, long since rebuilt as a spa hotel, was still inhabited by a landlord, a wealthy Englishman named – what was it again – Rice? Rumour had it he'd impregnated a peasant, then evicted her whole family. She had left, never to be seen again. And from that moment the landlord's family fortunes were ruined. The Big House fell into disrepair; the Englishman's father was forced to sell his orchard. Nobody knew what had happened to the peasant girl. Nobody ever knew what happened to peasant girls.

But Mandy did. And now she knew from which cliffs the peasant girl had thrown her lover's sapling. She now knew where the curse began.

Suddenly she had it. The Rys family curse. The three banshees. The reason all of those bad apples had been shaken off our fallen family tree. She understood how to break the curse.

It all came from the sapling. The magical Rys Russet, the lucky *Lendemain*. What had Gerald's mother told him, all those generations ago? *The juice of these apples runs in your blood. Plant the tree on your land and your children's blood shall run with it too.*

That was what Gerald had failed to do. That was what Mandy had to do now, and she set off to find it. To find the sapling.

Mandy believed there was a curse on our family, but for the longest time she didn't think to break it. She didn't believe it would ever hurt quiet, nerdy Deena, Rachel's protégée. She didn't imagine that it could reach Ida, so far from our family, a Nolan, not a Rys. For all her research, she didn't understand that the curse didn't work like that. Nobody was immune from being branded. Bad apples, the lot of us.

But she understood that soon enough. The moment

she knew I had inadvertently come out to my father, she knew the curse would come to me too.

Mandy did write one of the letters. The note she left on her bed before she disappeared. I was the first to read it, but already her tearstains had blurred the words. I had missed a single letter at the end of the last word: a crucial letter, a letter that changed everything.

Daughter.

Daughters.

Going to the end of the world. Give all my love to my daughters.

I suppose my mother was never quite sure she would return. I suppose that was why she wrote the note, left her bedroom pristine, her things tidied, her loose ends tied.

It seemed an impossible task. For all my mother knew, the sapling had been thrown into the Atlantic, left to rot at the bottom of the seabed, seaweed-tangled, fed by salt and bleached seal bones. But something pushed Mandy onwards. Guided her car to the cliffs just over yonder, close to where our ancestor once lived and loved and was betrayed with her unborn son swirling in the depths of her.

Three voices urged my mother on.

Cliffs are a bitch to climb backwards. Hand under foot and foot over hand she scaled them, down, down, trying to keep from falling. She could see something far below. Further than most had ever thought to look, to search, to photograph. A sharp jut of rock and a dark spill of soil so unlike the muck and mud of the cliffs. And, at its edge, a branch. Not a peace offering. Not a laurel. A thin and spindly, barely living tree. But it was alive. After all these years. Impossibly, it lived.

Mandy scrambled to reach it. Her footing grew erratic, her blistered hands sore. Her muscles screamed surrender. The sea was stormy. The wind was fierce. One gust was all it took. She fell.

Perhaps she slept. Perhaps she died. She couldn't tell. The three old women told her, after, that they'd found her. Found her car parked by their cliff (they didn't hold to notions like national parks; no, this land was their land, bound to their family name). Found her lying half alive by the remains of an apple tree, miles and miles down the rock and steep slope, the breakneck fall of the storm-swept cliffs.

How the three old biddies dragged her back up was a mystery, but Mandy suspected it involved a rope, a pulley and a great grey bull.

She came to in a cottage with a thatched roof and whitewashed walls built from the ruins in which her ancestors met, secretly, in the night. She'd been out for days. Out of time, out of mind.

'Rest,' said the old ladies. 'Recuperate. Gather back your strength.'

Their voices sounded familiar. She allowed herself to trust them.

When she was well enough to get up from the slouchy couch in the cottage living room, Mandy had connected it all. She slipped out of the house in the dead of night and walked for miles through the darkness to take the nearest bus to Dublin.

She didn't imagine they'd have buried her. Them, her family, the ones who'd known how many times she'd run away before. Who hadn't batted an eyelid. Who'd barely called the Guards.

The family that thought she was dead.

How would you know if you were dead? Could you feel it? As an ache – a physical sensation that left behind a hole inside you? Could you sense it as a smell – salty like the sea, or tart like apples? Would you know it in the way you somehow know you are asleep, in dreams?

Nobody seemed to see her. She was sidestepped by pall-bearers, looked over by the blank-faced family, assumed to be a distant relative from out of town. After walking all the way into said town in a storm of rain, umbrella-less, childless, lifeless, the only person who saw her could well have been a ghost herself. A mirror reflection, sitting up by the angels on O'Connell Street, looking like the sisters (the daughter and the sister) she had supposedly left behind.

Mandy began to doubt herself. She had a lump on her head the size of a hen's egg and her extremities were still tinged blue in the cold. Nobody saw her. Nobody looked at this woman, bedraggled, drenched, shivering in the downpour. Maybe the mourners were right. The priest on his pulpit, the newspaper print in black and white. Maybe Mandy Rys had died on that cliff. Maybe she was a ghost after all.

On the bus back to Donegal, no one would meet her eye. She passed through their vision as though she was invisible, and whether it was because she looked wretched, or because she was just a ghost, she couldn't tell.

Could dead women break curses? Did ghosts have any more stories to share?

Mandy sneaked back up to the cottage, searched the whole place when the banshees were away. When she heard them coming – carrying something heavy between them, with difficulty and great care – she hid under the tree in the old ruins behind their house, at the edge of the cliff: the ancient crumbling cottage from which her family curse had come, with nothing but the knowledge of everything she had done wrong.

And a spindly, ancient, half-alive tree in the corner, lopsided in a cracked clay pot.

Mandy barely had time to touch the tree when the cliffside called to her.

Mandy, Mandy, a wailing on the wind.

Follow, follow.

Mandy followed and in the dark she found me, the only one screaming and screaming her name.

34. *Le Lendemain*

The end of the world, 2012

Beside Mandy – beside us – was a small tree. Damp leaves, dull bark, soil half spilling out of a cracked clay pot.

'It's the sapling,' I whispered. 'It's the Rys family curse.'

'*Le Lendemain*,' said Mandy. 'The next morning.'

However long a life story takes to tell was the time it took them to find us. We were in the last place you'd think to look: a tumbledown ancient ruin, roofed by a gnarled hawthorn tree, facing nothing but the edges of cliffs and the sea. But they found us.

Three banshees stood silhouetted in the storm.

They were family. They were ghosts. They were ancient battle goddesses.

They had the answers. They were the keepers of the curse.

Three grey ladies screaming the voices of those who could not speak, scratching their limbs to wake them, warn them. The screams of new babies in the air. Blood on the sheets. Blood on clean knickers. Girls bending their backs over heat and steam and dangerous machines, washing, always washing, the blood from their clothes. Girls alone in overseas hotel bathrooms, bleeding bright red on new pyjamas, washing the bottoms under hotel-room taps, washing, always washing. Bleeding, always bleeding. Left alone to wash and bleed.

And where did that leave me?

That left me in the trembling arms of my mother, who shielded her eyes from the glare of the banshees' torch beams.

The three witches clicked their tongues. They said, 'Well, there you are,' as if we'd only stepped out for a bit of air and a chat. 'Come on back inside. The open door will let the heat out.'

They sounded so certain that there was nothing strange about our situation that we followed without a word.

The hallway between the little kitchen and the main room was tight, was narrow, could only fit one body at a time. The first banshee led us, followed by me, followed by the second, followed by Mandy, followed by the third.

At the sound of our footsteps, I could hear the others rising from the threadbare couches, upsetting the rickety coffee table, spilling the tea.

'Did you find her?' Rachel's voice was raw and ragged. She sounded like an old woman.

I knew I was wet by the way my hair hung cold and heavy against my cheeks, with how Mandy's jumper was a weight on my chest, by how I could barely feel my feet. There was a strange, loud clicking sound reverberating round the cottage, which I realized with a shock was coming from my chattering teeth.

Rachel ran over with the bull-hair blanket, bundled me close to the fire before sitting right in front of me, looking at me and smacking me, once, hard across the cheek. Then she grabbed me and held me to her heart so tightly the heat of it warmed me better than the turf fire spluttering with occasional raindrops in the hearth.

I tried to push myself away, but still she held me.

'Rachel, what the *fuck*?' My voice was muffled, cracked, barely angry. 'You *hit* me.' It had felt less like a blow and more like the kind of smack you'd give somebody who'd fainted, a wake-up call, a return. Still, it smarted, in more ways than one.

'I was sure you'd jumped.' Her voice was as muffled as mine, lost in the thick tangles of my hair. 'I was sure you'd followed Mandy. After everything I said. You don't *do* that. You don't just fucking run out into the storm and off a cliff. You *don't do* that.'

I finally untangled myself from my sister. Aunt. From my aunt. 'I *didn't* do that.' I gestured down at my body – cold, yes, but also clearly alive. 'Obviously.'

Finn knelt beside me. His eyes were red, ringed with deep shadows. 'What were you doing out there then?' he asked. I realized I had scared him.

'I went to find Mandy.'

'Deena—' he said.

'And I did.'

'Deena—'

Rachel saw something in my expression that stopped her, made her hold out a hand to cut Finn short. 'Wait,' she said. 'You what?'

As if she had only been waiting for her cue, Mandy stepped out of the hallway.

How do you react, seeing a sister you thought had died? A sister you'd buried, had barely begun to mourn? It had been three days since Mandy's funeral, just over a week since she'd disappeared. Ida's mouth hinged open and her eyes filled with tears. Finn rubbed his own eyes as though the appearance of a dead woman was some kind of speck in his vision, a trick of the light. Cale moved closer to him on the couch, bent to whisper in his ear.

Rachel stood. 'Where were you?' she said.

'Here.' Mandy's voice shook. 'I've been here.'

'Are you going to explain why you let us all think you were dead?'

Mandy pressed her lips together in a gesture so reminiscent of her sister it made me catch my breath.

'I'm going to explain everything,' she said.

Mandy told her whole story again, history repeating itself over and over in the main room of the tiny cottage, and, as she spoke, the storm died slowly, the wind stopped wailing, the rain stopped dripping in through the cracks around the windows. The three banshees floated into the living room, shared the longest couch. Rachel stood in front of the fire, with me at her feet like a cat.

'A concussion,' she said flatly when Mandy was done. 'Why then didn't *these three* call me? Were they concussed too?' She nodded sharply at the banshees, who bared their sharp teeth.

Mandy leaned against the wall of the doorway, still not quite with us in the room. 'I didn't have my phone,' she said. 'Or my mind really, if I'm honest.'

'I'll say,' Rachel mumbled. She sat and poured out more tea, then switched, suddenly and inexplicably, into her usual bustling self. 'Would you ever come in and get warm, Mandy! Look, you're soaked to the skin. There's room in front of the fire with Deena. Here, have some tea. Hand round the biscuits, would you, Ida? Mind you don't spill crumbs off the plate.'

Ida knelt at Mandy's side and offered her a biscuit. Her hand trembled and the plate shook crumbs into the moth-eaten carpet.

Mandy took her daughter's hand instead of the biscuit. 'Hello, Ida,' she whispered.

'Hello.' Ida's voice was quiet, hesitant, unlike the cool, blunt way of speaking I thought was her usual and had only just about become accustomed to.

This wasn't the tear-filled embrace of a reunion I had been expecting.

At that moment, I realized that endings are rarely ever endings. I had come all this way – *we* had come all this way, me and Ida – to find our mother. And we had. Ida had never really met her mother before. I had been told from birth she was my sister. For us both, Mandy had been dead for almost a week. For Ida, she was already twice gone, and how could she be sure her absent mother wouldn't just leave again?

In the end, this didn't feel like an ending at all.

'So this is it,' I said. 'The stories have been told. This must mean that the curse is broken.'

Rachel didn't ask what I meant. Her eyes rested on the pile of letters on the little coffee table and I understood that she had read them when Mandy and I were out in the storm. We were on the same branch now, the lot of us. We'd climbed all the way up our family tree.

'Almost.' Three voices spoke at the same time, hitting each syllable like a single set of vocal cords, one mind branched into three. 'Takes more than a cuppa tea to break a curse.'

'You're family,' said Rachel. 'Aren't you? Like Mandy said. Relatives of Mary Ellen's.'

'Yes,' replied the banshees. 'And no.'

Finn stood and took an envelope from the windowsill, which was covered in keys and hairbrushes and toothpicks, things dug out of pockets. He held it up. It was a bill of some kind, addressed to a Ms Boyle, World's End, Donegal.

Ida let out a small laugh. '*Going to the end of the world?*' she quoted.

'Where else?' said the banshees. 'What else would you call this place?'

Outside the window, dawn swept over the cliffs, shining on the raindropped cobwebs, the spindly fallen trees, the flooded rocky fields. The wilderness stretched forever on every side but one, and on that side there was only ocean.

'So you *are* Boyles, like Mary Ellen,' said Ida.

'See, Deena? They aren't banshees. There's always an explanation.'

'And not a supernatural one,' Rachel said. 'There are no banshees. You don't really believe that.' She gestured towards the three old women. '*They* don't actually believe they're banshees anyway.'

'Oh, don't we?' The banshees' eyes wrinkled with mirth. 'Who do you believe *you* are?'

'What do you mean?'

'We meant what we said. Who do *you* believe you are?'

Rachel sighed, said patiently, 'I'm just me.'

'Exactly,' the three grey ghosts said together. 'You don't have to believe in who you are. You just are.' Together they grinned.

They were no great-great-aunts of ours. They were witches; they were goddesses; they were three banshees ready to scream our deaths. To warn us. To help us. So the same thing that happened to the bad apples of our family didn't keep on happening again and again.

My mother was not my mother. My sister was really my aunt. The girl I thought was my niece was my sister.

Going to the end of the world. Give all my love to my daughters.

Here we were now, together at last, here at the end of the world.

*

The storm had died down as quickly as it had come. We stepped out of the cottage into a calm, still day in which bright, shining puddles reflected the blue of the sky.

'Pathetic fallacy,' said Finn, 'is when the weather reflects the mood of a play or a story. Sometimes it's nothing but a metaphor: a girl walks sad and lonely in the rain. Sometimes it's an omen: the storm signals a battle about to be won.'

The past could be the present; my best friend's words could have been mine, spoken at a funeral for my eldest sister, who turned out to be my mother and not really dead at all.

'Maybe the storm isn't a battle,' I said. 'Maybe it just represents confusion: you battle through it to the truth.'

'*You* battle through it,' the three banshees said in their eerie synchronicity.

Mandy and Rachel and I said, 'We all do.'

From the ruined cottage, we took the sapling. It had lived for over a hundred years, alongside our family history, waiting to be found, to be rescued, to be planted.

'It'll never work,' said Rachel, watching me and Mandy fetch shovels from the shed. 'This land is barren. It's all rock and sand. The air is salty and harsh and the wind is almost constant.'

'Some apples like that,' said the banshees, watching

from the arch of the kitchen door. 'That's exactly the kind of air some apples need.'

We carried the tree to the cliff where I had stood just hours before, where Mandy had started the long climb down last week, where Mary Ellen had tried to destroy it over a century ago. We kept well away from the edge and stuck our spades into the hard land as if to dig a grave.

We kicked at the old clay pot that housed the sapling until it shattered under all our feet. We lowered the spindly trunk into the hole, threw earth over its roots, patted it down until there was black, sandy dirt under all our fingernails, like we'd dug up a treasure, a long-buried secret, a family curse.

We stood back, breathless and salty with sweat. The sea air was on our lips and our tongues, but was soon replaced by an overwhelming smell of apples.

The sapling took root. Within minutes, as we stood in a circle and watched in disbelief, the Rys Russet, *le Lendemain*, grew into a tree.

It takes about seven years to grow an apple tree, in the right conditions. This one shot up at our feet. The trunk widened, the branches multiplied, broke into buds. The buds flowered and grew apples large enough to harvest.

'That's impossible,' breathed my family.

34. Le Lendemain

'Now,' said the banshees, coming in a cluster from the door of their cottage. '*Now* the curse is broken.'

'*The juice of these apples runs in your blood,*' said Ida. '*Plant the tree on your land and your children's blood shall run with it too.*'

As one, Mandy and Rachel stretched an arm out to pick an apple each from the bottom branches of the tree. They were tall but had to stand on tiptoe to reach them. Mandy handed hers to Ida, Rachel hers to me. They were the perfect mix of tart and sweet. They tasted like every story in our family history. They tasted like endings.

'So this is how you break a curse,' said Finn, impressed, eyes wide and arms folded, watching us.

'Oh no,' said the banshees together. 'Not really.'

I threw an apple underarm to Cale and it landed straight in the palm of her hand. Ida grinned and tossed one to Finn. The banshees clustered round Rachel and Mandy, and the unlikely lot of us shared the apples from our family tree.

We were connected, all of us, by blood and beyond blood. Cale's ancestor and mine had been lovers. Finn and I became best friends because we were both queer. Ida seemed like a *nice, normal girl* on paper, but Mandy was her mother. Maybe we were all bad apples, no matter what we did. But maybe it wasn't just us.

'There are no bad apples,' I said into the crisp, sweet silence. 'Are there?'

The three banshees grinned with all their teeth. 'Now you're getting it,' they told me.

'What do you mean?' said Mandy.

'I mean, this isn't just our family. It's our whole country. Cale's ancestor, Ann Gorman, was thrown out of her home for who she loved. The same would have happened to Cale. If Finn was born a hundred years ago, he'd have been an outcast too: you don't hear of many biracial, bisexual boys in Irish history. But I bet there are stories like these in almost every family. As you said the day you left. If you're considered rotten by the rest of the family, by the rest of society, you're doomed.'

Rachel threw her apple core over the cliffs and into the sea. 'The past just keeps on repeating itself,' she said.

The banshees grinned as though we'd made them proud, as though this was a conclusion they had been leading us towards all along.

'The curse isn't on our family,' I said slowly, thinking as I spoke, speaking with more than just my own voice. 'It's on every woman in this country. Kept in shame and silence for generations. Kicked out, locked up, taken away. Their children sold in illegal adoptions; their babies buried in unmarked graves. Forced pregnancies and back-street abortions, eleven a day on the boat to England only to come home to rejection and stigma. Insults and prayers and keeping up appearances – and how do you break a curse like that?'

We were all crying again, the lot of us. Our tears salted the earth and fed the tree, made the apples taste like the sea.

'You tell the story,' said Mandy slowly. 'You tell your story and the story of your family. You speak your truth. You shatter the stigma. You hold your head up to the world and speak so that everyone else who was ever like you can recognize themselves. Can see that they aren't alone. Can see how the past will only keep repeating itself as long as we're kept powerless by our silence.'

'Yes,' said Rachel, stunned. 'Yes.'

I wrapped an arm round Rachel's waist and Ida tucked herself under Mandy's shoulder. Our family tree, in full bloom, heavy with good, ripe apples, swayed, deeply rooted, in the salty sea breeze.

35. *How to break a family curse*

Dublin, 2012

When we got home, funeral flowers still crowded the porch. Our fridge was full of food left over from the wake: the home-made quiches and shepherd's pies, the tarts and bakes, stale sandwiches still cut into triangles, wilted lettuce lolling out of them like tongues. The neighbours' curtains twitched as we walked up to the front door; loud gasps sounded from behind them.

Turned out it *was* a bit embarrassing when Mandy showed up at the door. I tried not to smirk too deeply as I gloated.

When word got back to the family, our phones rang off the hook. We silenced the ringers and helped Mandy unpack her boxes into what had been the spare room, but was now her room, our father be damned. Her shoes cluttered the floor and her cigarette ash dusted the windowsills, her hair mingled with ours in the shower drain.

When they received no answer, the family came knocking. Perhaps they expected to find Mandy filthy and matted, covered in earth, fingernails broken and bleeding from having scratched her way out of the grave. Instead, she opened the door halfway through breakfast in jeans and a T-shirt, holding a slice of toast in one hand.

'So it's true,' the family said in wonder.

Rachel appeared behind her sister, reached round her and slammed the door in the gawping faces of our family. Mandy's laughter followed them back down the garden path.

When our father came, we were ready for him. He didn't ring the doorbell, just let himself in with his key. In the kitchen, Rachel was making breakfast. Mandy was at the table on her laptop, alternating typing furiously and swearing at the hold music on her phone (having been dead for a week was turning out to be a bureaucratic nightmare). I was attaching a rainbow pin to the collar of my school shirt.

We heard his heavy footsteps in the hall but didn't look up. He stood in the doorway for a long time before speaking.

'What do you think you're playing at?' was the first thing he said to the daughter he thought had died.

Mandy tucked her phone between her shoulder and her ear, finished typing two-handed. 'Trying to get my driving licence reactivated,' she said. 'Hi, Dad.'

'One of the three of ye is going to tell me what's going on *right now*.'

'It was all a mistake,' I told him. 'Mandy isn't dead. Clearly. Or else she's currently the world's most boring ghost.'

'Ha,' said Mandy.

'Will you have some eggs?' Rachel asked our father. Her father. My grandfather. 'I'm making rashers too, or you can have some of that squeaky Greek cheese Deena likes instead.'

Our father's face got progressively redder, a volcano about to erupt. '*I don't want fucking cheese!*' he bellowed. 'I want you to tell me what this slut is doing in my kitchen.'

Silence fell like a cast-iron pan on the stovetop.

Rachel took a breath, cracked another egg. 'It's not your kitchen, Dad,' she said calmly. 'If you don't want breakfast you can just have coffee, and if you only want to insult us you can leave. I've to drive Deena to school in fifteen minutes. I'd advise you to take that time to talk to your eldest daughter.'

'Aren't you happy to see me?' asked Mandy.

Our father's face was a traffic light, a stop sign,

a warning. 'I'm happy to see you didn't kill yourself,' he said. 'But your blatant disrespect is—'

'Wow,' said Mandy. 'The bar's set low.'

'There,' I said, my pins in place. 'What do you think?'

The pins were a late birthday present from Cale, who had sent them by post the moment she got home, in an envelope sealed with a purple lipsticked kiss. One was an enamel rainbow flag. The other was a round pink badge that said POLITE YOUNG LESBIAN. I took a picture to send to our group chat, even though my face was burning with the force of my grandfather's gaze, even though my hands were shaking at the thought of wearing them to school.

My grandfather spluttered. The red of his face deepened to purple. He didn't seem to be able to speak. Finally, he choked out, 'This isn't over.' When he left, he slammed the door.

My heart hammered like the reverberations. 'Well. That's it. We can kiss this house goodbye.'

'Oh, don't be silly,' said Rachel, soaking the frying pan before sitting down to eat. 'The house is in our name. As per Mum's will. And, right now, I'm changing the locks.'

Fifteen minutes later, Rachel pulled up at the school.

'You sure you're ready for this?' Mandy asked from the front passenger seat.

'Nope.'

'That's the spirit. Knock 'em dead.'

I straightened the pins on my shirt collar and walked into the school hall ten minutes early for Friday assembly. I had lost my invisibility; a crowd of eyes watched me. News spread fast, and it had been five days since my sister had returned from the dead. I messaged my friends a running count of the whispers and rumours until the vice-principal bustled in and called for us to please stand for morning prayers.

Stay strong, Finn messaged, his usual parting words.

I tucked my phone back into my pocket and as the sea of girls rose around me I stayed seated, head held high, sitting on my shaking hands and hoping my face wouldn't go up in flames.

Afterwards, I waited by the doors for the two sixth years who had organized last week's protests. I handed them the leaflets I'd had Rachel print the day before. A record of sources and numbers. A list of every Magdalene laundry, every church-sanctioned mother-and-baby home, every Christian Brother industrial school ever opened in the country, alongside the recent dates that each had closed. A call for our school to secularize our education. A student petition to separate church and state.

Please stand up to do away with morning prayers, it said. It garnered almost two hundred signatures before it was confiscated, but pictures of the leaflets made their way online, were circulated so widely our school ended up, again, on local news pages:

SCHOOLGIRLS' CONFISCATED HISTORY OF MAGDALENE LAUNDRIES GOES VIRAL

SECONDARY-SCHOOL STUDENTS DEMAND ACCOUNTABILITY OF THE CHURCH

BEYOND GOSSIP AND SELFIES: TEEN GIRLS PETITION FOR SEPARATION OF CHURCH AND STATE

I carried their stories with me – Mary Ellen and Ann, Julia, Rachel and Mandy. They were less of a weight and more a reminder that the truth could be hard to hear, but was the only thing that brought us together.

'That and the banshees,' said Ida, flicking through the letters I'd written in Mandy's handwriting, propped up on one elbow on my bed. She was visiting for the weekend, had decided she'd drop by every month or so. 'Someone has to keep an eye on this crazy family,' she'd said.

Cale had also persuaded her grandparents to let her visit regularly, though it wasn't to keep an eye on anybody's family.

'I wonder – are all legends kinda warped?' I said to Ida. 'The scream of a banshee is supposed to foretell a death, but really it's a warning. They're supposed to be evil ghosts, but they only ever wanted to help. At least I think so.'

'I bet if the banshees were men, the myths wouldn't have got it wrong.'

'Huh.' I watched her touch Mary Ellen's name, Julia's. 'It's always the fault of the women, isn't it?'

'They weren't the ones who wrote history.'

'True. But they found ways to pass their stories down.'

We'd typed up our family history. We'd sent it to my grandfather, to the rest of our family who weren't Ryses, but who needed to be told nonetheless. Probably there were similar stories in the history of my grandmother's side of the family. Mandy agreed that, curse or no curse, she'd start her new research there.

We'd sent our stories to Lizzie, Julia's sister, now a very old lady. We'd sent them to her children and great-grandchildren, who were of an age with me and Ida. They'd got in touch, contributed stories of their own. We planned to meet in Sligo all together, a Rys family reunion, to honour the lives of those who came before.

We invited my grandfather but did not expect him to come.

'OK,' said Ida, gathering up the letters. 'Time to go.'

35. How to break a family curse

We met Finn at the wooden bridge, walked down the path by the Dollymount Strand to the statue of Mary where Cale was waiting. On the mosaic stones at the base of the statue she had set out her candles and crystals, her unlabelled glass bottles full of a sweet, cloudy liquid. We took each other's hands and I stood to say my prayer.

'Our Lady, Star of the Sea, watch over the boats to England. Watch over the planes. Bless the places with clinics and small pills, bless the bleeding women. Bless their tears and their relief. Our Lady, Star of the Sea, watch over the women. Watch over their passage home and erase their shame. Watch over the journeys, eleven every day, as it was in the beginning and hopefully will not always be, amen.'

I twisted my hands out of my friends' grips, took two steps and threw myself into the water. I surfaced, newly baptized by the sea at Dublin Bay.

In a heartbeat, my friends emptied their pockets, left their phones and their wallets with the candles, and with three great jumps, their screams like banshees echoing across the Irish Sea, followed me.

Author's Note

Dublin, 2018

I wrote the first draft of this novel in a very different Ireland to the one in which I write this now. In June 2016, when I first sat down to plot and research the history of the Rys women, about a year before I would start writing it all into Deena's story, excavations were beginning to be carried out under the Mother and Baby Homes Commission of Investigation on the site of the Bon Secours Mother and Baby Home in Tuam, County Galway.

In the 1970s, two schoolboys found human remains in the grounds of the old home. The church vehemently denied that the remains were linked to the home and said that what the boys had found was most likely a famine grave. In 2012, local historian Catherine Corless began a self-funded investigation into the deaths of babies and children in the Bon Secours Mother and

Baby Home. She uncovered the names of 796 infants and children who had died in the home between 1925 and 1961, paid €4 each for every death record of those 796 children, and discovered that none of them were buried in local cemeteries. The children's and babies' death records suggested that many had died of malnutrition and neglect. Catherine Corless put forward the idea that the remains found in the 1970s were not part of a famine grave, but were those of the children who'd died in the home, who were then buried in an unmarked grave in a vault in an old septic tank.

Seven hundred and ninety-six children means that one child died in that one mother-and-baby home every two weeks. This is not fiction. This is not a story. This all happened in living memory.

This novel was, in part, fuelled by rage.

The last Magdalene laundry in Ireland closed in 1996. It's estimated that about 30,000 to 35,000 women and girls were incarcerated in these Catholic-run institutions, with over 11,000 since 1922. Some were sent by social workers because their families could not care for them, some from reformatory schools, some by the police. Many were transferred straight from mother-and-baby homes after they'd given birth. Some were sent because they had suffered abuse or mental illness. Some accounts are from women who were sent because they were disobedient, because they were too pretty, for having a boyfriend, for being gay.

Most of the history of the Magdalene laundries relies on first-person accounts because, in a series of strange coincidences, almost all of the records of these places held by church officials are either missing or were mysteriously destroyed before official investigations could be carried out.

There is still no separation of church and state in Ireland. It was only in 2018 that our constitutional ban on blasphemy was repealed. It is only in 2019 that primary schools' 'baptism barrier' will be removed, meaning that schools will no longer be allowed to deny non-Catholic children a place on the basis of religion (or lack thereof). It is only in 2019 that a pregnant person* will be able to access safe, legal abortion in this country.

All the Bad Apples is set in 2012, the year in which Savita Halappanavar died in a maternity hospital in Galway after having been denied the abortion that would have

---

* Throughout this novel, I have used the words *mother* and *women* when talking about people who can become pregnant because the focus of the book was on the women in Deena's family in particular, but I want to emphasize that trans men, genderqueer and non-binary folks – not just cis women – can and do get pregnant, and need to be included in the continuing fight for reproductive rights.

saved her life. When she requested a termination, after having learned that she was suffering a septic miscarriage, she was reportedly told that 'Ireland is a Catholic country'.

Up until May 2018, when the people of this Catholic country – fuelled by a grassroots feminist movement that called for a referendum – voted overwhelmingly in favour of repealing the eighth amendment, abortion was illegal in Ireland, punishable by up to fourteen years in prison. This included abortion in cases of pregnancy as a result of incest or rape, abortion in the case of fatal foetal abnormalities and, until 2013, abortion in cases where the pregnancy was directly endangering the pregnant person's life.

The eighth amendment of the constitution of the Republic of Ireland gave equal right to life to the pregnant person and the unborn. After a High Court trial known as the 'X case' (*Attorney General* v. *X*) in 1992 – in which a fourteen-year-old girl, suicidal because of a pregnancy as a result of rape, was initially restrained from leaving the state for a period of nine months so as to stop her accessing abortion services overseas – pregnant people were granted the freedom to travel to procure an abortion, and the freedom to obtain information about abortion services overseas. It is estimated that since 1992 eleven women travelled outside the country every day to terminate their pregnancies legally.

This is a different Ireland but the past is still so close. The stigma. The shame. The silence of generations complicit in the institutional abuse and neglect of its people.

The places in this book are not all real places, but they are inspired by real places. The characters are not real people, but they are inspired by real people's stories.

There's great power in sharing stories. In connecting. In speaking truths. In bringing abuses to light. To read real stories of people who have had to travel to procure abortions, please visit *In Her Shoes: Women of the Eighth* (https://www.facebook.com/InHerIrishShoes), a Facebook page created to share anonymous stories of real people travelling abroad for abortions. To read real-life accounts of survivors of Magdalene laundries and mother-and-baby homes, please visit the Magdalene Oral History Project created by the Justice For Magdalenes group (jfmresearch.com/home/oralhistory project).

Cry. Rage. Speak out. Break the stigma. Break the curse.

If you or someone you know have been affected by any of the issues raised in this book, please remember you're not alone. The following organizations might help:

UK AND IRELAND
The Samaritans: 116 123 / www.samaritans.org / jo@samaritans.org – confidential twenty-four-hour helpline

IRELAND
Health Service Executive (HSE) My Options:
  1800 828 010 / www2.hse.ie/unplanned-pregnancy
  – freephone helpline and support for unplanned
  pregnancy and abortion information
Rape Crisis Network Ireland: 1800 778 888 /
  www.rapecrisishelp.ie – twenty-four-hour helpline
  for help and support on sexual violence
Dublin Rape Crisis Centre: 1800 778 888 /
  www.drcc.ie – twenty-four-hour helpline for help
  and support on sexual violence
BeLonGTo: 01 670 6223 / belongto.org – for services,
  advice and support for LGBTI+ youths from the ages
  of sixteen to twenty-three
National LGBT helpline: 1890 929 539 / www.lgbt.ie
  – for confidential help and support

UK

British Pregnancy Advisory Service (BPAS): www.bpas.org /
0345 730 4030 – for abortion care services and
support

Rape Crisis UK: www.rapecrisis.org.uk – for help and
support on sexual violence

Switchboard: www.switchboard.lgbt / 0300 330 0630
– confidential LGBT+ helpline and support

Acknowledgements

This book would not exist without an entire orchard of the best bad apples an author could wish for.

To Natalie Doherty, Naomi Colthurst and Kathy Dawson, my magical editors, thank you for believing in this ambitious project, and for growing it from a spindly sapling into the book I imagined it could be but could never have written without your invaluable insight and expertise. Thank you for raging with me. To my agent, Claire Wilson, thank you for championing this story from a seed, and, as always, for your advice, guidance, and kindness.

To Wendy Shakespeare, Harriet Venn, Lindsay Boggs, Regina Castillo, Lindsey Andrews, and to the stellar teams at PRH UK and Penguin Teen USA, thank you for making my stories into beautiful books.

To my parents, Cathy and Frank, and siblings, Claire, Kevin and Thomas, who are the most loving, nurturing, supportive family ever to produce an author who writes such dysfunctional families, thank you for being the roots that allow me to stand strong whatever the weather; I'm proud, as ever, to be a bad apple on this family tree. To my faves, Fleur, Aoife and Jess, thank you for your incredible support; this book owes a great debt to deep friendships. And to my daughters, my two witch babies, thank you for the magic and the whimsy, for challenging me and teaching me, and for a love I didn't know was possible.